Praise for
MAUREEN F. MCHUGH
and
NEKROPOLIS

"Maureen F. McHugh is one of the finest
U.S. fiction writers working today."
Minneapolis Star-Tribune

"A rich, multi-faceted portrait of a future society with roots
deep into the past . . . McHugh has long shown a talent
for immersing the reader in her characters' lives. The multiple
viewpoints in **NEKROPOLIS** work brilliantly to build a larger
picture of a world, as they reveal what it means to be an
individual . . . in a place and time very different from our own."
Locus

"As good as anything she's written before . . . McHugh conveys
the ambivalence of Hariba and Akhmim's lives . . . with
sympathy, eloquence, and power . . . Her disquieting tale
proves how provocative good science fiction can be."
Cleveland Plain Dealer

"A well-realized set of sympathetic but imperfect characters . . .
McHugh's Morocco . . . is very real, but ultimately it is Hariba,
Akhmim, and their heartbreaking, impossible relationship
that the reader will remember."
Publishers Weekly (*Starred Review*)

"Spare and lucid prose that reveals extraordinary compassion
for the marginal and the exiled."
Mary Doria Russell

"Maureen McHugh has mastered the trick
of astonishing the reader."
Washington Post Book World

Also by Maureen F. McHugh

CHINA MOUNTAIN ZHANG
HALF THE DAY IS NIGHT
MISSION CHILD

NEKROPOLIS

MAUREEN F. McHUGH

An Imprint of HarperCollinsPublishers

This is a work of fiction. Names, characters, places, and incidents are products of the author's imagination or are used fictitiously and are not to be construed as real. Any resemblance to actual events, locales, organizations, or persons, living or dead, is entirely coincidental.

EOS
An Imprint of HarperCollins*Publishers*
10 East 53rd Street
New York, New York 10022-5299

Copyright © 2001 by Maureen F. McHugh
ISBN: 0-380-79123-4
www.eosbooks.com

First Eos trade paperback printing: November 2002
First Eos hardcover printing: September 2001

The Library of Congress has catalogued the hardcover edition as follows:

McHugh, Maureen F. Nekropolis / Maureen F. McHugh.
    p.   cm.
    ISBN 0-380-97457-6 (hardcover)
    1. Morocco—Fiction.   I. Title.
    PS3563.C3687 N44 2001
    813'.54—dc21   2001033525

Eos Trademark Reg. U.S. Pat. Off. and in Other Countries, Marca Registrada, Hecho en U.S.A.
HarperCollins® is a trademark of HarperCollins Publishers Inc.

Printed in the U.S.A.

10 9 8 7 6 5 4 3 2 1

This novel was made possible by support from Bob *(and is lovingly dedicated to him).*

✴ Acknowledgments

A lot of people helped with this book, and I'll undoubtedly forget someone, the way I forgot to thank Astrid Julian for her
tremendous help on *Mission Child*, but here goes.

Thanks to Arla Myers, who patiently listened to me outline this
book on a seven-hour car ride back home from a convention. Without her and that car ride, this book wouldn't have happened. To
Jennifer Brehl, my patient and long-suffering editor. To Greg Feeley
and Sean Stewart, who said important things about this book and
about writing in general. To the Cleveland East Side Writers—Sarah
Willis, Charlotte Van Stolk, Charlie Oberndorf, Pat Brubaker, Paul
Ita, Erin O'Brien Nowjack, and Lori Maddox. You guys are the best.
To Sandy Dijkstra, who made me write two books when I only
wanted to commit to one. To Gardner Dozois, who published the be-
ginning of this book when other people had turned it down. To
Smith and Shelly, who are constitutionally incapable of doubting me.

Note: The Morocco of this book, while based on the country of the
same name, is entirely a fictional creation. Someday I'd like to visit
the real place. Until then, please forgive the errors of fact and feeling inflicted on the place and people for the purposes of this story.

NEKROPOLIS

1.
Paper Flowers

How I came to be jessed. Well, like most people who are jessed, I was sold. I was twenty-one, and I was sold three times in one day, one right after another; first to a dealer who looked at my teeth and in my ears and had me scanned for augmentation; then to a second dealer where I sat in the back office drinking tea and talking with a gap-toothed boy who was supposed to be sold to a restaurant owner as a clerk; and finally that afternoon to the restaurant owner. The restaurant owner couldn't really have wanted the boy anyway, since the position was for his wife's side of the house.

The jessing itself happened rather quickly, at the first dealer's. There was a package with foreign writing on it, from the north across the sea, so even the letters were strange and unreadable. He made me lean my head back and open my mouth, and he sprayed the roof of my mouth with an anesthetic. Then he opened the package and took out the tool to do the jessing. Watching him, I had leaned my head forward a bit and closed my mouth. "Lean back," he said. I leaned back again and looked at the ceiling. The roof of my mouth felt thick, as if I had drunk something that scalded it, except of course that it didn't hurt. I felt the pressure of something pressed against the roof of my mouth and there was a sound like a *phffft*.

I was more afraid when he'd done it than I'd been before. It was done. I couldn't back out. The jessing process was happening somewhere in my brain and I was changing. Jessing is supposed to enhance natural loyalties, but right then I wasn't feeling loyal to much of anything—even my mother's voice was raw on my nerves. Scared! I was so scared I could feel the sweat under my arms.

I wasn't really sold, of course. It's just that the medicine they use to do the jessing is made in the E.C.U., not here in Morocco. It's black-market and costs. The dealer has to get paid a lot, and that money goes against the bond that I owe to my owner. Not really owe, it's more money than I'll ever make unless maybe I save everything, never buy as much as a pair of earrings, and work for fifty years. And besides, when you're jessed, you're not supposed to want to leave. You're supposed to be trustworthy.

Sitting with the gap-toothed boy at the second dealer's, I still didn't feel loyal. I felt irritable and annoyed and nervous. I had expected never to feel that way again. I had expected my loyalty would be absolute, like the loyalty of a soldier, or a saint.

When Mbarek-salah came and hired me, I still didn't feel anything, not even when the dealer pronounced the trigger words. I didn't know at the time that the actual jessing process takes weeks, sometimes even months. I never felt like a soldier, though. I learned the sad fact that I couldn't give my life away, that anywhere I went, there I was. If a girl asked me tomorrow if she should be jessed, I don't know what I'd say. It's not a bad life. It's better than being an old maid in the Nekropolis, the part of the old city where I grew up. I'd have to ask her: What are you leaving?

I have been with my present owner since I was twenty-one. I'm twenty-six now. I was a good student, I got good marks in math and literature, so I was bonded to oversee cleaning and supplies. That's better than if I were a pretty girl and had to rely on looks. Then I would be used up in a few years.

I like my owner, like my work. But now I'd like to go to him and ask him to sell me.

"Hariba," he'd say, taking my hand in his fatherly way, "Aren't you happy here?"

"Mbarek-salah," I'd answer, my eyes demurely on my toes. "You are like a father and I have been only too happy with you." Which is true even beyond being jessed, praise God. I don't think I'd mind being part of Mbarek's household, even if I were unbound. Mostly Mbarek pays no attention to me, which is how I prefer things. I like my work and my room.

It would all be fine if it weren't for the new one.

I have no problems with AI. I don't mind the cleaning machine, poor thing, and as head of the women's household, I work with the household intelligence all the time. I may have had a simple, rather conservative upbringing, but I've come to be pretty comfortable with AI. The Holy Injunction doesn't mean that all AI is abomination. But AI should not be biologically constructed. AI should not be made in the image of humanity.

It's the mistress's *harni*. It's a very expensive, very pretty toy, the kind of thing that the mistress likes. It cost more, far more than my bond. For what it costs my widowed mother could stop selling funeral wreaths and live comfortably in her old age.

It comes over to our side sometimes—the master says that since it isn't human, it's allowed. There is no impropriety— it's never alone with the mistress. In fact, now, after having it a couple of months, she pretty much ignores it, which would be virtuous if she did it out of any sense of morality, but the truth is it's like a lot of other things; her little lion dog with the overbite—nasty little thing that Fadina, her body servant, had to feed and bathe until they got rid of it—the house in the country that they bought and only used twice and then sold. She got bored with it.

It thinks of itself. It has a name. It has gender.

It thinks it's male. And it's head of the men's side of the house. It thinks we should work together.

It looks human male and has curly black hair and soft honey-colored skin. It flirts, looking at me sideways out of black vulnerable eyes. Smiling at me with a smile that isn't in the slightest bit vulnerable. "Come on, Hariba," it says, "we work together. We should be friends. We're both young, we can help each other in our work."

I don't bother to answer.

It smiles wickedly. (Although I know it isn't wicked, it's just something grown and programmed. Soulless. I'm not so con- servative that I condemn cloning, but it's not a clone. It is a bio- logical construct. I've never seen one before, they're expensive and rare.) "Hariba," it says, "I think you are too pure. A Holy Sister."

"Don't sound foolish," I say.

"You need someone to tease you," it says, "you're very solemn. Tell me, is it because you're jessed?"

I don't know how much it knows. Does it understand the process of jessing? "The Second Koran says that just as a jessed hawk is tamed, not tied, so shall the servant be bound by affection and duty, not chains, with God's blessing."

"Does the Second Koran say it shouldn't make you sad, Hariba?"

Can something not human blaspheme?

In the morning Mbarek calls me into his office. He offers me tea, fragrant of mint, which I sip. He pages through my morning report, nodding, making pleased noises, occasionally slurping his tea. Afternoons and evenings Mbarek's at his restaurant. I've never been in it, but I understand it's an exceptional place.

"What will you do this afternoon?" he asks.

It's my afternoon free. "My childhood friend Ayesha and I will go shopping, Mbarek-salah."

"Ah," he says, smiling. "Spend a little extra silver," he says. "Buy yourself earrings or something. I'll see the credit is available." He's a good man. He never holds that money against my bond. A generous man is a wealthy man, as it says in the Second Koran.

I murmur my thanks. He makes a show of paging through the report, and the sheets of paper whisper against each other.

"And what do you think of Akhmim, the *harni*? Is he working out?"

"I don't spend much time with it, Mbarek-salah. Its work is with the men's household."

"You're an old-fashioned girl, Hariba, that's good." Mbarek-salah holds the report a little farther away, striking a very dignified pose in his reading. "*Harni* have social training, but no practice. The merchant recommended to me that I send it out to talk and meet with people as much as possible. I would like you to help me with this, daughter."

I wriggle my toes. He has stopped referring to it as if it were a person, which is good, but now he's going to try to send it with me. "I must meet my friend Ayesha at her home in the Nekropolis, Mbarek-salah. My mother lives across the street. Perhaps it's not a good place to take a *harni*." The Nekropolis is a conservative place. A lot of the people who live there are poor people who have left farms and small towns to come to the city.

Mbarek-salah waves his hand airily. "Everything is in order, Hariba," he says, referring to the reports in front of him. "My wife has asked that you use a little more scent with the linens."

His wife thinks I am too cheap. Mbarek-salah likes to think that he runs a frugal household. He does not; money hemorrhages from this house, silver pours from the walls and runs down the street into the pockets of everyone in this city.

I hope Mbarek will forget about the *harni,* but he doesn't. There's no respite. I must take it with me.

It's waiting for me after lunch. I'm wearing lavender and pale yellow, with long yellow ribbons tied around my wrists, and I cover my hair with a lavender veil.

"Jessed, Hariba," it says. "You wouldn't have me along if you weren't."

Of course I'm jessed. I always wear ribbons when I go out. "The Second Koran says ribbons are a symbol of devotion to the Most Holy, as well as an earthly master."

It runs its long fingers through its curly hair, shakes its head, and its golden earring dances. Artifice, the pretense of humanity, although I guess even a *harni*'s hair gets in its eyes. "Why would you choose to be jessed?" it asks.

"You wouldn't understand," I say. "Come along."

It never takes offense, never worries about offending. "Can you tell the difference between the compulsion and your own feelings?" it asks. Jessing changes the unruly brain, makes us feel the loyalty that we should. If I've chosen to have myself changed to feel loyalty, then it isn't really compulsion. And it makes service easier, if it's something my brain wants me to do.

"Jessing only heightens my natural tendencies, and makes a servant as trustworthy as kin, praise God," I say.

"Then why are you sad?" it asks.

"I am not sad!" I snap.

"I'm sorry," it says immediately. Blessedly, it's silent while we go down to the train. I point which direction we're going and it nods and follows. I get a seat on the train and it stands in front of me. It glances down at me. Smiles. I fancy it looks as if it feels pity for me. (Artifice. Does the cleaning machine feel sorry for anyone? Even itself? Does the household intelligence? The body chemistry of a *harni* may be based on humanity, but it's carefully calculated.)

It wears a white shirt and its skin is smooth. I look at the floor.

The train lets us off at the edge of the Nekropolis, and we climb the steps from the underground platform, past the unfortunate poor who live in the tunnels. I toss a coin onto a woman's skirt. We come up on the big plaza outside the Moussin of the White Falcon. Mourners in white stand outside the Moussin and I can faintly smell the incense on the hot air. The sun is blinding after the cool dark train and the white Moussin and the mourners' robes are painful to look at. They're talking and laughing. Often, mourners haven't seen each other for years if a family is spread all across the country. The Moussin of the White Falcon is especially large, and services go on all the time. It's because it's on the edge of the Nekropolis. The Nekropolis was a cemetery long before it was a place to live, and the first people who lived there were beggars, hiding in the tombs.

I look quickly, but I don't see my mother. If my mother sees me with the *harni*, she'll be upset. She is a poor woman, and she doesn't like AI, and it would worry her that I had to live in a household with something like the *harni*. I hurry through the cemetery gate into the Nekropolis. I hope she's not home, since Ayesha lives across the street.

The *harni* looks around, as curious as a child or a jackdaw.

I grew up inside the Nekropolis. We didn't have running water. It was delivered every day in a big lorritank and people would go out and buy it by the liter, and we lived in three adjoining mausoleums instead of a flat, but other than that, it was a pretty normal childhood. I have a sister and two brothers. My mother sells paper funeral decorations. The Nekropolis is a very good place for her to live. No long train rides every day from the countryside. The part we lived in was old. Next to my bed were the dates for the person buried behind the wall, 2073 to 2144. All of the family was dead years ago. No one ever came to this death house to lay paper flowers and birds.

Our house always smelled of cinnamon and the perfume my mother used on her paper flowers and birds. In the middle death house there were funeral arrangements everywhere and when we ate we would clear a space on the floor and sit, surrounded. When I was a little girl, I learned the different uses of papers: how my mother used translucent tissue for carnations, stiff satiny brittle paper for roses, and strong paper with a grain like linen for arrogant falcons. As children we all smelled of perfume, and when I stayed the night with my friend Ayesha, she would wrap her arms around my waist and whisper in my neck, "You smell good."

I'm not waiting for the *harni*. It has to follow, it has no credit for the train ride. If it isn't paying attention and gets lost, it can walk home.

When I glance back a block and a half later, it's following me, its long curly hair wild about its shoulders, its face turned artlessly toward the sun. Does it enjoy the feeling of sunlight on skin? Probably, that's a basic biological pleasure. It must enjoy things like eating.

Ayesha comes out, running on light feet. "Hariba!" she calls. She still lives across from my mother, but now she has a husband and a pretty four-year-old daughter, a chubby child with clear skin the color of amber and black hair. Tariam, the little girl, stands clinging to the doorway, her thumb in her mouth. Ayesha grabs my wrists and her bracelets jingle. "Come out of the heat!" She glances past me and says, "Who's this?"

The *harni* stands there, one hand on his hip, smiling.

Ayesha drops my wrists and pulls a little at her rose-colored veil. She's startled, thinking of course that I've brought a handsome young man with me. Only a rich man can keep separate households for himself and his wife, but Ayesha is a modest person who wouldn't go around unescorted with a young man who wasn't her husband.

"It's a *harni*," I say and laugh, shrill and nervous. "Mbarek-salah asked me to bring him."

"A *harni*?" she asks, her voice doubtful.

I wave my hand. "You know the mistress, always wanting toys. He's in charge of the men's household." "He" I say. I meant "it." "It's in charge." But I don't correct myself, not wanting to call attention to my error.

"I'm Akhmim," it says smoothly. "You're a friend of Hariba's?"

I look across the street, but the door to my mother's house is shut. She must not be home. Praise God. My little brother Nabil is never home in the day.

Here I am, standing on the street in front of my mother's house, and the *harni* is pretending to be a man. It has no respect for my reputation.

"Ayesha," I say, "let's go."

She looks at the *harni* a moment more, then goes back to her little girl, picks her up, and carries her inside. Normally I'd go inside with her, sit, and talk with her mother, Ena. I'd hold Tariam on my lap and wish I had a little girl with perfect tiny fingernails and such a clean, sweet milk smell. It'd be cool and dark inside and we'd eat pistachios and drink tea. Then I'd go across the street to see my mother and youngest brother, Nabil, who's the only one who lives at home now.

The *harni* stands in the street, away from me, looking at the ground. It seems uncomfortable. It doesn't look at me; at least it has the decency to make it appear we aren't together.

Ayesha comes out, bracelets ringing. While we shop in the souk, she doesn't refer to the *harni*, but as it follows us, she glances back a lot. I glance back and it flashes a white smile. It seems perfectly content to trail along, looking at the souk stalls with their red canopies like married women's veils.

"Maybe we should let him walk with us," Ayesha says as she stops at a jewelry stall. "It seems rude to ignore him."

I laugh, full of nervousness. "It's not human."

"Does it have feelings?" Ayesha asks.

I shrug. "After a fashion. It's AI."

"It doesn't look like a machine," she says.

"It's not a machine," I say, irritated with her.

"How can it be AI if it isn't a machine?" she presses.

"Because it's manufactured. A technician's creation. An artificial combination of genes, grown somewhere."

"Human genes?"

"Probably," I say. "Maybe some animal genes. Maybe some that they made up themselves, how would I know?" It's ruining my afternoon. "I wish it would offer to go home."

"Maybe he can't," Ayesha says. "If Mbarek-salah told him to come, he'd have to, wouldn't he?"

I don't really know anything about *harni*.

"It doesn't seem fair," Ayesha says. "*Harni*," she calls, "come here."

He tilts his head, all alert. "Yes, mistress?"

"Are *harni* prescripted for taste?" she inquires.

"What do you mean, the taste of food?" he asks. "I can taste just like you do, although"—he smiles—"I personally am not overly fond of cherries."

"No, no," Ayesha says. "Colors, clothing. Are you capable of helping make choices? About earrings, for example?"

He comes to look at the jewelry, and selects a pair of gold and rose enamel teardrops and holds them up for her. "I think my taste is no better than the average person's," he says, "but I like these."

She frowns, looks at him through her lashes. She's got me thinking of it as "him." And she's flirting with him! Ayesha! A married woman!

"What do you think, Hariba?" she asks. She takes the earrings, holds one beside her face. "They're pretty."

"I think they're gaudy."

She's hurt. Honestly, they suit her.

She frowns at me. "I'll take them," she says. The stallman names a price.

"No, no, no," says the *harni*, "you shouldn't buy them. This man's a thief." He reaches to touch her, as if he'd pull her away, and I hold my breath in shock—if the thing should touch her!

But the stallman interrupts with a lower price. The *harni* bargains. He's a good bargainer, but he should be, he has no compassion, no concern for the stallkeeper. Charity is a human virtue. The Second Koran says, "A human in need becomes every man's child."

Interminable, this bargaining, but finally the earrings are Ayesha's. "We should stop and have some tea," she says.

"I have a headache," I say. "I think I should go home."

"If Hariba's ill, we should go," the *harni* says.

Ayesha looks at me, looks away, guilty. She should feel guilt.

I come down the hall to access the household AI and the *harni*'s there. Apparently busy, but waiting for me. "I'll be finished in a minute and out of your way," it says. Beautiful fingers, wrist bones, beautiful face, and dark curling hair show-ing just where its shirt closes; it's elegantly constructed. Lean and long-legged, like a hound. When the technician con-structed it, did he know how it would look when it was grown? Are they designed with aesthetics in mind?

It takes the report and steps aside, but doesn't go on with its work. I ignore it, doing my work as if it weren't there, standing so it's behind me.

"Why don't you like me?" it finally asks.

I consider my answers. I could say it's a thing, not some-thing to like or dislike, but that isn't true. I like my bed, my things. "Because of your arrogance," I say to the system.

A startled hiss of indrawn breath. "My . . . arrogance?" it asks.

"Your presumption." It's hard to keep my voice steady. Every time I'm around the *harni,* I find myself hating the way I speak.

"I . . . I am sorry, Hariba," it whispers. "I have little experi-ence. I didn't realize I'd insulted you."

It sounds sad. I'm tempted to turn around and look at it, but I don't. It doesn't really feel pain, I remind myself. It's a thing, it has no more feelings than a fish. Less.

"Please, tell me what I've done?"

"Your behavior. This conversation, here," I say. "You're al-ways trying to make people think you're human."

Silence. Is it considering? Or would it be more accurate to say processing?

"You blame me for being what I am," the *harni* says. It sighs. "I can't help being what I am."

I wait for it to say more, but it doesn't. I turn around, but it's gone.

*   *   *

After that, every time it sees me, it makes some excuse to avoid me if it can. I don't know if I'm grateful or not. I'm very uncomfortable.

My tasks aren't complicated. I see to the cleaning machine and set it loose in the women's household when it won't inconvenience the mistress. I'm jessed to Mbarek, although I serve the mistress. I'm glad I'm not jessed to her; Fadina is and she has to put up with a great deal. I'm careful never to blame the mistress in front of Fadina. She knows that the mistress is unreasonable, but of course, emotionally she is bound to affection and duty.

On Friday mornings the mistress is usually in her rooms, preparing for her Sunday *bismek*. On Friday afternoons she goes out to play the Tiles with her friends and gossip about husbands and the wives who aren't there. I clean on Friday afternoons. I call the cleaning machine and it follows me down the hallway like a dog, snuffling along the baseboards for dust.

I open the door and smell attar of roses. The room is different from the way it usually looks. Today there's a white marble floor veined with gold and amethyst, covered with purple rugs. There are braziers, low couches, and huge open windows looking out on a pillared walkway, like some sheik's palace, and beyond that vistas go down to a lavender sea. It's the mistress's current *bismek* setting. A young man is reading a letter on the walkway, a girl stands behind him, her face is tear-stained.

Interactive fantasies. The characters are generated from lists of traits, they're projections controlled by whoever is game-mistress of the *bismek* and fleshed out by the household AI.

Everyone else comes over and becomes characters in the setting. There are poisonings and love affairs. The mistress's setting is in ancient times and seems to be quite popular. Some of her friends have two or three identities in the game.

Before this game, the *bismek* settings all came from her foreign soap operas—women who were as bold as men, and improbable clothing and kissing and immoral technology. The characters all had augmentation, which is forbidden, of course. There was technology everywhere, and people talking to each other through AI interfaces. It was fascinating, but I hated it. I hated living with the temptation, I hated the shallowness of it all. No one in those stories ever had to make a real decision about their lives, and they all had jobs creating simulations and beautiful clothes or were personalities in some sort of interface.

She usually turns it off when she goes out. The little cleaning machine stops in the doorway. It can read the difference between reality and the projection, but she has ordered it never to enter the projection because she says the sight of the thing snuffling through walls damages her sense of the alternate reality. I reach behind the screen and turn the projection off so I can clean. The scene disappears and all that's left is the mistress's rooms and their bare white walls—something no one ever sees except me. "Go ahead," I tell the machine and start for the mistress's room to pick up things for the laundry.

To my horror, the mistress steps out of her bedroom. Her hair is loose and long and disheveled and she is dressed in a day robe, obviously not intending to go out. She sees me in the hall and her face darkens, her beautiful, heavy eyebrows folding toward her nose, and I instinctively start to back up.

"Oh, mistress," I say, "I'm sorry, I didn't know you were in, I'm sorry, let me get the cleaning machine and leave, I'll just be out of here in a moment, I thought you had gone out to play the Tiles, I should have checked with Fadina, it is my fault, mistress—"

"Did you turn them off?" she demands. "You stupid girl. *Did you turn Zarin and Nisea off?*"

I nod mutely.

"O Holy One," she says. "Ugly, incompetent girl! Are you completely lacking in sense? Did you think they would be there and I wouldn't be here? It's difficult enough to prepare without interference!"

"I'll turn it back on," I say.

"Don't touch anything!" she shrieks. "FADINA!" Fadina is always explaining to me how difficult it is for the mistress to think up new scenarios for her friends' participation.

I keep backing up, hissing at the cleaning machine, while the mistress follows me down the hall, shrieking, "FADINA!" and because I'm watching the mistress, I back into Fadina coming in the door.

"Didn't you tell Hariba that I'd be in this afternoon?" the mistress says.

"Of course," Fadina says.

I'm aghast. "You did not!" I say.

"I did, too," Fadina says. "You were at the access. I distinctly told you and you said you would clean later."

I start to defend myself and the mistress slaps me in the face. "Enough of you, girl," she says. And then the mistress makes me stand there and berates me, reaching out now and then to grab my hair and yank it painfully because of course she believes Fadina when the girl is clearly lying to avoid punishment. I cannot believe that Fadina has done this to me; she is in terror of offending the mistress, but she has always been a good girl, and I'm innocent. My cheek stings, and my head aches from having my hair yanked, but, worse, I'm angry and very, very humiliated.

Finally we are allowed to leave. I know I should give Fadina a piece of my mind, but I just want to escape. Out in the hall, Fadina grabs me so hard that her nails bite into the soft part under my arm. "I told you she was in an absolute frenzy about Saturday," she whispers. "I can't believe you did that! And now she'll be in a terrible mood all evening and I'm the one who will suffer for it!"

"Fadina," I protest.

"Don't you 'Fadina' me, Hariba! If I don't get a slap out of this, it will be the intervention of the Holy One!"

I have already gotten a slap, and it wasn't even my fault. I pull my arm away from Fadina and try to walk down the hall without losing my dignity, the cleaning machine snuffling behind. My face is hot and I'm about to cry. Everything blurs in tears. I duck into the linens and sit down on the hamper. I want to leave this place, I don't want to work for that old woman. I realize that my only friend in the world is Ayesha and now we are far apart and I feel hurt and lonely and I just sob.

The door to the linens opens and I turn my back, thinking, Go away, whoever you are.

"Oh, excuse me," the *harni* says.

At least *it* will go away. But the thought that the only thing around is the *harni* makes me feel even lonelier. I cannot stop myself from sobbing.

"Hariba," it says hesitantly, "are you all right?"

I can't answer. I want it to go away, and I don't.

After a moment, it says from right behind me, "Hariba, are you ill?"

I shake my head.

I can feel it standing there, perplexed, but I don't know what to do and I can't stop crying and I feel foolish. I want my mother. Not that she would do anything other than remind me that the world is not fair. My mother believes in facing reality. "Be strong," she always says. And that makes me cry harder.

After a minute, I hear the *harni* leave and, awash in self-pity, I even cry over that. My feelings of foolishness are beginning to outweigh my feelings of unhappiness, but perversely enough I realize that I'm enjoying my cry. That it has been inside me, building stronger and stronger, and I didn't even know it.

Then someone comes in again and I straighten my back again and pretend to be checking towels. The only person it could be is Fadina.

But it's the *harni*, with a box of tissues. He crouches beside me, his face full of concern. "Here," he says.

Embarrassed, I take one. If you didn't know, you would think he was a regular human. He even smells of clean man-scent. Like my brothers. I don't really have to dislike *him*. He didn't pick what he is.

I blow my nose, wondering if *harni* ever cry. "Thank you," I say. I can't not say, "Thank you."

"I was afraid you were ill," he says.

I shake my head. "No, I'm just angry."

"You cry when you are angry?" he asks.

"The mistress is upset at me and it's Fadina's fault, but I

had to take the blame." That makes me start to cry again, but the *harni* is patient and he just crouches next to me in among the linens, holding the box of tissues. By the time I collect myself, there is a little crumpled pile of tissues and some have tumbled to the floor. I take two tissues and start folding them into a flower, like my mother makes.

"Why are you nice to me when I'm mean to you?" I ask.

He shrugs. "Because you don't want to be mean to me," he says. "It makes you suffer. I'm sorry that I make you uncomfortable."

"But you can't help being what you are," I say. My eyes are probably red. *Harni* never cry, I'm certain. They are too perfect. I keep my eyes on the flower.

"Neither can you," he says. "When Mbarek-salah made you take me with you on your day off, you weren't even free to be angry with him. I knew that was why you were angry with me." He has eyes like my brother Fhassin (who had long eyelashes like a girl, just like the *harni*).

Thinking about Mbarek-salah makes my head ache a little and I think of something else. I remember and cover my mouth in horror. "Oh no."

"What is it?" he asks.

"I think . . . I think Fadina did tell me that the mistress would be in, but I was . . . was thinking of something else and I didn't pay attention." I was standing at the access, wondering if the *harni* was around, since that was where I was most likely to run into him.

"It is natural enough," he says, unnatural thing that he is. "If Fadina weren't jessed, she would probably be more understanding."

He's prescripted to be kind, I remind myself. I should not

ascribe human motives to an AI. But I've been mean to him and he is the only one in the whole household sitting here among the linens with a box of tissues. I fluff out the folds of the flower and put it among the linens. A white tissue flower, a funeral flower.

"Thank you . . . Akhmim." It is hard to say his name.

He smiles. "Don't be sad, Hariba."

I'm careful and avoid the eye of the mistress as much as I can. Fadina is civil to me, but not friendly. She says hello to me, politely, and goes on with whatever she is doing.

It is Akhmim, the *harni*, who stops me one evening and says, "The mistress wants us for *bismek* tomorrow." It's not the first time I've been asked to stand in, but usually it's Fadina who lets me know and tells me what I'm supposed to do.

Anymore I try to be kind to Akhmim. He's easy to talk to, and, like me, he's alone in the household.

"What are we supposed to be?" I ask.

The *harni* flicks his long fingers dismissively, "Servants, of course. What's it like?" He hasn't been here that long, so this is the first time he's been asked to participate.

"*Bismek?*" I shrug. "Playacting."

"Like children's games?" he asks, looking doubtful.

"Well, yes and no. The mistress's *bismek* been going on a couple of years now and there are hundreds of characters," I say. "The ladies all have roles, and you have to remember to call them by their character names and not their real names, and you have to pretend it's all real. All sorts of things happen; people get in trouble, and they all figure out elaborate plots to get out of trouble and people get strange illnesses and everybody professes their undying affection. The mistress threw her best friend in prison for a while. Fadina said that was very popular."

He looks at me for a moment, blinking his long eyelashes. "You're making fun of me, Hariba," he says, doubtful.

"No," I say, laughing, "it's true." It is, too. "Akhmim, no one is ever really hurt or uncomfortable."

I think he can't decide whether to believe me or not.

Saturday afternoon I'm dressed in a pagan-looking robe that leaves one shoulder bare. And makes me look ridiculous, I might add. I'm probably a server. Projections are prettier than real people, but they can't very well hand out real food.

I arrive early at the mistress's quarters. The scent of some heavy, almost bitter incense is overwhelming. The cook is laying out real food, using our own service, but the table is too tall to sit at on the floor—more like a European table—and there are candles and brass bowls of dates to make it look antique. Without the projection the elaborate table looks odd, since the room is empty of furniture. Akhmim is helping, bringing in lounging chairs so the guests can recline at the table. He's dressed in a white robe that comes to his knees and brown sandals that have elaborate crisscross ties, and, like me, his shoulder is bare. Unlike me, the *harni* looks graceful. He glances up at me and smiles and I'm embarrassed to be seen by a man with my shoulder and neck bare. Remember, I think, Akhmim is what he is; he's not really a man or he wouldn't be here.

"Hariba," Akhmim says, "Fadina says that the mistress is in a terrible mood."

"She's always in a terrible mood when she's nervous," I say.

"I'm nervous."

"Akhmim," I say, laughing, "don't worry!"

"I don't understand any of this playing pretend," he wails softly.

I take his hand and squeeze it. If he were a man, I wouldn't touch him. I've never touched him before. His hand is warm and human. "You'll do fine. We don't have to do much anyway, just serve dinner. You can manage that, probably better than I can."

He bites his lower lip, and I'm suddenly reminded of my brother Fhassin—I could almost cry. But I just squeeze his hand again. I'm nervous, too, but not about serving dinner. I have avoided the mistress since the incident with the cleaning machine.

Fadina comes in and turns on the projection, and suddenly the white marble room glows around us, full of servants and musicians tuning up. I feel better, able to hide in the crowd. Akhmim glances around. "It *is* exciting," he says thoughtfully.

There are five guests. Fadina greets them at the door and takes them back to the wardrobe to change. Five middle-aged women, all come to pretend. I tell Akhmim their character names as they come in so he knows what to call them.

The musicians start playing; projected characters, women and men, recline on projected couches. I know some of their names. Of course, they have projected servers and projected food. I wish I knew what the scenario was. Usually Fadina tells me ahead of time, but she doesn't talk much to me these days. Pretty soon the mistress comes in and the real guests all find the real couches where they can talk to each other. First is bread and cheese, already on the table, and Akhmim has to pour wine—not real wine, of course—but I can just stand there, next to a projected servant, thank God. Even this close, she seems real, exotic with her pale hair. I ask her what her name is and she whispers, "Miri." Fadina is standing next to the mistress's couch, she glares at me. I'm not supposed to make the household AI do extra work.

The first part of the meal is boring. The mistress's friends get up once in a while to whisper to each other or a projection, and projections do the same thing. There's some sort of intrigue going on, people look very tense and excited. Akhmim and I glance at each other and he smiles. While I'm serving, I whisper to him, "Not so bad, is it?"

The two lovers I turned off are at this dinner; I guess they are important characters right now. The girl is apparently supposed to be the daughter of one of the mistress's friends.

Almost two hours into the dinner—after a course of clear soup, then a luncheon of lamb in pastry with pistachios that smells so good my stomach rumbles, and finally an orange sorbet—the girl says loudly to her lover, "I can't stand this anymore! You have to choose!" All the projections look over— of course the *bismek* ladies have been watching the two lovers all through the meal.

"What are you talking about?" the boy says, although he looks guilty—it's obvious he knows.

"Don't you pretend!" the girl says.

"Nisea," he says, "you are making a scene."

"No, I'm not," she says, and stands up. "I'm going home." But she sways, beautiful in her long gown, and then her eyes roll back in her head and she falls to the marble floor, thrashing, her heels beating against it. The projected characters rush to the girl. The one of the mistress's friends who is the "mother" of the girl behaves with theatrical dignity in the circle of real women—since she can't really touch the girl. The male lover is hysterical, kneeling and sobbing. It makes me uncomfortable, both the seizures and the reactions. I look for Akhmim. He is standing against the wall, holding a pitcher of wine, observing. He looks delighted. The girl's lover reaches the table and picks up her wineglass while everybody else watches him. Only an idiot would fail to realize that it's supposed to be important. The "mother" shrieks suddenly, "Stop him! It's poison!" and there is more agitated activity but they are too late. The lover drinks down the wine. The "mother" is "held back" by her friends.

I'm embarrassed by the way these women play with feelings. I look over at Akhmim, but he is just watching. I wonder, what does he think?

There's a call for a physician, projections rush around. There is a long, drawn-out death scene for the girl, followed by an equally long death for the lover. The women are openly sobbing, even Fadina. I clasp my hands together, squeeze them, look at the floor. I glance up and everyone is clustered around the lovers' bodies, both unnaturally beautiful in death. Finally everything is played out and the projected characters shut off. They sit around the "dining room" and discuss the scenario and how masterful it was. The mistress looks drained but pleased. One by one the women pad back to the wardrobe and change, then let themselves out until only the mistress and the "mother" are left.

"It was wonderful," she keeps telling the mistress.

"As good as when Hekmet was ill?" the mistress asks.

"Oh yes. It was wonderful!" Finally they go back to change, Fadina following to help, and Akhmim and I can clear the dishes off the table.

"So what did you think?" I ask. "Was it what you expected?"

Akhmim shrugs. "I didn't know what to expect."

I stack plates and dump them on a tray. Akhmim boosts the tray, balancing it at his shoulder like a waiter. He's really much stronger than he looks. "You don't like it," he says finally.

I shake my head.

"Why not? Because it's not real?"

"All this violence," I say. Nobody would want to live this way. Nobody would want these things to happen to them." I'm collecting wineglasses, colored transparent blue and rose like soap bubbles.

He stands looking at me, observing me the way he did the women, I think. What do we look like to *harni*? He's beautiful, the tray balanced effortlessly, the muscles of his bare arm and shoulder visible. He looks enough like an infidel in his white robe, with his perfect, timeless face. Even his long curly hair seems right.

I try to explain. "They entertain themselves with suffering."

"They're only projections," he says.

"But they seem real. The whole point is to forget they're projections, isn't it?" The glasses ring against each other as I collect them.

Softly he says, "They are bored women. What else do they have in their lives?"

I want him to understand how I'm different. "You can't tell me it doesn't affect the way they see people. Look at the way the mistress treats Fadina!" Akhmim tries to interrupt me, but I want to finish what I'm saying. "She wants excitement, even if it means watching death. Watching a seizure, that's not entertaining, not unless there's something wrong. It's decadent, what they do, it's . . . it's sinful! Death isn't entertainment."

"Hariba!" he says.

Then the mistress grabs my hair and yanks me around and all the glasses in my arms fall to the floor and shatter.

Sweet childhood. Adulthood is salty. Not that it's not rewarding, mind you, just different. The rewards of childhood are joy and pleasure, but the reward of adulthood is strength.

I'm punished, but it is light punishment, praise God. The mistress beats me. She doesn't really hurt me much. It's noisy and frightening, and I cut my knee where I kneel in broken glass, but it's nothing serious. I'm locked in my room and only allowed punishment food: bread, mint tea, and a little soup. But I can have all the paper I want, and I fill my rooms with flowers. White paper roses, ice-pale irises with petals curling down to reveal their centers, snowy calla lilies like trumpets, and poppies and tulips of luscious paper with nap like velvet. My walls are white and the world is white, filled with white flowers.

"How about daisies?" Akhmim asks. He comes to bring me my food and my paper.

"Too innocent," I say. "Daisies are only for children."

Fadina recommended to the mistress that Akhmim be my jailer. She thinks that I hate to have him near me, but I couldn't have asked for better company than the *harni*. He's never impatient, never comes to me asking for attention for his own problems. He wants to learn how to make flowers. I try to teach him, but he can't learn to do anything but awkwardly copy my model. "You make them out of your own head," he says. His clever fingers stumble and crease the paper or turn it.

"My mother makes birds, too," I say.

"Can you make birds?" he asks.

I don't want to make birds, just flowers.

I think about the Nekropolis. Akhmim is doing his duties and mine, too. He's busy during the day and mostly I'm alone. When I'm not making flowers, I sit and look out my window, watching the street, or I sleep. It is probably because I'm not getting much to eat, but I can sleep for hours. A week passes, then two. Sometimes I feel as if I've got to get out of this room, but then I ask myself where I'd want to go and I realize that it doesn't make any difference. This room, the outside, they're all the same place, except that this room is safe.

If there's anyplace I want to go, it is the Nekropolis. Not the real one, the one in my mind, but it's gone. I was the eldest, then my sister, Rashida, then my brother Fhassin, and then the baby boy, Nabil. In families of four, underneath the fighting, there's always pairing, two and two. Fhassin and I were a pair. My brother. I think a lot about Fhassin and about the Nekropolis, locked in my room.

I sleep, eat my little breakfast that Akhmim brings me, sleep again. Then I sit at the window or make flowers, sleep again. The only bad time is late afternoon to early evening, when I've slept so much that I can't sleep anymore and my stomach is growling. I'm fretful and teary. When Akhmim comes in the evening with dinner, he bruises my senses until I get accustomed to his being there. His voice has many shades, his skin is much more supple, much more oiled, and textured than paper. He overwhelms me.

Sometimes he sits with his arm around my shoulders and I lean against him. I pretend intimacy doesn't matter because he is only a *harni*, but I know that I'm lying to myself. How could I ever have thought him safe because he was made rather than born? I understood from the first that he wasn't to be trusted, but actually it was me who couldn't be trusted.

He's curious about my childhood. To keep him close to me, I tell him everything I can remember about growing up, all the children's games, teach him the songs we skipped rope to, the rhymes we used to pick who was it, everybody with their fists in the center, tapping a fist on every stress as we chanted:

ONCE my SIS-ter HAD a HOUSE,
THEN she LEFT it TO a MOUSE,
SING a SONG,
TELL a LIE,
KISS my SIS-ter,
SAY good-BYE.

"What does it mean?" he asks, laughing.

"It doesn't mean anything," I explain, "it's a way of picking who's it. Who's the fox, or who holds the broom while everybody hides." I tell him about fox and hounds, about how my brother Fhassin was a daredevil and one time to get away he climbed to the roof of Ayesha's grandmother's house and ran along the roofs and how our mother punished him. And of how we got in a fight and I pushed him and he fell and broke his collarbone.

"What does Ayesha do?" he asks.

"Ayesha is married," I say. "Her husband works. He directs lorritanks, like the one that delivers water."

"Did you ever have a boyfriend?" he asks.

"I did, his name was Aziz."

"Why didn't you marry?" he asks. He's so innocent.

"It didn't work," I say.

"Is that why you became jessed?"

"No," I say.

He's patient, he waits.

"No," I say again. "It was because of Nouzha."

Then I have to explain.

Nouzha moved into the death house across the street, where Ayesha's grandfather had lived until he died. Ayesha's grandfather had been a soldier when he was young and to be brave for the Holy he had a Serinitin implant, before they knew they damaged people's brains. When he was old, he didn't remember who he was anymore. When he died, Nouzha and her husband moved in. Nouzha had white hair and had had her ears pointed and she wanted a baby. I was only twenty, and trying to decide whether I should marry Aziz. He had not asked me, but I thought he might, and I wasn't sure what I should answer. Nouzha was younger than me, nineteen, but she wanted a baby and that seemed terribly adult. And she had come from outside the Nekropolis, and had pointed ears, and everybody thought she was just a little too good for herself and maybe a little shameless.

We talked about Aziz and she told me that after marriage everything was not milk and honey. She was very vague on just what she meant by that, but I should know that it was not like it seemed now, when I was in love with Aziz. I should give myself over to him, but I should hold some part of myself private, for myself, and not let marriage swallow me.

Now I realize that she was a young bride trying to learn the difference between romance and life, and the conversations seem obvious and adolescent, but then it seemed adult to talk about marriage this way. It was like something sacred, and I was being initiated into mysteries. I dyed my hair white.

My sister, Rashida, hated her. Nabil made eyes at her all the time, but he was only thirteen. Fhassin was seventeen and he laughed at Nabil. Fhassin laughed at all sorts of things. He looked at the world from under his long eyelashes, girlish in his hard sharp-chinned face with his monkey grin. That was the year Fhassin, who had always been shorter than everybody, grew tall. He was visited by giggling girls, but he never took any of them seriously.

But Nouzha and Aziz and everything on our street really was outside, not inside the family where everything mattered. In the evenings we sat on the floor in the middle of our three death houses and made paper flowers. We lived in a house filled with perfume. I was twenty, Rashida was nineteen. Nobody had left my mother's house, and we never thought that was strange. But it was, the way we were held there.

So when did Fhassin stop seeing her as silly and begin to see Nouzha as a person? I didn't suspect it. The giggling girls still came by the house, and Fhassin still grinned and didn't really pay much attention. He and Nouzha were careful, meeting in the afternoon when her husband was building houses outside the Nekropolis in the city and the rest of us were sleeping.

I think Fhassin did it because he was always a daredevil, like walking on the roofs of the death houses, or the time when he was ten that he took money out of our mother's money pot so he could sneak out and ride the train. He was lost in the city for hours, finally sneaking back onto the train and risking getting caught as a free-farer.

No, that isn't true, The truth must be that he fell in love

with her. I was never really in love with Aziz; maybe I've never been in love with anyone. How could I understand? I couldn't stand the thought of leaving the family to marry Aziz. How could Fhassin turn his back on the family for Nouzha? But some alchemy must have transformed him, made him see her as something other than a silly girl—yes, it's a cliché to call her a vain and silly girl, but that's what she was. For her it was probably like this. She was married, and it wasn't very exciting anymore, not nearly as interesting as when her husband was courting her. Fhassin made her feel important—look at the risk he was taking—for her. For her!

But what was going on inside Fhassin? Fhassin despised romantic love, sentimentality.

Her husband suspected, came home, and caught them. The neighborhood swarmed out into the street to see my brother, shirtless, protecting Nouzha, whose hair was all unbound around her shoulders. Fhassin had a razor, and was holding off her screaming husband. The heat poured all over his brown adolescent shoulders and chest. We stood in the street, sweating. And Fhassin was laughing, deadly serious, but laughing. He was alive. Was it the intensity? Was that the lure for Fhassin? This was my brother, who I had known all my life, and he was a stranger.

I realized then that the Nekropolis had become a foreign place, and I didn't know anyone behind the skinmask of their face.

They took my brother and Nouzha, divorced her from her husband for the adultery trial, flogged them both, then dumped them in prison for thirteen years. I didn't wait for Aziz to ask me to marry him—not that he would have now. I let my hair go black. I became a dutiful daughter. I hated my life, but I didn't know how to escape. When I was twenty-one, I was jessed, impressed to feel duty and affection to whoever would pay the fee of my impression.

I try to explain, but Akhmim doesn't understand. He has to go. I cry when he's gone.

Finally, after twenty-eight days, I emerge from my room, white and trembling like Iqurth from the tomb, to face the world and my duties. I don't know what the mistress has told Mbarek, but I'm subjected to a vague lecture I'm sure Mbarek thinks of as fatherly. Fadina avoids meeting my eyes when she sees me. The girl who works with the cook watches the floor. I move like a ghost through the women's quarters. Only the mistress sees me, fastens her eyes on me when I happen to pass her, and her look is cruel. If I hear her, I take to stepping out of the hall if I can.

Friday afternoon the mistress is playing the Tiles, and I take the cleaning machine to her room. I have checked with Fadina to confirm that she's not in, but I can't convince myself that she's left. Maybe Fadina has forgotten. Maybe the mistress hasn't told her. I tiptoe in and stand, listening. The usual projection is on—not *bismek*, but the everyday clutter of silks and fragile tables with silver lace frames, antique lamps, paisley scarfs, and cobalt pottery. The cleaning machine won't go in with a projection on. I stop and listen, no sound but the breeze through the window hangings. I creep through the quarters, shaking. The bed is unmade, a tumble of blue and silver brocade. That's unusual, Fadina always makes it. I think about making it, but I decide I'd better not. Do what I always do or the mistress will be on me. Best do only what's safe. I pick up the clothes off the floor and creep back and turn off the projection. The cleaning machine starts.

If she comes back early, what will I do? I stand by the projection switch, unwilling to leave, even to put the clothing in the laundry. If she comes back, when I hear her, I'll snap on the projection machine. The cleaning machine will stop and I'll take it and leave. It's the best I can do.

The cleaning machine snuffles around, getting dust from the windowsills and tabletops, cleaning the floor. It's slow. I keep thinking I hear her and snapping on the projection. The machine stops and I listen, but I don't hear anything, so I snap the projection off and the cleaning machine starts again. Finally the rooms are done and the cleaning machine and I make our escape. I have used extra scent on the sheets in the linen closet, the way she likes them, and I have put extra oil in the rings on the lights and extra scent in the air freshener. It's all a waste, all that money, but that's what she likes.

I have a terrible headache. I go to my room and wait and try to sleep until the headache is gone. I'm asleep when Fadina bangs on my door and I feel groggy and disheveled.

"The mistress wants you," she snaps, glaring at me.

I can't go.

I can't not go. I follow her without doing up my hair or putting on my sandals.

The mistress is sitting in her bedroom, still dressed up in saffron and veils. I imagine she has just gotten back. "Hariba," she says, "did you clean my rooms?"

What did I disturb? I didn't do anything to this room except pick up the laundry and run the cleaning machine, is something missing? "Yes, mistress," I say. Oh my heart.

"Look at this room," she hisses.

I look, not knowing what I'm looking for.

"Look at the bed!"

The bed looks just the same as it did when I came in, blankets and sheets tumbled, shining blue and silver, the scent of her perfume in the cool air.

"Come here," the mistress commands. "Kneel down." I kneel down so I'm not taller than she is. She looks at me for a moment, furious and speechless. Then I see it coming, but I can't do anything, up comes her hand and she slaps me. I topple sideways, mostly from surprise. "Are you too stupid to even know to make a bed?"

"Fadina always makes your bed," I say. I should have made it, I should have. Holy One, I'm such an idiot.

"So the one time Fadina doesn't do your work you are too lazy to do it yourself?"

"Mistress," I say, "I was afraid to—"

"You *should* be afraid!" she shouts. She slaps me, both sides of my face, and shouts at me, her face close to mine. On and on. I don't listen, it's just sound. Fadina walks me to the door. I'm holding my head up, trying to maintain some dignity. "Hariba," Fadina whispers.

"What?" I say, thinking maybe she has realized that it's the mistress, that it's not my fault.

But she just shakes her head, "Try not to upset her, that's all. Just don't upset her." Her face is pleading, she wants me to understand.

Understand what? That she's jessed? As Akhmim says, "We are only what we are."

But I understand what it's going to be like, now. The mistress hates me, and there's nothing I can do. The only way to escape is to ask Mbarek to sell me off, but then I'd have to leave Akhmim. And since he's a *harni*, he can't even ride the train without someone else providing credit. If I leave, I'll never see him again.

The room is full of whispers. The window is open and the breeze rustles among the paper flowers. There are flowers everywhere, on the dresser, the chairs. Akhmim and I sit in the dark room, lit only by the light from the street. He comes in the evening to visit me, like my brother sneaking to see another man's wife. He's sitting with one leg underneath him. Like some animal, a panther, indolent.

"You'll still be young when I'm old," I say.

"No," he says. That is all, just the one word.

"Do you get old?"

"If we live out our natural span. About sixty, sixty-five years."

"Do you get wrinkles? White hair?"

"Some. Our joints get bad, swell, like arthritis. Things go wrong." He's quiet tonight. Usually he's cheerful.

"You're patient," I say.

He makes a gesture with his hands. "It doesn't matter."

"Is it hard for you to be patient?"

"Sometimes," he says. "I feel frustration, anger, fear. But we're bred to be patient."

"What's wrong?" I ask. I sound like a little girl, my voice all breathy.

"I'm thinking. You should leave here."

The mistress is always finding something. Nothing I do is right. She pulls my hair, confines me to my room. "I can't," I say, "I'm jessed."

He's still in the twilight.

"Akhmim," I say, suddenly cruel, "do you want me to go?"

"*Harni* are not supposed to have 'wants,' " he says, his voice flat. I have never heard him say the word *"harni."* It sounds obscene. It makes me get up, his voice. It fills me with nervousness, with aimless energy. If he is despairing, what is there for me? I leave the window, brush my fingers across the desk, hearing the flowers rustle. I touch all the furniture, and take an armload of flowers, crisp and cool, and drop them in his lap. "What?" he says. I take more flowers and throw them over his shoulders. His face is turned up at me, lit by the light from the street, full of wonder. I gather flowers off the chair, drop them on him. There are flowers all over the bed, funeral flowers. He reaches up, flowers spilling off his sleeves, and takes my arms to make me stop, saying, "Hariba, what?" I lean forward and close my eyes.

I wait, hearing the breeze rustle the lilies, the poppies, the roses on the bed. I wait forever. Until he finally kisses me.

He won't do any more than kiss me. Lying among all the crushed flowers, he will stroke my face, my hair, he will kiss me, but that's all. "You have to leave," he says desperately. "You have to tell Mbarek, tell him to sell you."

I won't leave. I have nothing to go to.

"Do you love me because you have to? Is it because you are a *harni* and I'm a human and you have to serve me?" I ask. He's never said that he loves me, but I know.

He shakes his head.

"Do you love me because of us? Of what we are?" I press. There are no words for the questions I'm asking him.

"Hariba," he says.

"Do you love the mistress?"

"No," he says.

"You should love the mistress, shouldn't you, but you love me."

"Go home, go to the Nekropolis. Run away," he urges, kissing my throat, gentle. Moth wing kisses, as if he has been thinking of my throat for a long time.

"Run away? From Mbarek? What would I do for the rest of my life? Make paper flowers?"

"What's wrong with that?"

"Would you come with me?" I ask.

He sighs and raises up on his elbow. "You shouldn't fall in love with me."

This is funny. "This is a fine time to tell me."

"No," he says, "it is true." He counts on his fine fingers, "One, I'm a *harni*, not a human being, and I belong to someone else. Two, I have caused all of your problems; if I hadn't been here, you wouldn't have had all your troubles. Three, the reason it is wrong for a human to love a *harni* is because *harni*-human relationships are bad paradigms for human behavior, they lead to difficulty in dealing with human-to-human relationships—"

"I don't have any human-to-human relationships," I interrupt.

"You will, you're still young."

I laugh at him. "Akhmim, you're younger than I am. Prescripted wisdom."

"But wisdom nonetheless," he says solemnly.

"Then why did you kiss me?" I ask.

He sighs. It is such a human thing, that sigh, full of frustration. "Because you're sad."

"I'm not sad right now," I say. "I'm happy because you are

here." I'm also nervous. Afraid. Because this is all strange and even though I keep telling myself that he's human, I'm afraid that underneath he is really alien, more unknowable than my brother. But I want him to stay with me. And I'm happy. Afraid but happy.

My lover. "I want you to be my lover," I say.

"No." He sits up. He's beautiful, even disheveled. I can imagine what I look like. Maybe he doesn't even like me, maybe he has to act this way because I want it. He runs his fingers through his hair and his earring gleams in the light from the street.

"Do *harni* fall in love?" I ask.

"I have to go," he says. "We've crushed your flowers." He picks up a lily, whose long petals have become twisted and crumpled, and tries to straighten it out.

"I can make more. Do you have to do this because I want you to?"

"No," he says very quietly. Then more clearly, like a recitation, "*Harni* don't have feelings, not in the sense that humans do. We are loyal, flexible, and affectionate."

"That makes you sound like a smart dog," I say, irritated.

"Yes," he says, "that is what I am, a smart dog, a very smart dog. Good night, Hariba."

When he opens the door, the breeze draws and the flowers rustle and some tumble off the bed, trying to follow him.

"Daughter," Mbarek says, "I'm not sure that this is the best situation for you." He looks at me kindly. I wish Mbarek did not think that he had to be my father.

"Mbarek-salah?" I say. "I don't understand, has my work

been unsatisfactory?" Of course my work has been unsatisfactory—the mistress hates me. But I'm afraid they have
somehow realized what is between Akhmim and me—although I don't know how they could. Akhmim is avoiding me
again.

"No, no"—he waves his hand airily—"your accounts are in
order, you have been a good frugal girl. It's not your fault."

"I . . . I'm aware that I have been clumsy, that perhaps I
have not always understood what the mistress wished, but,
Mbarek-salah, I'm improving!" I'm getting better at ignoring her, I mean. I don't want him to feel inadequate. Sitting
here, I realize the trouble I've caused him. He hates having
to deal with the household in any but the most perfunctory
way. I'm jessed to this man, his feelings matter to me. Re-
jection of my services is painful. This has been a good job.
I've been able to save some of my side money so that when
I'm old I won't be like my mother, forced to struggle and
hope that her children will be able to support her when she
can't work anymore.

Mbarek is uncomfortable. The part of me that is not jessed
can see this is not the kind of duty that Mbarek likes. This is
not how he sees himself; he prefers to be the benevolent pa-
triarch. "Daughter," he says, "you have been exemplary, but
wives . . ." He sighs. "Sometimes, child, they get whims, and
it's better for me, and for you, if we find you some good position with another household."

At least he hasn't said anything about Akhmim. I bow my
head because I'm afraid I will cry. I study my toes. I try not to
think of Akhmim. Alone again. O Holy One, I'm tired of being
alone. I'll be alone my whole life, jessed women do not marry.
I can't help it, I start to cry. Mbarek takes it as a sign of my loy-

alty and pats me gently on the shoulder. "There, there, child, it'll be all right."

I don't want Mbarek to comfort me. The part of me that watches, that isn't jessed, doesn't even really like Mbarek, and at the same time I want to make him happy. I gamely sniff and try to smile. "I . . . I know you know what is best," I manage. But my distress makes him uncomfortable. He says when arrangements are made he'll tell me.

I look for Akhmim, to tell him, but he stays in the men's side of the house, away from the middle where we eat, and far away from the women's side.

I begin to understand. He didn't love me, it was just that he was a *harni* and it was me . . . I led him to myself. Maybe I'm no better than Nouzha, with her white hair and pointed ears. I work, what else is there to do? And I avoid the mistress. Evidently Mbarek has told her he is getting rid of me, because the attacks cease. Fadina even smiles at me, if distantly. I would like to make friends with Fadina again, but she doesn't give me a chance. I'll never see him again. He isn't even that far from me and I'll never see him again.

There's nothing to be done about it. Akhmim avoids me. I look across the courtyard or the dining room at the men's side, but I almost never see him. Once in a while he's there, with his long curly hair and his black gazelle eyes, but he doesn't look at me.

I pack my things. My new mistress comes. She is a tall gray-haired woman, slightly pop-eyed. She has a breathy voice and a way of hunching her shoulders, as if she wished she were actually very small. I'm supposed to give *her* my life? It's monstrous.

We're in Mbarek's office. I'm upset. I want desperately to leave, I'm afraid of coming into a room and finding the mistress. I'm trying not to think of Akhmim. But what is most upsetting is the thought of leaving Mbarek. Will the next girl understand that he wants to pretend he is frugal, but that he really is not? I'm nearly overwhelmed by shame because I have caused this. I'm only leaving because of my own foolishness and I have failed Mbarek, who only wanted peace.

I will not cry. These are impressed emotions. Soon I'll feel them for this strange woman. O Holy, what rotten luck to have gotten this woman for a mistress. She wears bronze and white—bronze was all the fashion when I first came and the mistress wore it often—but this is years later and these are second-rate clothes, a younger woman's clothing and not suited for a middle-aged woman at all. She's nervous, wanting me to like her, and all I want to do is throw myself at Mbarek's feet and embarrass him into saying that I can stay.

Mbarek says, "Hariba, she has paid the fee." He shows me the credit transaction and I see that the fee is lower than it was when I came to Mbarek's household. "I order you to accept this woman as your new mistress."

That's it. That's the trigger. I feel a little disoriented. I never really noticed how the skin under Mbarek's jaw was soft and lax. He's actually rather nondescript. I wonder what it must be like for the mistress to have married him. She's tall and vivid, if a bit heavy, and was a beauty in her day. She must find him disappointing. No wonder she's bitter.

My new mistress smiles tentatively. Well, she may not be fashionable, the way my old mistress was, but she looks kind, praise God. I hope so, I would like to live in a kind household. I smile back at her.

That's it. I'm impressed.

My new household is much smaller than the old one. I must be frugal; there's a lot less money in this house. It's surprising how accustomed I've gotten to money at Mbarek's house; this is much more like the way I grew up.

I inventory the linens and clean all the rooms from top to bottom. My mistress sits at the table and watches me scrub the counters and clean the grime that has collected in the cracks.

"Things are different in a big house, I assume," she says. Her name is Zoubida. That's what she wants me to call her, but it feels too informal, so I don't call her anything at all.

"Yes, ma'am," I say. "A lot more people."

I open the cold box. "Do you want to keep any of this?" I'll be cooking.

She waves her hand. "Oh no, keep what you need."

It is full of half-eaten things that I am afraid to keep. Some of them are really old. I empty it out and scrub it, the cold wafting out as I do. Then I put back the handful of things I'm certain aren't spoiled. I wash out the sink.

I make a salad of chicken and greens and oranges for lunch. It's something that the old mistress used to like. The new master shuffles in, the backs of his slippers flattened by tromping on them. "What's this?" he says.

"It's a recipe from her old house," my mistress says.

He looks at it doubtfully. He's not a salad eater, I suspect.

"For dinner, I can make couscous," I say.

He nods and tastes the salad gingerly.

"Did you eat this a lot at your last place?" my mistress asks.

"Oh, not me," I say. "But my mistress liked it."

I'll eat chickpeas later, after I clean up after lunch.

The master seems pleased by the salad and eats every bit. "Hariba," he says while I'm picking up the plates, "how do you stop a lawyer from drowning?"

"I don't know, sir."

"Take your foot off his neck," he says, and laughs, watching me with watering eyes.

I laugh, too. He is always telling me dreadful jokes, but the mistress wants us to get along. I always laugh.

The master shuffles off to go meet some friends at a coffee house. The mistress doesn't seem to know what to do with herself.

"I would like to clean all the cupboards," I say.

"Why don't you sit for a moment and have some tea?" she says. Watching me work makes her nervous.

"Oh, really, I'm not thirsty," I say. "But thank you, ma'am."

I don't know what to do with her. I don't want to make her uncomfortable. "Have you always lived here, ma'am?" I ask.

She tells me all about her family, starting stories and losing track, and getting names mixed up. But I pretend to follow and be interested. I take everything out of the cupboards and wash them. Things are incredibly dusty!

"Before you we had a girl who came in during the day and went home at night," the mistress says.

She didn't seem to do much.

I shop and make couscous and chickpea soup for dinner.

The daughter is sixteen. Her name is Tereze. She has her hair hennaed and she wears Indian filagree and a blue dot in the middle of her forehead to look like an emancipated Indian woman. Girls are all dressing like Indian gender terrorists. She has a phone card flipped open and is talking to one of her friends.

"Stop talking on the phone. Now," her mother says.

She rolls her eyes. "My mother wants me to stop talking," she says to the phone. "So what do you think, should we tell her or not?"

The mistress reaches over and grabs the phone card from her and crumples it up.

"That had more than half an hour left on it!" the girl says.

"Then you should have listened to me," the mother says. "I got my credit chip statement today. There are a lot of charges on here that I didn't make."

"I'll pay you back," the daughter says.

"Pay me back! This is more than you get in a month!"

"You want me to dress like a beggar!" the girl says. What a tongue she has in her. "If you gave me enough, I wouldn't have to take your credit chip!"

"We're not made out of money!" her mother says.

"You have enough money for *her*!" the girl says. "I should be in school with that money!"

"School is a waste with you!" the mistress says. "Your marks are terrible! If you got decent marks, I could see spending the money!"

"I hate you!" the daughter shrieks. "You never give me a chance!"

Akhmim. I think of him all the time. Rather than listen, I think of telling Akhmim about the daughter, about the master.

Emboldened by my mistress's approval, I rearrange the furniture. I take some things she has—they are not very nice—and put them away. I reprogram the household AI. It is very limited, insufficient for anything as complicated as *bismek*, but it can handle projections, of course. I remember the things my old mistress used to like and I project cobalt blue vases and silver-framed pictures. Marble floors would overwhelm these rooms, but the ivory tile I pick is nice.

My mistress is delighted. It is wonderful to work for someone who is easy to please.

My days are free on Tuesday and half-a-day Sunday. Tuesday my mistress apologizes to me. They are a little tight on credit and she cannot advance my leisure allowance until Sunday, do I mind?

Well, a little, but I say I don't. I spend the afternoon making flowers.

When I make flowers, I think of Akhmim and myself on the bed, surrounded by crushed carnations and irises. It isn't good to think about Akhmim. He doesn't miss me, I'm sure. He's a *harni,* always an owned thing, subject to the whims of his owners. If they had constructed him with lasting loyalties, his life would be horrible. Surely when the technician constructed his genes, he made certain that Akhmim would forget quickly. He told me that *harni* do not love. But he also told me that they did. And he told me he didn't love the mistress, but maybe he only said that because he had to, because I don't like the old mistress and his duty is to make humans happy.

I put the blue and white and silver paper flowers in a vase. My mistress thinks they are lovely.

Long lilies, spiked stamens, and long petals like lolling tongues. Sometimes feelings are in me that have no words and I look at the paper flowers and want to rip them to pieces.

On Sunday my mistress has my leisure allowance. Mbarek used to add a little something extra, but I realize that in my new circumstances I can't expect that. I go to the Moussin of the White Falcon, on the edge of the Nekropolis, to listen to the service.

Then I take the train to the street of Mbarek's house. I don't intend to walk down the street, but of course I do. And I stand outside the house, looking for a sign of Akhmim. I'm afraid to stand long, I don't want anyone to see me. What would I tell them, that I'm homesick? I'm jessed.

I like to take something to do on the train so the ride isn't boring. I've brought a bag full of paper to make flowers. I can earn a little money on the side by making wreaths. Anything I earn on my own I can keep. I'm not allowed to give it to my mistress, that's against the law. It's to protect the jessed that this is true.

In the Nekropolis we lived in death houses, surrounded by death. Perhaps it isn't odd that I'm a bit morbid, and perhaps that is why I pull a flower out of my bag and leave it on a windowsill on the men's side of the house. After all, something did die, although I can't put in words exactly what it was. I don't really know which window is Akhmim's, but it doesn't matter, it's just a gesture. It only makes me feel foolish.

Monday I wake early and drink hot mint tea. I take buckets of water and scrub down the stone courtyard. I make a list of all the repairs that need to be done. I take the mistress's news printouts and bundle them. She saves them; she subscribes to several news services and she feels that they might be useful. My old mistress would have quite a lot to say about someone who would save news printouts. The mistress goes out to shop and I clean everything in her storage. She has clothes she should throw out, things fifteen years old and hopelessly out of date. (I remember when I wore my hair white. And before when we used to wrap our hair in our veils, the points trailing to the backs of our knees, We looked foolish, affected. How did I get to be so old when I'm not even thirty?)

I put aside all the things I should mend, but I don't want to sit yet. I run the cleaning machine, an old clumsy thing even stupider than the one at Mbarek's. I push myself all day, a whirlwind. There is not enough in this house to do, even if I clean the cleaning machine, so I clean some rooms twice.

Still, when it is time to go to sleep, I can't. I sit in my room making a funeral wreath of carnations and tiny, half-open roses. The white roses gleam under my desklight like satin.

I wake up on my free day, tired and stiff. In the mirror I look ghastly, my hair tangled and my eyes puffy. Just as well the *harni* never saw me like this, I think. But I won't think of Akhmim anymore. That part of my life is over, and I have laid a flower at its death house. Today I will take my funeral wreaths around and see if I can find a shop that will buy them. They are good work, surely someone will be interested. It would just be pocket money.

I take the train all the way to the Nekropolis, carefully protecting my wreaths from the other commuters. All day I walk through the Nekropolis, talking to stallkeepers, stopping sometimes for tea. When I have sold the wreaths, I sit for a while to watch the people and let my tired mind empty.

I'm at peace, now I can go back to my mistress.

The Second Koran tells us that the darkness in ourselves is a sinister thing. It waits until we relax, it waits until we reach the most vulnerable moments, and then it snares us. I want to be dutiful, I want to do what I should. But when I go back to the train, I think of where I'm going; to that small house and my empty room. What will I do tonight? Make more paper flowers, more wreaths. I'm sick of them. Sick of the Nekropolis.

I can take the train to my mistress's house or I can go by the street where Mbarek's house is. I'm tired, I'm ready to go to my little room and relax. O Holy One, I dread the empty evening. Maybe I should go by Mbarek's street just to fill up time. I have all this empty time ahead. Tonight and tomorrow and this week and next month and down through the years, unmarried, empty, until I'm an old dried-up woman Evenings folding paper. Days cleaning someone else's house. Free afternoons spent shopping a bit, stopping in tea shops because my feet hurt. That is what lives are, aren't they? Attempts to fill our time with activity designed to prevent us from realizing that there is no meaning? I sit at a tiny table the size of a serving platter and watch the boys hum by on their scooters, girls sitting behind them, clutching their boyfriends' waists with one hand, holding their veils with the other, while the ends stream and snap behind them, glittering with the shimmer of gold (this year's fashion).

So I get off the train and walk to the street where Mbarek lives. And I walk up the street past the house. I stop and look at it. The walls are pale yellow stone. I'm wearing rose and sky blue, but I have gone out without ribbons on my wrists.

"Hariba," Akhmim says, leaning on the windowsill, "you're still sad."

He looks familiar and it is easy, as if we do this every evening. "I live a sad life," I say, my voice even. But my heart is pounding. To see him! To talk to him!

"I found your token," he says.

"My token," I repeat, not understanding.

"The flower. I tried to watch every day. I thought you'd come and I missed you." He disappears for a moment, and then he is sitting on the windowsill, legs and feet outside, and he jumps lightly to the ground.

I take him to a tea shop. People look at us, wondering what a young woman is doing unescorted with a young man. Let them look. "Order what you want," I say, "I have some money."

"Are you happier?" he asks. "You don't look happier, you look tired."

And he looks perfect, as he always does. Have I fallen in love with him precisely because he isn't human? I don't care, I feel love, no matter what the reason. Does a reason for a feeling matter? The feeling I have for my mistress may be there only because I'm impressed, but the *feeling* is real enough.

"My mistress is kind, praise God," I say, looking at the table. His perfect hand, beautiful nails and long fingers, lies there.

"Are you happy?" he asks again.

"Are you?" I ask.

He shrugs. "A *harni* doesn't have the right to be happy or sad."

"Neither do I," I say.

"That's your fault. Why did you do it?" he asks. "Why did you choose to be jessed if it makes you unhappy?"

"It's hard to find work in the Nekropolis, and I didn't think I would ever get married."

He shakes his head. "Someone would marry you. And if they didn't, is it awful not to get married?"

"Is it awful to be jessed?" I ask.

"Is it?"

"I thought," I say, and then I don't know what to say. "I thought if I was jessed, I wouldn't care. I thought it would be easy if I was jessed. I thought I would be *owned*. I mean, my heart would be owned. You know, I wouldn't need to make choices. I didn't understand it. I thought I would be happy. But it isn't like that. Jessing doesn't make me like it, it just makes it really awful if I leave."

How can he understand how our choices are taken from us? He doesn't even understand freedom and what an illusion it really is.

"Run away," he says.

Leave the mistress? I'm horrified. "She needs me; she can't run that house by herself and I cost her a great deal of money. She made sacrifices to buy me."

"You could live in the Nekropolis and make funeral wreaths," he points out. "You could talk to whomever you wished and no one would order you around."

"I don't want to live in the Nekropolis," I say.

"Why not?"

"There is nothing there for me!"

"You have friends there."

"I wouldn't if I ran away."

"Make new ones," he says.

"Would you go?" I ask.

He shakes his head. "I can't."

"What if you could make a living, would you run away?"

"No," he says, "no."

Our tea comes. My face is aflame with color, I don't know what to say. I don't know what to think.

"I'm jessed," I say. "If I run away, do you know what will

happen to me? I'll be sick. I might die. My own body will turn against me. Maybe, eventually I'll get well. I'm afraid. I don't want to be sick. I don't want it to happen."

"Oh, Hariba," he says softly, "I'm sorry. I shouldn't say these things to you."

"I didn't think you could have these feelings," I whisper.

He shrugs again. "I can have any feelings," he says. "*Harni* aren't jessed."

"You told me to think of you as a dog," I remind him. "Loyal."

"I'm loyal," he says. "You didn't ask who I was loyal to."

"You're supposed to be loyal to the mistress."

He drums the table with his fingers, *taptaptaptap taptaptap-tap.* "*Harni* aren't like geese," he says, not looking at me. His earring is golden, he is rich and fine-looking. I had not real-ized at my new place how starved I had become for fine things. "We don't impress on the first person we see." Then he shakes his head. "I shouldn't talk about all this nonsense. You have to go. I have to go back before they miss me."

"I could steal you away."

"No," he says. "You said you will get sick. You might die." But he would go with me. I can see it in his face. What is there for him at Mbarek's? The mistress ignores him. It is me he has bonded to. It is me he loves.

No one has ever loved me like he does. I am already dead if I stay with my mistress. I realize that I've been thinking about death. I really want to die.

"Maybe we are already dead, living this way," I say.

He doesn't understand me, not at all.

"We have to talk more," I say.

"We have to go," he insists. Then he smiles at me and all the unhappiness disappears from his face. He doesn't seem human anymore, he seems pleasant; *harni*. I get a chill. He's alien. I understand him less than I understand people like my old mistress. We get up and he looks away as I pay.

Outside Mbarek's house I tell him, "I'll come back next Tuesday." On Tuesday I get my spending money.

It's good I got so much cleaning done before I saw Ahkmim because I sleepwalk through the next few days. I leave the cleaning machine in the doorway, where the mistress almost trips over it. I forget to set the clothes in order. I don't know what to think.

I hear the mistress say to the neighbor, "She's a godsend, but moody. One day she's doing everything, the next day she can't be counted on to remember to set the table."

What right does she have to talk about me that way? Her house was a pigsty when I came.

What am I thinking? What is wrong with me that I blame my mistress? Where is my head? I feel ill, my eyes water, and my head fills. I can't breathe, I feel heavy. I must be dutiful. I used to have this feeling once in a while when I was first jessed, it's part of the adjustment. It must be the change from Mbarek. I have to adjust all over again.

I find the mistress, tell her I'm not feeling well, and go lie down.

The next afternoon, just before dinner, it happens again. The day after that is fine, but then it happens at midmorning of the third day. It is Tuesday and I have the day off. My voice is hoarse, my head aches. What is wrong with me?

I know what is wrong with me. I'm trying not to think about what I'm planning because if I let myself think, the jessing will fight with me. I'm trying to be two people, one a good girl and the other a secret, hidden even from my own self.

I'm afraid. I don't want to die. Although I don't mind the idea of being dead, just dying. Inside me is a tiny part that would like it all to stop, to end.

I wonder if I am trying to commit suicide. I'm crazy. But if I think about it, then the sickness comes on me, worse and worse. I can't stand it here and I can't go away.

I go to the Moussin in the afternoon, lugging my bag, which is heavy with paper, and sit in the cool dusty darkness, nursing my poor head. I feel as if I should pray. I should ask for help, for guidance. The Moussin is so old that the stone is irregularly worn and through my slippers I can feel the little ridges and valleys in the marble. Up around the main worship hall there are galleries hidden by arabesques of scrollwork. Ayesha and I used to sit up there when we were children. Above that, sunlight flashes through clerestory windows. Where the light hits the marble floor, it shines hard, hurting my eyes and my head. I rest my forehead on my arm, turned sideways on the bench so I can lean against the back. With my eyes closed I smell incense and my own scent of perfume and perspiration.

There are people there for service, but no one bothers me. Isn't that amazing?

Or maybe it is only because anyone can see that I'm impure.

I'm tired of my own melodrama. I keep thinking that people are looking at me, that someone is going to say something to me. I don't know where to go.

I don't even pretend to think of going back to my room. I get on the train and go to Mbarek's house. I climb the stairs from the train—these are newer, but like the floor of the Moussin they are unevenly worn, sagging in the centers from the weight of this crowded city. What would it be like to cross the sea and go north? To go to Spain? I used to want to travel, to go to a place where people had yellow hair, to see whole forests of trees. Cross the oceans, learn other languages. I told Ayesha that I would even like to taste dog, or swine. She thought I was showing off, but it was true, once I would have liked to try things.

I'm excited, full of energy and purpose. I can do anything. I can understand Fhassin, standing in the street with his razor, laughing. It is worth it, anything is worth it for this feeling of being alive. I have been jessed, I've been asleep for a long time.

There are people on Mbarek's street. I stand in front of the house across the street. What am I going to say if someone opens the door? *I'm waiting to meet a friend.* What if they don't leave, what if Akhmim sees them and doesn't come out? The sun bakes my hair, my head. *Akhmim, where are you? Look out the window.* He's probably waiting on the mistress. Maybe there is a *bismek* party and those women are poisoning Akhmim. They could do anything, they own him. I want to crouch in the street and cover my head in my hands, rock and cry like a widow woman from the Nekropolis. Like my mother must have done when my father died. I grew up without a father, maybe that's why I'm wild. Maybe that's why Fhassin is in prison and I'm headed there. I pull my veil up so my face is shadowed. So no one can see my tears.

Oh, my head. Am I drunk? Am I insane? Has the Holy One, seeing my thoughts, driven me mad?

I look at my brown hands. I cover my face.

"Hariba?" He takes my shoulders.

I look up at him, his beautiful familiar face, and I'm stricken with terror. What is he? What am I trusting my life, my future to? O Holy One, I'm afraid. What if I die?

"What's wrong?" he asks. "Are you ill?"

"I'm going insane," I say. "I can't stand it, Akhmim, I can't go back to my room—"

"Hush," he says, looking up the street and down. "You have to. I'm only a *harni*. I can't do anything, I can't help you."

"We have to go. We have to go away somewhere, you and I."

He shakes his head. "Hariba, please. You must hush."

"We should be free," I say. My head hurts very badly. The tears keep coming, even though I'm not really crying.

"I can't be free," he says. "That was just talk."

"I have to go now," I say. "I'm jessed, Akhmim. It's hard, but if I don't go now, I'll never go."

"But you said you'll get sick," he says.

"I can't live this way," I say, and it is true. If I don't do something, I'll die.

"Your mistress—"

"DON'T TALK ABOUT HER!" I shout. If he talks about her, I won't be able to leave.

He looks around again. We are a spectacle, a man and a woman arguing on the street.

"Come with me, we'll go somewhere, talk," I say, all honey. He can't deny me, I see it in his face. He has to get off the street. He'd go anywhere. Any place is safer than this.

He lets me take him into the train, down the stairs to the platform. I clutch my indigo veil tight at my throat. We wait in silence. He has his hands in his pockets. He looks like a boy from the Nekropolis, standing there in just his shirt, no outer robe. He looks away, shifts his weight from one foot to the other, ill at ease. Human. Events are making him more human. Taking away all his certainties.

"What kind of genes are in you?" I ask.

"What?" he asks.

"What kind of genes?"

"Are you asking for my chart?" he says.

I shake my head. "Human?"

He shrugs. "Mostly. Some artificial sequences."

"No animal genes," I say. I sound irrational because I can't get clear what I mean. The headache makes my thoughts skip, my tongue thick.

He smiles a little. "No dogs, no monkeys."

I smile back, he's teasing me. I'm learning to understand when he teases. "I have some difficult news for you, Akhmim. I think you are a mere human being."

His smile vanishes. He shakes his head. "Hariba," he says. He's about to talk like a father.

I stop him with a gesture. My head still hurts.

The train whispers in, sounding like wind. Oh, the lights. I sit down, shading my eyes, and he stands in front of me. I can feel him looking down at me. I look up and smile, or maybe grimace. He smiles back, looking worried. There is a family of Gypsies at the other end of the car, wild and homeless and dirty. We are like them, I realize.

At the Moussin of the White Falcon we get off. Funny that we are going into a cemetery to live. But only for a while, I think. Somehow I will find a way we can leave, if I live. We'll go north, across the sea, up to the continent, where we'll be strangers. I take him through the streets and stop in front of a row of death houses, like Ayesha's family's, but an inn.

"There are inns here?" Akhmim asks.

"Of course," I say. "People come from the country to visit their families. People live in the Nekropolis, we have stores and everything."

I give Akhmim money and tell him to rent us a place for the night. "Tell them your wife is sick," I whisper. I'm afraid.

"I don't have any credit. If they take my identification, they'll know," he says.

"This is the Nekropolis," I say. "They don't use credit. Go on. Here you are a man."

He frowns at me, but takes the money. I watch him out of the corner of my eye, bargaining, pointing at me. Just pay, I think, even though we have very little money. I just want to lie down, to sleep. And finally he comes out and takes me by the hand and leads me to our place. A tiny room of rough whitewashed walls: a bed, a chair, a pitcher of water, and two glasses.

"I have something for your head," he says. "The man gave it to me." He smiles ruefully. "He thinks you're pregnant."

My hand shakes when I hold it out. He puts the white pills in my hand and pours a glass of water for me. "I'll leave you here," he says. "I'll go back. I won't tell anyone that I know where you are."

"Then I'll die," I say. "I don't want to argue, Akhmim, just stay until tomorrow." Then it will be too late. "I need you to take care of me, so I can get better and we can live."

"What can I do? I can't live," he says in anguish. "I can't get work!"

"You can sell funeral wreaths. I'll make them."

He looks torn. It is one thing to think how you will act, another to be in the situation and do it. And I know, seeing his face, that he really is human because his problem is a very human problem. Safety or freedom.

"We will talk about it tomorrow," I say. "My head is aching."

"Because you're jessed," he says. "It's dangerous. What if we don't make enough money? What if they catch us?"

"That's life," I say. I'll go to prison. He'll be sent back to the mistress. Punished. Maybe made to be conscript labor. Maybe they will put him down, like an animal.

"Is it worth the pain?" he asks in a small voice.

I don't know, but I can't say that. "Not when you have the pain," I say, "but afterward it is."

"Your poor head." He strokes my forehead. His hand is cool and soothing.

"Yes," I say. "Change causes pain."

Is it worth dying for?

2.
Ties

In the beginning there was paradise, and then I was sent out into the world of men.

The first and last lesson they teach us is that we aren't human. But we know it. Humans are rigid and *harni* bend. Humans have only one shape. I'm bent around Hariba. Hariba is full of sharp angles and unexpected soft places. She thinks that no one gets in, but for a *harni*, Hariba is . . . is . . . in the crèche we would have said that Hariba is half-open. There is space there, empty. That is what makes it easy to love her. When I am with her, there is the constant anxiety that I'm not making her happy, and when I see her look of love, something within me leaps up, relieved and delighted.

I've gone into that dim, secret space and it has brought me here, to the place of the human dead. Hariba is sick. And I'm helpless.

She sits in the bed in the cool room with the sheet over her knees, and folds paper into flowers. There are lilies on long stalks that she curls into wreaths, then she fills them with tiny flower cups. She names the flowers for me; canna lily, narcissus, rose, impatiens. They are all paper white. She ties them up with long white satin ribbons like the kind she used to wear around her wrists. While she does it, she's happy and I'm happy to sit with her.

Then the headaches come back and she lies on her side with her knees to her chin, whimpering. The room feels warmer, the air heavier. Her face shines with sweat and long trails of black hair stick to her forehead. Then she's closed, no space for me, and the headaches fill her and at the same time there is this need, this terrible need, that I can't satisfy. I found her in the street that way, outside the master's house, and that's how she brought me here, with that terrible need.

I stay with her and hold the bucket when she's sick. "I'm sorry," she says. "I'm sorry."

"Shhhh," I say. "Shhhhh." I wipe her face with a cloth. The room smells of sweat and vomit and someone who has been in bed too long.

Need. We need money to have a safe place and she needs to be safe.

While she sleeps, I take the wreaths and I go out into the Nekropolis, to the Moussin of the White Falcon. I can bring her back money. It's a good day, hot and bright. The square in front of the Moussin is crowded with people; some of them are empty, some of them complicated by grief and need. It is in their voices and their faces, in the way their hands shape themselves empty. Women hunch their backs around the emptiness and wail.

Lots of people are set up to sell wreaths, and most of them have lots of wreaths and banks of flowers. Dry and baking heat. The kind that heats to the bone. I spread out a towel and put my wreaths down. I only have six—two as wide across as my arm and full of the sweep and curve of the canna lilies and four smaller ones with roses. Across from me, a woman sits on a cloth, with wreaths and falcons with their paper wings spread all around her, and makes more things. Humans are only complete like this, when they are doing something that makes their minds and hands busy, when they are doing something that makes them solve puzzles. I like to watch this woman because *harni* are never complete alone and so there is something peaceful and at the same time disquieting about it. Humans say they are happy when they have things, but hands and mind in concert make them complete.

A tall boy squats near me with single flowers for sale. He's looking at my wreaths.

"My wife makes them," I say, "but she's sick, so she can't make many."

He nods. "They're very nice. Very good work. How much?"

I shrug. "I don't know. How much should I ask?"

He considers. "Five for the big ones and three for the small," he says. "That's what I'd ask." He's pleased that I asked and his pleasure is like warmth. Like heat.

"Thank you," I say.

"From the Mashahana," he says absently. It's what Hariba says when you thank her. I'll remember to say it.

Mourners come and some of them already have flowers, but some of them look at the wreaths. "How much?" they ask and I say, "Five for the large ones and three for the small." I sell three of the small ones, and then, as the shadows are lengthening over the square, both of the large ones. One of the large ones goes to a man who is pleased with himself. One goes to a woman who is needy.

"It is a beautiful piece," I say to the woman. "Canna lilies and roses and lemon leaves. My wife makes them. She's sick."

She nods. Her veil is white with a stripe of blue. She's a widow, I think.

"Who is it for?" I ask.

"My son," she says hoarsely and there's the sharpness of her pain, a terrible wave of feeling. She's hollow.

"Is he sad, now?" I ask. That's a center for her pain, that she isn't needed anymore, and she cries silently as she hands me the money. She's empty and anything I do will make her crack. Instead of letting her put the money in my palm, I take her hand, and then cover it with my other hand and she stands there with her eyes closed and the tears running down her face. She's captured by touch, still as an animal. She stands, shocked and holding it in, and then she breaks; first her knees giving way so she sinks, and then her back bending, curving until she's on her knees and her forehead slowly, achingly slowly, comes down until it touches my hands clasped around hers, and she sobs. "Sweet boy," she sobs. "Sweet, sweet boy."

"Yes," I whisper, feeling her strange pleasure at her pain.

"Sweet boy."

The widow's name is Myryam and she takes me to a café and buys me a drink of cold orange bitters. She's hungry to be touched, but doesn't dare take my hand. It's hard to be a widow and to go without touch and it's drying her up inside and out. Her son was twenty-five when he crashed a lorry into a bridge abutment and after weeks and weeks of pain, finally died. She shows me a picture of a plump, smiling boy with well-oiled black hair and a shirt so white it hurts the eyes.

"He's handsome," I say.

"He is," she says. "That was taken when he got his certificate to drive a lorry. He was happy. I was happy for him. His father wanted him to do books, but he wasn't good at math. He wasn't interested. He was very smart about something when he was interested, but numbers, he said he didn't care. He got a certificate to be a lorry driver and then he could be out talking to people. He loved people."

She rises like bread in a warm kitchen, talking of her son and touching the corners of her eyes with her veil.

"Maybe you can give me some advice?" I ask.

"You're like my own sweet boy," she says and we bask in the pleasure of each other's company.

"My wife makes wreaths, but she's ill and she can't make many anymore. I need to find work, but I don't know where to start."

Myryam's thoughtful. "You could be a waiter. You'd be good at it, I think. Let me ask around." She's comfortable now. We fit together like key and lock. "You're someone's good son," she says.

The sun is going down and the dry air is cooling. The breeze stirs, swirling the dust in the street, curls and hollows, empty and full. "I have to go," I explain, "my wife's alone . . ." I walk home through the empty streets, thinking of Myryam and things I can do for her. Ask her advice and call on her to see how she's doing. She'd like that.

The light's on, but the room feels cool. Hariba's sitting on the bed, shivering and crying. "Where did you go!"

"I went to the Moussin," I say. I sit down next to her. Her skin is hot and dry, her hair lank and oily. "I sold all of the wreaths you made but one."

"I didn't know where you'd gone!" Hariba says. "You were gone!"

"I'm here now," I say and hold her and stroke her hair. "Sweet girl, I'm here now."

"I was scared," she says. "I thought you'd gone back."

"I'm sorry," I say. Oh, I feel bad. "I'm sorry, sweetheart."

"I thought you'd gone back to Mbarek-salah. I thought you'd left me here to die."

"Shhh," I say. "Shhh, you're not going to die. I'll take care of you."

"You're just a baby here," she whispered. "I've got to take care of things."

"I met a woman, a widow, at the Moussin. She bought your great big wreath, the one with the canna lilies and the roses and the lemon leaves?"

Hariba looks up at me and nods. I wipe at the tear stains with my thumb.

"Her son was killed in a lorry accident, oh, a year ago, maybe. She bought your wreath for him. She's going to help me find a job, maybe as a waiter. Do you think I'd be a good waiter?"

"I don't know," Hariba says. She rests her head against my chest. "Maybe. You didn't tell her, did you? You didn't tell her about us?"

"No, sweetheart. I told her my wife was ill."

Shyly, Hariba says, "You told her I was your wife?"

I kiss her forehead. Ah, I've said the right thing. "Of course. Now you go to sleep so you can feel better."

"I'm not going to get better," she says.

"It always feels that way when we're sick. When we're sick, we can't remember what it's like to feel good. Now lie down." She's prickly and unhappy. My poor Hariba.

"Do *harni* get sick?" she asks.

"Of course we do," I say. "We get sick, we fall down and hurt ourselves. Just like you."

That's what she wants. Humans always want us to be human, but we aren't. I sit and watch her go to sleep.

I share 98 percent of my DNA with Hariba, but so does a chimpanzee, and I know Hariba wouldn't like to think she had run away with a chimpanzee. I'm not, though, I'm a *harni*. 98 percent is a number, 2 percent is a number, these are numbers I've been taught, but they don't explain differences.

I was born in a crèche. I was the only male in a sibling group of five. More humans want female *harni* than male, so there are eight females to every male. I had four sisters just like myself. We were all one, in the way of *harni*, almost indistinguishable, until we were five years old and we had to start sleeping in separate beds and going to different classes so we would differentiate. We cried. We were cast out of paradise and after that we were never whole again. I learned that my sisters had names—Isna, Sardalas, Dakhla, and Kenitra—and the more they went each to her separate classroom, the more they changed in different directions. Our teachers had trouble telling us apart, but the other *harni* in the crèche didn't. And because I was a boy, I changed most of all. I learned I had a name. I learned I was alone.

Before we were separate, we didn't play like humans.

After we were separated, we would mimic each other a lot. And sometimes we'd play pretend. We'd play that my sisters had been sold to a human, and because I was the boy, I had to be the rich man who bought them. I'd sit in the chair and order them to do things for me: "Brush my hair," or "Bring me my shoes." Then they would go off to their room, which was usually Isna's bed because it was closest to the wall and farthest from the door, and they would pile on top of each other like mice keeping warm and lie together, happy in the touch and smell of each other. Alone in the chair, I'd feel the air on my skin and the way the edge of the seat cut into my thighs, until I couldn't stand it. I'd say that I was coming to inspect their quarters and when I pretended to find them, they would take me in and teach me *harni* ways, until I declared I'd never be human again. and then I'd curl up with them on the narrow bed and smell the milky smell of us all together.

Of course, humans can't be *harni*. They try when they have sex, even if they don't know what they're trying for, but they're always apart and always alone. Once I grew up, I was always alone, too, but the difference is, I remember when it wasn't that way.

Hariba says it's silly to go to the Moussin with only one wreath. Her need tears at me, little hooks tugging while her demand that I be human, be the *man*, and take care of things pushes me away and out.

"Myryam might be there," I explain. "She's going to help me find a job to support us."

"No, no, no, no, no," Hariba murmurs.

"Lie down," I say, soft. "I'll sit here until you go to sleep."

But Hariba can't sleep. "Am I going to die?" she asks.

"No," I say, "you're going to get better."

Her head aches. She's miserable.

"Do you want me to get a doctor?" I ask.

"No," she says fiercely, "no doctor. A doctor would know that I'm jessed and that I ran away."

"Okay," I promise. "I won't call a doctor."

She's soothed and she pushes the pillow away and lays her cheek against the sheet. She doesn't close her eyes. They are vacant and bruised. I rub her back. She's wearing a cotton shift and it's damp and transparent—two white chalky tablets have broken her fever for a bit of time, making her perspire. The vertebrae are like the bones of a snake, a ridge under her sand-colored skin. They curl down into the small of her back and curve up over her shoulders to twist where her head is turned and disappear into her hair.

"You go on," she says absently, far away.

She can't be made happy. I sit for a while, hopeless and hopeful until she dozes. Finally freed, I pull the sheet over her and kiss her on the temple, and leave her lying there.

Outside on the street the hot dry wind curls the dust into a devil, turning and turning, and I follow it to the souk to buy rice. Maybe Hariba can keep it down. She was worried that I was leaving. I'll surprise her by coming back early and feed her sweet milky chai, spoonful by spoonful.

A woman without a veil is bargaining with a man about oranges and there is something familiar about her that makes me stop. Then I realize, it isn't that she's familiar because I know her, it's because she's a *harni*.

I haven't seen another *harni* since I left the crèche.

She cocks her head and flirts with the stallman while he fills her bag with oranges. He puts an extra in for her.

She turns around and sees me. She's enough like me to be my sister—although she isn't my crèche-mate.

"Why are you here?" she asks.

"I'm with someone, but she's sick," I say. "I want to get her some rice and chai."

"I know where to buy it," she says.

I want to touch her and she wants to touch me, to collapse together skin to skin and feel someone else, but we're here in this human souk, so I follow her between the marketmen. She reaches back with one slim hand and catches my wrist, her skin dry and warm, and takes me behind a stall into a space just wide enough for us and we wrap ourselves around each other. I smell her skin and her hair and her dry, slightly cinnamon smell. She nuzzles the base of my neck, smelling me. Relax. Relax, her scent says to me. We are one.

We stay there only a few moments, and then I follow her out to buy chai and rice.

"I'm in trouble," I say. "Hariba has run away—she's jessed—and we don't have any money."

"I'll come back here tomorrow," the *harni* says in answer. She gives me an orange. I want to embrace her again, to feel safe. I want to take her with me back to Hariba.

She takes me to a stallman who sells fragrant basmati rice, and then we leave the souk and find a tea shop where I can buy chai.

"Do you live near here?" I ask her.

"My owner does," she says.

"In the Nekropolis?"

She shrugs. "I come shopping at this time most days."

"Tomorrow?" I ask.

"Tomorrow," she promises.

She doesn't wear a veil because she's a *harni* and therefore not a decent woman. Her hair runs down her back like a hot black tongue, shining in the sun. I remember the touch of her dry hand. The inside of the tea shop is cool and smells of mint and cinnamon. Hariba has to eat.

I have to buy a cup since I didn't bring one, but they have green tea chai, which Hariba likes better than black tea chai. It's milky, spiced, and sweet.

"Hariba," I whisper when I get home.

"Akhmim?" she asks.

"I brought you some chai."

"Ohhh, Akhmim," she says, grateful I've come back. "I can't, I can't drink it, I'll get sick."

"Drink a little," I say. "You have to have something."

I sit on the bed and coax her with spoonfuls, as if feeding a child. I push her hair back off her face. "Akhmim," she says, "I'm afraid. What are we going to do?"

"I'm here," I say. "I'll take care of you."

It is the right thing to say, and her little happiness, her relief, softens the room.

In the late afternoon I go to the Moussin of the White Falcon, but Myryam doesn't come that evening.

At night I lay down in bed next to Hariba, craving the touch of someone. For a few minutes she lets our skin touch. Her skin is hot and alive. Supple and smooth and faintly damp. I can smell the rich odor of her unwashed hair. I think of the *harni* in the souk and of her touch. I close my eyes. I'm calm. Lonely, but not quite as lonely with Hariba here beside me.

After a few minutes, Hariba shifts, moving a little away. She can't sleep against me, nor can she stand it if I sleep against her. She can only allow so much touch.

The next morning the souk is full of wind and dust and women wrap their veils around their faces to keep the grit out of their teeth. I wait for my *harni*. Skin of my skin, bone of my bone, where are you?

At last I see her. Her hair is tied up, but pieces have escaped and blow around. She holds her hand up to the side of her face, trying to block the dust.

She beckons me and I follow her back to the tea shop. I'm hoping that we'll go behind a stall again, but with the wind so bad the cotton cloths snap and bell and there is no sensible place for us to hide. It's too easy to imagine the shape of our bodies in the full-bellied cloth and the stallman thinking we were human lovers.

The tea shop lets us get out of the wind, at least.

I'm hungry, but after paying for our room, I don't have very much money left. I ask for mint tea. The *harni* sits down across from me. No one here has ever seen a *harni*, no one here even knows to think we might not be human.

"You need something to eat," she says. She signals the waiter and tells him to bring us flaky dough pockets filled with beans and orange and figs. "And a pot of black tea with milk," she adds.

She leans forward. "I can get you work," she says.

"Ah," I say, relieved. "What?"

"You can rent yourself as a servant," she says. "For a

few hours at a time. My owner can help you. He does it with me."

"Do you think I could do it?"

She shrugs. "It isn't hard."

"What? I'd help when they needed more people?" I'm thinking of the mistress's *bismek* games. "Serve food?"

"No," she says, "sex. Humans are always looking for someone to have sex with them."

Hariba isn't. Sex frightens her, although she loves to be kissed. But I'm relieved, sex is easy. "You mean like a prostitute."

She nodded. "But you mustn't call us that. My owner gets angry when you do." She flips her hair over her shoulder. She has a high, strong nose and beautiful eyes. Humans would think she's lovely. I'm happy to just be with her. It's much easier than trying to anticipate Hariba's feelings. She doesn't require me to talk, and I don't require her to talk. Being close to her makes me itch. I want skintouch. I want to smell her. If we could just go somewhere and curl up together, my happiness would be complete.

"Can we go somewhere?" I say.

" 'Can we go somewhere?' " she mimics me, sounding plaintive, and laughs with delight. *Harni* games.

I sit in my chair like a woman and flip my hair back.

We laugh together, and the sound blends until it sounds like one laugh, neither male nor female.

The *harni*'s house is on the edge of the Nekropolis, outside the wall. It's a real house on an old street. The house next door has a crumbling wall. There are bricks in the street and plastic sheeting to keep the wind out. The *harni*'s house looks strong and tight.

Her owner is a man of middle age, neither short nor tall, with hair that thins to a bare coin-sized patch at his crown. He's quick and has an oddly delicate way of using his hands. He's talking to a short man delivering oil and as he talks he taps his palm with one finger. His fingernails are beautifully manicured.

He turns to us, frowning, and then his eyebrows fly up and he says, "Ah!" To the oilman he says, "All right? All right?"

"Yes, Karim-salah," the oilman says.

Karim beckons to us to follow him across the courtyard to his office. "Yes, yes, yes," he says. "Sit down. Let me look at you. You're a *harni*, and you want to work for me. Yes?"

"Yes, Karim-salah," I say. I smile my best, but he's too distracted. There's no making him happy, he's busy, too busy, eyes on me, but his mind is everywhere.

"Have you had any experience serving people? For their pleasure? Yes? You understand?"

"Yes, I understand, but no, I've not . . . not really."

"Never mind," he says, "you're a *harni*. You're all perverted, like foreigners. Ebuyeth, you show him around? Then we will talk about money."

"Yes, Karim-salah," my *harni* says.

It's a very old-fashioned house. At the center is a courtyard with patterned tiles around the edges and porticos on all four sides. The shuttered windows are closed, but the louvers are open to let in the air and yellow draperies fill and sigh in the doorways. At two opposite corners are stairways and on the second and third floors are more covered walkways with more rooms opening off them.

"Up here," says the *harni* and lifts her robes to climb the stairs. "These two sides"—she gestures to the west and the north of the open courtyard—"these are women. That side"—she points towards the east—"that is for men and boys, and that"—she points to the south"—is for us. Fadima! Tabi! Everyone, I'm bringing a new one in!" she calls and pulls aside the draperies to the women's side. Two children are playing beside a big clay olive jar. A woman without a veil is sitting on a couch, putting henna on the backs of another woman's hands. There's a foreign hair wand on the floor, and magazines, and celebrity picture printouts taped to the walls.

"Karim says he doesn't have any money," says the one getting her hands painted. "But he goes and buys a *harni*."

"No," the *harni* says, "he is independent."

"Independent?" says the woman. "Who owns him?"

Who owns me, indeed? "My owner is Hariba," I say, "but she wishes to pretend we're free."

"Tabi!" they call. "Tabi! Come here!"

Three more women come from rooms. Tabi is a little woman with very round hips who has makeup stains on her pink robe. A bare-chested boy, painted like a girl but with his small nipples rouged, slides around the curtain and another boy, barely dressed but without paint, follows him. The unpainted boy has a water pipe and he draws on it.

"Put that down right here, Mouse," says one of the women, but he just smiles, chin tucked down and eyes cast sideways at her, and draws more smoke.

"You don't want to work for Karim," says one of the women.

Tabi rolls her eyes. "Mashahana. Karim is no better and no worse than any of them."

"How would you know? You've never worked anywhere else!"

"Neither have you," Tabi says.

"Are you jessed?" I ask.

They all laugh. "Of course not," says the one who is painting the other's hands. "We're not slaves. Except for the *harni*."

The painted boy says, "Do you think Karim will let us play some music?"

The women hoot. "Boy, do you want to pay for power out of your own pocket?"

"I bought power cells on Wednesday and he said he'd pay me back! He hasn't let us play the music system in a week," the boy says.

"The only music Karim likes is the clink of coins."

I had never seen a coin until I went to the souk with Hariba. I thought money was all electronic, but in the Nekropolis they still use cash.

"Karim is too stingy," one of the women says to no one in particular.

"You can always make your own music."

Another woman hums and gets up and dances a few steps.

My *harni* pulls my arm a little and we duck out of the draperies and go to her side, which is now, I assume, my side. She pulls back the drapery and a girl and a boy, coiled together on the rose-colored couch, unfold. They are very young, and despite the differences of their sex, alike as two young gazelles. They look at me, resting on their elbows, the boy's hand resting on the girl's thigh. The walls here are bare and the floor is stained but bare.

There is nothing to say, only skin. I sit down on the couch and we all touch and pet each other and I inhale young milky

skin with its faintly cinnamon scent. I slide my shoes off and
for the first time since I left the crèche to go to Mbarek-salah's,
I'm we.

The light's very bright when the draperies are pulled aside. I
can only blink and make out the silhouette.

"Mashahana, you *harni* are disgusting. Karim is looking for
you and the new one, Ebuyeth." It's Tabi.

I sit up, away from the comfort of touch, and the perspiration on my skin dries in the dusty air. I slip into my shoes. I'm
sorry Tabi doesn't like when we touch, but I can't help doing
it, even if it would make her happy.

"You know," she says, "I'd understand if you had sex, although Mashahana knows, we all get more of that than anyone wants, but this piling on top of each other is unnatural.
Like rats in winter."

I follow Ebuyeth.

"The more of you there are together, the worse it is," Tabi
says.

It's nice in a way, because she doesn't care if we answer or
not. She's not really talking to us at all.

Downstairs Karim is sitting at his desk, papers in front of him.

"You find it all satisfactory?" Karim says. "Okay? You will
get forty percent?" He touches the papers with the tip of a
stylus. "Which is fair, because I provide the place, and
arrange for the people to meet you and make sure that if
there is too much roughness you don't have to serve that
person again. I've never done anything like this, had someone here who wasn't part of my household. You understand,
I'm merely trying this out. If it doesn't work out, you will

have to leave." He taps his teeth with the stylus. "Come back this evening, at dusk."

The *harni* lets me out. I touch her hand, the warm, dry skin. I don't want to leave, but when I think of Hariba, I know she'll be upset.

It's afternoon and the day's nearly gone. The wind blows grit in my face and men go home bent against it, with their djellabas pushed against their legs. The sunlight is angled harsh against the buildings.

I only have a little money, enough to buy chai for Hariba, but maybe tomorrow I'll have more.

"Where have you been?" she says when I come in. She's sitting in the bed with her knees drawn up to her chin. Her face is bony and she's getting thin.

"I've work," I say. "I found some work."

"Ahhhh," she sighs. "What kind?" I've pleased her.

"Waiting tables at a club. But it's very late. At first I don't know how much money I will make. I'm going back tonight."

"Tonight?" she says. She doesn't want to be left here.

"It'll be okay," I promise. "How are you feeling? Are you getting better? I brought you some chai."

I sit next to her on the bed and feed her like a child. She'll take about half a cup and then she says no more, afraid it will make her sick.

"It's just on trial tonight," I say. "I don't know if I'll make any money at all."

"Will they give you dinner?" Hariba is ever-practical.

"Yes, I think they'll give me dinner." I lie down beside her where she sits. "I don't want to leave you here."

She smiles. "You're too good to me. Put your head on my lap." She strokes my forehead. "What's it like? This place?"

"It's on the edge of the Nekropolis, in a regular house, not a death house. The owner's name is Karim and he's a little fussy. He talks too much." I make my hand into a mouth and make it talk. "He's nice enough, though."

She laughs. "You charmed him, didn't you."

"I don't know," I say. "He doesn't notice much except Karim."

I make small talk with her and she's happy and even finishes her chai. Maybe she's adapting to not being jessed. I don't think Hariba has had a lot of happiness. Unless it sneaks up on her, she's wary of it. I have to ambush her to get her smiling.

"I'll make flowers for a while, when you're out," she says.

"And then when I come back, I pick up all these little snips of paper. It's just to make me work," I say.

"Yes," she says. "Work, my husband!"

"Your flowers are beautiful."

Hariba doesn't know how to flirt, but she loves it.

I leave her feeling good, sitting in the bed surrounded by sheets of paper. Soon I'll have money to buy her more paper and she can make crisp, dry roses and stiff tulips that shimmer like silk.

The wind is still blowing. I don't mind at first, but the wind wears at me until I'm glad to get to Karim's house. Inside the door, the heat of the day is still in the walls, warm and kind.

Karim is in his office, and he directs me upstairs. The courtyard has a string of lights—red, green, yellow, blue, white—shaped like candle flames. Upstairs the drapes have been pulled aside so the front rooms are all open, lit with soft lights, and everybody sits as if this were a play. The women

are all dressed in thin robes and their rosy nipples and the tri-
angles of their pubic hair are visible through the cloth.
They're all painted and their hair is curled. One of the boys
looks like a beautiful girl. His robe is nearly transparent, too,
except it has a panel of fabric that runs down the front from
neck to hem, hiding his sex.

The *harni* are all naked. The woman and the girl each
wear a gold chain necklace and slippers, but the boy wears
nothing at all. I take off my clothes. I'm glad it's warm in the
room.

The women are talking, in a desultory way, about nothing
really. "So then, what did your cousin say?" "He said it was
none of her business, anyway. He said what he did when he
was working was his business."

Karim comes upstairs. "Sit on that couch," he says to me,
pointing. "You're pretty old. Most people want a boy. Still,
we'll see. Tabi? Is everything all right?"

"Whoever sold you these figs stole your money," she says.

Karim goes back downstairs. Being a prostitute is a lot like
being a servant—nothing much happens. A little later a man
comes up the stairs and hands one of the women a length of
violet ribbon. She smiles up at him, takes him by the hand,
and leads him back into a room.

"Violet means oral sex," says Ebuyeth. "Blue means inter-
course, red means anal sex."

"Ahh," I say, pleased to be enlightened.

"For your customers, use that room," she says, and points
to a doorway on my left.

The next man comes with a blue ribbon for the *harni* girl.
She stands up. She's young; her body has hardly any
curves and her breasts are tiny, pointed things. She doesn't

look at the man, but keeps her head down, as if she were shy.

"Hello, Ubu Hraith-salah," she says in a little voice and leads him to a room.

A servant girl hurries upstairs and says, "Tabi, Fadima, Suyet, downstairs."

Tabi sighs and gets to her feet and the girls go. There are voices and music downstairs.

More men come up and take Ebuyeth, some of the other women, the painted boy dressed as a girl, and the other boy who is painted but wears trousers.

Finally a man comes up holding a red ribbon and stops in front of me. He holds out the ribbon to me. He's middle-aged and his face is heavily lined.

I take the ribbon and lead him to the room that my *harni* told me to use. I wonder how much money I'll make. The room is tiny and dim. There is a lamp covered with a red cloth and the whole room is red. The man's face is red, as if he stood in front of a fire. He's irritated with me. It'll be hard to make him happy—I'm not sure he wants me to.

"Do you want me to lie on the bed?" I ask.

"I want you to kneel. Face that way," he says.

On the table beside the bed there are jars and packages. He takes a wide-mouthed jar and and smears my ass with it. It's cold and the goose bumps stand up on the skin of my thighs. Then he pulls up his robes and, looking over my shoulder, I see that his cock is aroused. He smears it with the same gel. Then he gets on the bed, on his knees, and knee-walks until he is between my legs.

He puts the tip of it against me and pushes it in. I tighten up. "Relax," he snaps.

It hurts. The skin feels stretched. I relax as best I can. I can really only feel him at the opening, and inside a strange sensation, as if I need to defecate really badly. It hurts. I'm trying to figure out if he wants it to hurt or not.

He starts to move back and forth. I grit my teeth and kneel on the uneven surface of the bed. I feel as if I'm torn and I can't help making a cry, but he doesn't seem to notice. I drop my head and breathe out through my mouth—harsh breaths.

Finally he shudders and pulls out. He gets off the bed and walks out without looking back at me.

I don't know if I did well, or if I did badly and he's mad at me, but I hurt and I'm startled and not sure what to do. When I stand up, a little trickle of blood runs down the inside of my leg. I find a washcloth and dip it in cold water and try to clean myself up. I walk bowlegged back out to where the *harni* boy and Ebuyeth are sitting.

Ebuyeth takes me back to a place where I can clean up better and washes me, then puts a cold gel on that makes me feel numb. Then we lean together for a while. Skintalk.

We go back out and wait.

That night I have one more customer, but he wants oral sex. He's dark, darker than anyone I know, and his hair lies in tight curls against his head. He has fleshy, feminine lips. I think, From the way he is dressed, he drives a lorry or does some sort of construction work. He follows me into the little room. In the little room I catch the smell of him— unwashed male. His knuckles are grimy. When he drops his pants, the smell is stronger. He's wearing no underclothing.

He won't look at me.

Oral sex is easy, although a couple of times I choke. He grabs my head near the end and pumps away, but afterward he smiles at me and I smile back. He's pleased.

Some nights I don't have any customers and some nights I've five or six. Karim seems pleased enough by the arrangement. After the customers, I stay for a while with the *harni* before I go back to Hariba.

She's getting thinner. Her knee knobs are thicker than her thighs and her collarbones stand out like wings. Sometimes she has a few good hours, but then the headaches come back and she gets sick. The headache pills make her stomach hurt.

Two weeks after I start working, I find a death house we can rent. It's more comfortable than the hotel and not as expensive. The death houses are small and square, with thick walls where the coffins have been closed up in the masonry. Sometimes two death houses will be joined back-to-back. They have tiny windows and they're dark, but they are sturdy and cool in the day and warm at night.

"You'll feel better here," I tell Hariba. She's too frail to walk. I hired a pedicab to bring her here. But the death house makes her happy. "It's nice. It's a lot like the one I grew up in, but here, ours didn't have this carving on the lintel!" She holds her veil together, her fist tight against her chest. She points out things to me.

I settle her on her pallet with her lamp and her paper. There is a bank of solar collectors on the roof, and I buy a burner and a pot and a pan and we're all right, I think, for the moment. She's happier and I can feel the warmth of it.

The headache is bad and she has dry heaves. Then she lies

back and I stroke her damp forehead. "I'm not afraid to die," she says.

"Ask Tabi," Ebuyeth says in the evening. "Tabi might know what to do."

Tonight Tabi is wearing her pink robe, and she has rubbed rouge into her nipples. She's putting her hair up into a knot with a long tail hanging out of it. For a short woman she has a lot of hair.

"You look delicious," I say.

She accepts the compliment. Tabi doesn't dislike us, but she thinks we're very intelligent animals.

"I need your advice, Tabi," I say.

"If you're really going to talk to me, go put some clothes on," she says.

I go put on my shirt and come back.

She sighs and shakes her head.

"It's about my"—I'm not sure what to call Hariba—"my owner," I finally say. "She was jessed, and we ran away."

Tabi cocks her head at me. "That was stupid," she says.

"Yes," I say, "yes, I know. But she felt she had to."

"The poor thing thinks she's in love with you, doesn't she."

I shrug. "She's sick, all the time, because of the jessing. She has headaches and her stomach is sick and if she doesn't eat something, she'll starve to death."

Tabi lets her hair fall. "Why don't you just go back?"

"They would put her in prison, she says." They would put me down as unstable. I'm not ready to die.

Tabi stretches out one leg and studies it. "You might try hashish," she says finally. "It's good when your stomach is upset."

"Do you have some?" I ask.

"Ask Mouse," she says. "Mouse sells it."

Mouse sells me a bit no bigger than my thumb. "Do you have a pipe? I've got one you can have." Mouse's room is a dusty mess. It's a narrow room with a high window and there are clothes all over the floor—surprising because Mouse doesn't wear much, ever. I've never seen Mouse with shoes on, but there are a pair of sandals and three shoes. He rummages under the bed, his skinny ass in the air, then he looks into a wide-mouthed jar, like the kind housewives use to store oil. He pulls out a pair of scissors, a spool of ribbon with much of the ribbon off the spool and winding through the contents of the jar, a chopstick with a burned end, a much crumpled scarf, and a plastic toy truck the size of my hand before he evidently sees what he wants. "Here," he says.

The clay pipe is as long as my finger and it doesn't look as if it's ever been used. "How much?" I ask.

He shrugs. "I've got a bunch of them somewhere. Nothing. Are you going to smoke it?"

"No," I say, "it's for Hariba."

"Is she a *harni*?"

"No, she's human. She's sick and she can't eat. Tabi thought hashish would help her."

"It will, it's good for that. I was wondering because *harni* don't smoke hashish, I mean, not that I know of. She's not pregnant, is she?"

"No," I say.

"It's not good for pregnant women," he says, serious.

"Thank you," I say.

"Why don't *harni* smoke hashish?" he asks.

"I don't know."

"Does it work for you?"

I shrug. "Probably. Wine makes me drunk. But I think it isn't what we want. I think humans smoke hashish and drink wine because they're lonely, and even when they're together, they're still lonely, and they smoke and drink to forget."

"Maybe," Mouse says, looking into the jar. "Let me know if you need more." His voice seems to come from the jar.

I go back to the *harni* and wash Ebuyeth's hair and we all sit on the balcony in the last of the evening sun so it will dry. We sit all together so we all touch and I close my eyes and our skin is against skin. Then I forgot I-am-I and I'm just warm sunlight and skin and cinnamon scent.

The only time the boy and the girl are ever apart is when one or the other has a client. What would happen if we were allowed to grow up right? Without being separated in the crèche, without being taught where our skin ended and someone else's skin began. It would have been nice to find out.

It's too late for me, though. I'm aware of myself most of the time. I even enjoy being together in a *harni* pile as myself. Whenever there is "I" there is "other" and when they separated my siblings and me, I became "I" and lost all the rest to "other."

I like sex. I have one client who comes and does oral sex to me while I do oral sex to him, lying head to genitals on the bed. I like the feeling and I like coming. Like hashish and wine, in the moment of coming there is utter forgetfulness of self. But that's as close as humans ever seem to come to the merging of "I" and "other"—the momentary forgetfulness of separation, which isn't the same.

That's why humans are only happy when they are doing,

because when they're absorbed in something they forget the awful loneliness of being themselves.

"I brought you something," I tell Hariba in the morning. "Tabi said it would help you feel better."

"Who is Tabi?" she asks, sleepy.

"The owner's wife where I work," I say.

"Medicine," she says, sounded defeated.

"To help you not feel sick."

"If I feel sick, how can I take this medicine so I don't feel sick?" she says, but smiles a tired smile, trying not to be peevish.

"Ah," I say, "there's the secret. You smoke it."

She sits up and pushes her heavy hair back from her face. "What is it?"

"Hashish," I say, and push back a strand of hair that falls back across her forehead.

"Akhmim!" she says. "Hashish? Old men sit at hashish bars and smoke it, it's not a medicine!"

"Tabi said it would help," I say, coaxing and cajoling. With Hariba sick, it's hard to get moments of peace. I'm always anxious, trying to please, trying to satisfy.

"I . . . can't," she says. But I know I can get her to do it. She doesn't have the energy to resist. I sit on the bed next to her and she watches with dull eyes while I unpeel the foil from around the hashish. It's dark, resinous stuff. I put some in the bowl of the pipe and light a match, and, as I've seen men do, lay the lighted match across the bowl and carefully hand her the pipe.

She takes a draw and coughs out smoke. "It's *harsh*," she says, "and the smoke is *hot*."

"It's okay," I say. "Try again."

She manages to hold it a moment before coughing, and then she hands me the pipe, shaking her head. "I can't, Akhmim, I can't."

She lies back. Her eyes are watering and I wipe them with the edge of the sheet. "It's okay," I say. "It'll get better." Her plain square face is very dear to me. Sometimes it amazes me that we aren't the same thing, that she's human. Her otherness hits me most at moments like this when I'm understanding her well and I suddenly wonder how much of that understanding is just my assumptions of sameness, and then I wonder what she's really thinking and feeling. Her face becomes familiar and strange. She's really a stranger in my life, this human, who has turned everything upside-down.

She doesn't know I'm looking at the animal she is, human animal. I stroke her hand as a kind of apology. I live with her every day, in this place of animals. In a bit the strangeness will pass and she'll be just Hariba to me again.

"Try some more," I say.

"Akhmim," she protests weakly, "I can't."

But she does. After a bit, I can see that her pupils are big and dark. "I feel strange," she says.

"It's hashish."

"I know," she says, and pauses as if she were going to say something, but doesn't say anything.

"Have some rice."

"I wish we had something sweet," she says.

"How about a little milk and honey in your rice?" I offer. I make a kind of pudding of the rice, cooking it in milk and egg and sweetening it and even dusting a little cinnamon on top.

She eats it in tiny bites off the spoon, but she eats all of it, the whole bowl, and then, her shrunken stomach full, she falls asleep. I lie down next to her in the dim, cool death house, with the dates of the dead in the wall barely visible, and sleep, dreaming of sex and cinnamon.

In the evening she smokes more hashish, doing better this time. "I will become a regular rich man's wife," she says, "expecting my hashish." She's languid and happy and something rises within me, eased.

I buy some tangine to celebrate, but although she eats a little of it, the stew of pigeon and fruit in pastry is too rich for her. "Make me rice pudding," she begs, so I do, and watch to make sure she eats most of it before running out into the hot evening to go to Karim's house. I'm almost sad to go, it's nice to be with Hariba when she's smoked the hashish.

"Tabi," I say, coming up the stairs. "Tabi!"

Tabi is sitting in her room, peering into a mirror at her eye makeup. "It's too hot for all this rushing around," she says.

I kiss the top of her head. "Thank you, thank you. The hashish really helped."

Tabi smiles, genuinely pleased.

Mouse sells me more, and suggests that I buy a water pipe. "It cools the smoke," he says. "It'll be easier for her." He tells me where to buy one.

It's hot, so I'm glad to strip my clothes. I sit hip to hip with Ebuyeth, skin to skin, while the boy and the girl lie together on the couch, watching nothing with sleepy, empty eyes. Away from human needs is such a relief.

The girl is the busiest of all of us. Most nights she has an unending stream of customers. They come in looking for her.

Some are hopeful, some are hangdog, a few, here for their first time, are scared, but very few are happy.

My first customer is here for anal sex. I've learned a lot since the first night. Anal sex isn't that bad. I take him back into my little room with its red wash of light. I have a basin and a cloth and first I have him lie down and I soap his penis and clean it gently until it's standing for me. Then I use the gel, warming it in my hands before I put it on him. He watches me, his robe hiked up so that he is exposed and vulnerable, but he likes the feel of my hands. I don't feel as if he wants me to talk, and when I glance at him, he looks away. I don't look at him again.

He's not pretty, this one. His face is sunken in and he has a thin beard full of white and gray. His thighs are thin, his calves are poor. His breath smells.

When I've greased him up, I grease myself. I've learned to relax, and it's easy now. One customer told me a human can never relax the way a *harni* can—he said it so I'd know that he considered me no better than a slut by nature, so after that I'd act ashamed for him and he was pleased.

There is always some resistance at first, the customer must push past the tight ring of sphincter. That is where most of the feeling is for me. Once he is inside me, I feel him as a fullness, and deeper inside me, a pleasant excitement, if I'm not too tired to care.

This one sighs, "Ahhh," as he pushes inside me.

I think of Hariba and of how I'd like to sleep while he is pumping. As long as he doesn't come out of me unexpectedly, I don't have to think much to stay relaxed.

It's hard, working all night and tending to Hariba during the day. I'd like to sleep for a whole night. I'd like the smooth suppleness of skin, warm and living, lying next to me as I fell asleep. Maybe if I don't have many customers, I can sleep tonight.

That's what I think while he jerks and moans.

After midnight, we have soup and bread. The girl has a bad tooth and she soaks her bread until the crust is soft before eating it. I go downstairs and find Karim.

"Put a robe on if you come downstairs," he says absently.

"Yes, Karim-salah," I say. "The girl has a toothache."

"Wassyla?" he says.

I don't know her name. "The *harni*," I say.

"Holy One," Karim mutters. "Now a dentist bill. Can she still work?"

"I believe so," I say.

He gets up and I follow him down the hall, watching his heels lick at the hem of his robe as he walks. He comes upstairs. A rare enough thing. There is a flutter among the human girls. Ebuyeth sits with her hands in her lap. The girl and the boy gaze up mutely.

"Your tooth hurts?" he asks.

"Yes, Karim-salah," she says. I've rarely heard her voice. It's sweet and high.

"Open your mouth," he says, and takes her face in his hand to tilt her head back. "Which one?"

"One the left side," she says, "on the bottom."

"Her cheek is swollen," the boy says. I've heard his voice even less than the girl's. It might almost be hers, dropped an octave but still sweet.

She winces slightly when Karim touches her cheek.

"All right," Karim says, "enough for tonight. You go in back and go to sleep."

"Karim-salah," she says, "may I stay out here?"

He has already started to walk away and he turns around in a swirl of striped robe. He looks suspicious.

"I'll work, if you want," she says.

He frowns.

"She doesn't want to be alone," I say. "She's a *harni*, Karim-salah."

He looks at me, then at her, then at all of us, frowning. "All right," he says finally, and turns on his heel and goes downstairs. The girl stays with us all night, but no one has a ribbon for her, and when we aren't working, we stay touching her until finally, when the night is over, Tabi brings her an analgesic patch. There is the sharp smell of rubbing alcohol when she peels it open. I can still smell it over the cinnamon skin smell when we all curl up together to sleep for a few hours.

Hariba is ready for her hashish when I get home, and after I've gotten her to eat some sweet rice.

I think about ways to make things better, but I can't think of anything. I wouldn't give up being with the *harni*, and I can't leave Hariba alone and sick. Hariba brought me here, and I won't forget that, not even for the pleasure of *harni* company.

I watch her sleep on the bed. Her skin is dry. I'll get some of Tabi's oil and oil Hariba's skin until it's soft and supple and warm. I sleep and dream of men's bodies and the things that I can do that excite them, like a puzzle of organs and openings. It isn't a bad dream, just tiring.

"Akhmim?"

I'm walking near the Moussin of the White Falcon, looking for a shop that Mouse told me about where I can buy a water pipe to replace the little clay pipe I got from Mouse and some hashish. The hashish, he promises, is decently priced and I'll be glad to have made the trip.

"Akhmim?" It's the widow, Myryam, who bought Hariba's canna lily wreath.

"Hello! Hello!" I say, and her face melts with relief.

"I waited for you twice," she says and shakes a finger at me.

"Oh, pardon!" I say. "I found a job in the evenings and I haven't been able to wait there for you!"

She's pleased to have the excuse to forgive me. She asks me about my wife.

I lift my hands in a little helpless gesture.

"Ah," she says, "poor thing. Listen, then, I've found you a job. Not a real job at first"—she makes vague motions with her hands—"but there is a man that my brother knows, he needs someone to take care of visitors, show them places for a few hours."

I start to say that I've a job, but the hashish for Hariba is expensive. "Every day?" I say.

"No, not at first," she says. "Just once or twice a week. But you're such a decent young man, I'm certain there'll be more and more opportunities."

I think about it. The sun's hot and the air is so dry it makes your nose bleed. A few hours, maybe it would pay for the hashish.

The man that her brother knows is younger than I expected. "Myryam sent you?" he says. His name is Yusef. "Good. Have you lived here all your life?"

"No," I admit, "I used to live outside of here, about an hour and a half away."

"Hmm," he says. I feel his disappointment. "Well, you could follow Saad on a tour for a couple of days, assist, and we'll see if you pick up the spiel. You know this is only a couple of times a week?"

"Myryam told me." I smile to show this isn't any problem. That I like him.

"Saad is taking a group to the souk and the Moussin in"— he leans back to check the clock on the wall—"forty-five minutes. Can you go with him?"

"Sure," I say.

"It's not hard, if you're good with people. Some people can do it, some can't." He looks past me and out the door. "Some, like Saad, never get it right." He grins. "Oh, Saad, didn't see you standing there."

Saad is slight, with graying hair. He shakes his head, but he is smiling. "Taking half-naked foreigners to the Moussin isn't enough punishment. I have to have a boss who is a crazy man."

"It's a business for the insane," Yusef says.

"That's true," says Saad.

We drink mint tea and they complain about the people they take around. "Foreigners," Yusef says, "they aren't bad. You show them the Moussin, you tell them a couple of stories about martyrs, that's all they want."

The foreigners come on a big lorry-bus. I'm expecting the women to have on next to nothing, but they are decently, if oddly, covered. They wear long skirts and sandals colored like children's candy. The men wear white shin-length caftans over their bright shirts and sand-colored trousers. Their shoes are big, complicated things with laces and ties. They all look club-footed, but they walk all right.

They have a translator with them, a women with strands of windblown hair showing under her scarf. She comes up to us, her shoulders hunched and her mouth pinched. Her eyes are invisible behind big sunglasses. Then she smiles. "Yusef, Saad. We're not late?"

"Late?" Yusef says. "No, not at all."

"They all dressed for the Moussin. They're all right?"

"They are fine," Saad says. "They understand that the women can't go into the sanctuary?"

"Yes. Into the Moussin, but not the sanctuary."

The woman talks as if she were a man. I've never seen a foreigner before. Her skin is pink and delicate, but the wind's reddened her cheeks and roughed her up.

She turns and talks to them in their language, beckoning. The crowd straggles over. She introduces Saad, who greets them in their language. But that's all of it that he speaks. He outlines the tour, stopping to let her translate. I study the foreigners, their faces as pale as cheese. A few talk to each other, but most of them listen like schoolchildren, carefully watching Saad when he speaks although they don't understand him.

He takes them down the street to a tea shop and I follow. They sit down and the owner pours them watery mint tea.

"You said we wouldn't be coming here again," the foreign woman says.

Saad shrugs. "Yusef makes the decisions, I can only suggest."

"I get complaints about this place every time." She starts to say more, but someone calls out to her and she goes over to talk to them.

"It's not very good tea," Saad says to me, "but they don't really care."

It's not a very nice tea shop, either, but it's big enough for all of them. A regular tea shop would have been too busy anyway, there wouldn't have been enough chairs. They sip the indifferent tea while the owner shows them brass and silver bracelets to buy.

Eventually Saad has the foreign woman round them up again and we troop back up the street to the lorry-bus. It's a tall narrow thing with steps up. Saad directs me to the front seat, so high I look down on the driver. It's cool inside and the windows are like smoke, just cutting the glare of the day. The movement of the air raises goose bumps on the skin of my arms.

The city looks different from the bus—distant.

The foreigners smile at me as they climb on and file past. A couple say, "Good morning," badly. I say, "Good morning" back to them.

We go to the souk first, and Saad explains that we are going to go to the street of gold and then to look at carpets. They all get off in single file and clump at the edge of the bus. I get off the bus and the heat is like a blanket, welcome after the chill of the bus. Saad and the foreign woman walk off and the foreigners follow and so do I. I've never been to the street of gold.

It isn't like I pictured it. A street of gold should be a bit more astonishing, I think, but trash still collects in the gutters and most of the shops don't have much gold. I haven't walked very far before I'm hot—the bus is very cold.

Saad explains how the street of gold has been in the bazaar in one form or another for nearly two millennia. At one time there were four hundred jewelers working here, and beggars used to sift the dust for gold. They'd scoop up the dirt out of the street and put it in a pan and pour water over it, then they'd swirl the water around—he gestures to show the motion while the foreign woman translates—and the heavier gold flake would settle to the bottom of the flat pan.

I think it sounds impossible, but the foreigners seem to like it. Saad's a little like a *harni*. He lives off of making these people happy.

He tells them the names of some of the families who have been here four and five hundred years. He tells them how to tell good-quality gold from stuff that's been adulterated.

He tells them about the symbols of our country: the lion, the eagle, the goat, and the snake. "Watch for them in jewelry," he says. I wonder why anyone would want to come and be lectured at. He acts as if they are all children.

The foreigners disperse to shop.

"That's all?" I ask.

Saad shrugs. "They come to shop," he says. "The Moussin is different."

I walk down the street. Two women are trying to learn the price of something. They keep motioning for the jeweler to write it down, but he doesn't seem to understand.

"How much?" I ask him.

He's old, and his eyes disappear in wrinkles when he smiles.

I write the sum down on one of the women's minders. She's looking at a bracelet.

I pick up a smooth piece that ends in lion heads and open it. "This," I say.

She dutifully holds out her arm and I let it close around her wrist. It's hard to tell how old foreigners are. She is lovely and looks like a girl, but she has lines around her eyes and mouth, as if she's been kept artificially young.

She and her companion look at the bracelet, chattering. Her companion is older. I can tell that, even if her companion's hair is young and red.

She asks the shopkeeper how much for the bracelet. The sum he tells her is far too high—I write it on the slate, but draw a line through it and write down half the amount and show it to them.

The shopkeeper bargains with me. The amount we agree on is still way too high, but they are foreigners.

The woman is delighted and embarrassed. The older woman wants something, too, so I walk with them until she finds a bracelet she likes. It's flat and chased with a pattern of orange leaves and curliques.

When both women have their bracelets, I find Saad. I'm not sure how long we'll stay here. He's been watching me with the two women.

"If you do that for one," Saad says, "they'll all want it." But he's smiling. The foreign woman who translates smiles, too.

This is easy. These people want very much to be pleased.

But I'm not working with the *harni*. I'd rather sleep.

When I come back home, Hariba is shaking in fever. "Akhmim," she says, reaching out for me. Her need for me is nothing like the need of the two foreigners. Their need was simple and clean and it was easy to fill them up, but Hariba is sick. Frightened. When she needed love and attention, that was easy. When she sat with her fingers full of paper, folding flowers and trying to teach me the names, I'd say her name and it was like rain. She'd turn her face toward me.

"I'm here, Hariba," I say.

"It's all shaking," she says.

Her face is white and red and her hair clings to her back in damp rat tails. She's dehydrated.

"You need some tea," I say.

"We need to get outside," she says. "It's going to shake down on top of us!"

"What's going to shake down on top of us?"

"The roof!" she says.

"It's not shaking," I say, my voice as gentle as I can make it. "You have a fever. Lie back down."

"No!" she says, "Don't you feel it?" She grabs the sheet in her hands, wringing it, "O Prophet! Please, please, we have to get out!" I sit down next to her, holding her shoulders.

"It's okay," I say. "Hush now, it's okay." But my voice isn't getting through to her. I feel nervousness rising in me to match her fear.

"No," she says, and tries to push me away. She shoves hard, but I pull her close to me. She reaches up to touch my cheek, and grabs at my face with her nails. I rear back and she lunges away from her covers and she's past me and out into the street.

"Hariba!" I shout and chase her.

Her white sleeping robe is thin cotton and I can see her through it, almost as if she's naked. Poor Hariba would be mortified if she knew what she was doing, that she'd be dressed this way where strangers can see her. Her skin is brown where the damp cotton clings to her and she turns toward me and half-crouches, her face in anguish. She has her hands in front of her, pleading, but like claws.

"Hariba," I say. "Hariba." I croon it. "Hariba." She hears it and it speaks to something in her fever, but it's a tenuous thing and I'm afraid she'll run away from me. "Hariba," I say and slowly crouch down, sit down in the dust of the street. "Hariba."

She hesitates, partly I think because she has forgotten what she's running to or from. She sways.

"Hariba," I say again. Just her name. Long, and drawn-out, low, and almost a whisper.

I'm hypnotizing her with her name.

"Come back to me," I whisper.

She looks bemused.

"I'll help you," I whisper.

She shakes her head—and the movement unbalances her and she sits down in a heap.

I scrabble over to her—these are my good pants and they'll be dusty at work tonight, but what does it matter, since I don't wear clothes at work. Then again, I'm not sure I can leave her like this. What if I come home and find she's gone, wandering the streets in a fever dream?

"It's shaking," she says.

"Nothing's shaking," I say. "It's your poor fevered head."

"I'm cold," she says.

It's blisteringly hot, but there's a breeze. She's shivering and when I take her back inside, into the shade of our house, her teeth start chattering. I whisper her name and wrap her in blankets. There is no more wonderful sound to a human than their name.

"I'll make you some tea, Hariba, my Hariba," I say. "It will warm you up."

"When I close my eyes, I'm dreaming and I'm not even asleep," she says. At least my presence means something to her.

"I know, I know, sweet Hariba."

"Where's my mother?" she asks.

"Your mother? At her home."

"Take me home," she says.

"I can't," I say. The moment I say it I realize it's the wrong answer.

"Akhmim, take me home."

"Not this afternoon," I say. "Soon, but not this afternoon."

"I want to go home," she says. She's crying now.

"Your mother is probably selling wreaths," I say. "You rest now, we'll see your mother later." That soothes her. I should remember that.

She curls up on her side, wrapped in the blanket. I make mint tea and bring it to her.

"I don't want it," she says.

"You need it. Come on. It will warm you up."

She doesn't want it, but I sit and cajole and bully and lie. Sweat is trickling down my ribs, it's such hard work. But she sits up and sips tea. I keep at her, getting her to drink about half the cup.

"I'm hot," she says.

She lies down, and after a bit she starts moaning. I get a cloth and a bowl of water. "Come on," I say, and pull her cotton shift over her head. She raises her thin arms, listless as a child. I can see her sternum and the bones of her chest disappearing under her tiny breasts. She lies back down and I start to wipe her down with the cool water. Her nipples tighten up, but she doesn't acknowledge the cold.

She looks past me, as if I'm not even here.

And then she seizes.

She clenches her teeth and tightens all her muscles, her fingers in fists, and at first I think she's angry, but she starts going, "Unh, unh, unh," and I can see a sliver of white just under her half-closed eyelids.

"Hariba!" I say. "Hariba!"

She can't hear me for the storm in her. Is this the shaking she was afraid of? I keep calling her name, calling her, and then she relaxes. But she's empty, her eyes lolling white in her sockets for a few seconds, until she closes up as if she's in a deep sleep or a faint.

"Hariba," I whisper.

Eventually she opens her eyes. "Umm?" she says, her look vacant.

"Look at me," I say, and at first she doesn't, but finally she seems to make an effort and her eyes find me.

I push her tangled hair away from her face. "Just rest," I say, "I'm here." It's a relief, though, because for a few moments she doesn't have any need in her.

An hour later she has another brief seizure.

I don't go to work. I sit with her while the shadows lengthen, and I feed her sips of water. A little and a little more and a little more, until finally, around midnight, her fever breaks some and she falls into what seems to be a natural sleep.

Hariba's friend Ayesha answers the door, for which I'm thankful. "Yes?" she says, drawing her veil up over her mouth, thinking she's in the presence of a strange man, and then she recognizes me. "You!" she hisses. "What have you done with Hariba?"

I don't know what to say. "I . . . I haven't done anything with Hariba. She's sick, I need your help."

She glares at me. I think she's going to shout for help. "Please!" I say, "Hariba is sick and she wants her mother!"

"Take me to her," she says.

Ayesha doesn't speak to me while we walk. Her anger makes me nervous. I keep smiling at her, trying to get her to see that I don't mean any harm, that I'm just trying to help Hariba. I'm not bad, I want to say. "I've found some work," I explain. "And we rented a house like yours, like hers. She feels more at home. But she's sick, I think from the jessing." We turn onto our little street. "It's that one." I point. "That's where we're living."

Ayesha runs to the door and calls for Hariba.

"Here," Hariba answers in a small voice. It's early in the day and her fever is down this morning. She felt normal to my touch when I left to get Ayesha.

Ayesha runs inside and kneels beside her, stroking her face and calling her sweet names and crying.

"Akhmim?" Hariba says. "Why did you go get Ayesha?"

"Because you're sick, and you need your family."

"No," she shakes her head. "Ayesha, no, you mustn't tell anyone you saw me . . ." and then she dissolves into weak tears.

"You need a doctor," Ayesha says.

"No," Hariba says. "No, he'll tell the police! Akhmim can take care of me!"

"You need more care than I can give you," I say, kneeling down next to them. "I have to work, to take care of us."

Ayesha hisses at me, "Get away from her."

I sit back on my heels, unsure what I've done. Maybe I didn't know what to do and I've made Hariba more sick? "I've been trying to take care of her—"

"Shut up," Ayesha says.

Hariba cries wordlessly.

Ayesha says, "I'll go get Nabil."

"No!" Hariba says.

But it's all in motion.

Ayesha comes back with a small stocky man—I can see Hariba's face in his, although her hair is straight and his is in loose curls. They have a pedicab with them and they bundle her in.

"Akhmim!" she says. "Akhmim has to come with me!"

Ayesha stares at me in hate. Her brother doesn't even admit I exist. They take her away—she's too weak to do aything but cry for me.

I've failed. I've left her unhappy, and I can hear her calling me, even when she's out of sight.

I wish I were at Karim's. I wish I were with the *harni*.

3
Duty

All of my children are taller than me. Their father wasn't a particularly tall man, but my father and brothers were tall. Allah made me small so I wouldn't need much, I always said. I gave it all to my children. Fhassin was tall. Even Rashida, my second daughter and the smallest one, she is bigger than me. But look at what has happened. I've lost one. Fhassin is dead to us all, though I pray for him. I think it was because he was my favorite and no matter how much you hide it, children know. And now Hariba comes home, sick and in disgrace.

I go over it in my mind. What did I do wrong? Was it only because they grew up without a father? The youngest, Nabil, wasn't born when his father died.

I am sitting in the door of my sister's house—my grand-niece climbs onto my lap and holds out her chubby fist and breathes, "Look." She uncurls her fist to show me a raisin stuck with crumbs. She has a biscuit in her other hand. She smells of crumbs and sour food. She closes her fist again. Opens it again and breathes, "Look."

"I see," I say.

Sarai, for that is her name, puts the raisin down in the doorway, deliberate and thoughtful. She looks at it, her hand splayed open suspended in the air. She reaches back down to pick it up and her palm squishes it against the floor. She fumbles and picks it up and it is covered with dust. She raises it toward her mouth and I say, "Sarai, no."

She looks at me, considering. Watching me, she brings it toward her mouth again.

"No," I say again. I expect her to try to put it in her mouth anyway, and then I'll take it from her and she'll cry. Instead she holds it out to give it to me. I open my hand and she drops it in.

My sister has a cat and it has had a litter of kittens. Skinny, long-legged things with heads too small for their bodies. Sarai sees a kitten and toddles after it. The kittens are half-wild things. They can take care of themselves. I throw the dirty raisin into the street.

My youngest daughter is pregnant. I want to have grandchildren, but am I ready again for babies? Am I ready to still myself and to slow myself for her little ones? When Hariba was a year old and Rashida was on the way, I remember crouching on the floor, bulky with child, and saying to Hariba, "No, no, no. Sharp. Don't touch." I remember that moment, not because of what I said but because I realized how many hours of my life I had already spent slowing my mind down, and thinking of nothing but this child, and that I would have years of children ahead of me. I loved her. I loved her too much, the way when she was sitting she would roll onto one hip and put her hand on the floor, trying to decide if she should crawl or walk, if the speed of walking was worth the difficulty of getting up and the danger of falling down. But I wanted to talk to someone, and my husband and I, we were new to the neighborhood then and I didn't know anyone. Women can only survive if they have other women who understand, who know what it's like when you've been saying "no" all day to a toddler and you are tired of her anger and her unreasonableness, when you have become nothing but "no" and "no" and "no." Don't climb that, don't go out there, don't walk away from me, don't eat that, don't pick that up. Hours of "no"s. Years of "no"s. And you're tired because you have the baby and your home and your life and the baby has nothing but itself.

I didn't love Hariba when she was born. I thought she would come out of me and I would love her. When she was born, I looked at her and I was frightened. We were living in my husband's family's flat over the barbershop and his mother and his sister and my mother were all there and they put her on my swollen belly. Her face was flat and creased, you could barely see her eyes and I thought I would see her and become a mother at that moment. But I didn't feel she was mine. She was dangerous, so frail, I was afraid I would do something wrong. Did she feel that denial in me? After she was born, I grew so sad and tired that I could barely get out of bed, and Samil, my poor husband, would come home to find nothing cooked, nothing done, and me sitting on the bed, holding the baby.

She had an empty mother those first months. I had nothing to fill her with. When Rashida was born, I had friends. They came to the birthing. We would trade children, give each other a break sometimes. Hamet would come over with her boy on her hip and say, "Talk to me! I need an intelligent voice or I'll go mad!" She was plump and pretty and desperate, and we'd laugh. In the death houses it was a city of women and children and old people during the day. It was full of mess and crumbs and noise. Then it would start to get dark and the men would come home. Samil would say to the little ones, "Stop making that racket!" and I'd shush them. The doors of the death houses would be open and bars of light would come from them, and between the bars of light would be purple shadows. The sound of cutlery on plates. The smell of charcoal and flatbread and rice.

In my memory those nights are calm, quiet, and still, but in my memory I'm always looking at the glow of other houses. It wasn't nearly that simple. Hamet came to me one day with a cloth bag and said, "Please, keep this for me. Don't ask me anything, just keep it." I took the cloth bag and looked inside and there was a gun, a shiny plastic-looking thing, oddly heavy. I looked at her, looked into her face. Ibrahim, her husband, he might have had a temper, what did I know? I had never seen her with bruises on her face, but I'd heard them argue. I had heard everyone argue, everyone had heard Samil and me argue. We lived at elbows. Her face was calm, closed. I could feel the fear in the way her face was so serene. I put the bag away where the babies wouldn't find it and didn't even tell Samil. A few months later she asked for it back. "I'll take that bag back now," she said. "Thank you for keeping it." I gave it back to her. I don't know why it was okay, or if Ibrahim had missed it and made her give it back. We talked, but we weren't close beyond the concerns of motherhood.

When Samil died and I had three babies and the fourth on

the way, Hamet sat with me. All she said was "You'll get through this." I didn't want someone to tell me I'd get through it. But she was right. Still, for months I was hollow again, until my baby was born. Hariba and Fhassin, both infants with a mother hollowed by fear or grief. Is that where it happened?

I'm thinking about this when Nabil brings Hariba to my sister's house in the pedicab. I'm thinking of her as a baby, all round-faced, so that I'm even more shocked by this thin girl. When she went to be jessed, I was saddened for her because who would marry a jessed girl? She would never have children. But I didn't ever think my children might die before me.

The skin under Hariba's eyes is purple and full of fluid, but the rest of her is nothing. Her hair is brittle and full of broken ends. She see me and she starts to cry, reaching out from the pedicab with her thin arms. I reach up to hug her. "Child of my heart," I say. I don't know where the words come from, formal and frightening to a sick young woman, I'm sure.

"Mama," she sobs, and coughs, choking on her own sorrow.

"It's okay," I soothe. "Mama's here now. Hush, my girl, hush." Words, meaningless words, like petting a dog. To her little brother I say, "Get her in! Get her in! She doesn't need to be out in the street like this!" It takes the two of us supporting her under her thin arms to get her inside.

"Mama," she says, "Akhmim needs to come see me."

"Shhhh," I say. "Come lie down. You need to lie down."

We help her into the cool darkness of my sister's house and help her lie down on the bed we've made for her in the back.

My sister is making cheese. Her daughter is diapering a baby. The house has the ammonia smell of diapers. Hariba is crying silently, tears coming unheeded. Hariba was always proud. The others were always complaining, "Mama, Hariba is bossing me around." "Mama, Hariba is telling me what to do." The oldest child always grows up too fast, has too much responsibility and too little fun. I would come home from selling flowers and find her, her dark eyebrows knit into a terrible line, willing them to behave. I was always telling her, "You watch them, Hariba. You have to be the little mother." They weren't allowed to go outside while I was gone, and I was afraid she would let them. She was only six. I remember frightening her, telling her if she let them go out, men would take her sister and sell her.

"Don't be angry when you turn your face to her," my sister Zehra would say. I was always afraid and it made me fierce with Hariba. Zehra puts the press on her cheese and comes to crouch beside my daughter with me.

I pet Hariba and hush her.

I had to work. We had to eat. There was nothing to be done for it. A child needs a mother, but a child also needs food, a roof. When they could go to school, it was better, it wasn't all on her. What else could I do? It was what had to be, and there's no sense crying over it. Nothing would change if I did it again. Our children are hostages to the world.

"Little one," I say.

She falls asleep.

"Is she going to die?" Nabil asks.

"No," I say and my sister Zehra hisses at my son through her teeth. I'm not sure, though. It's instinct to tell your children it will all be okay, and my youngest boy has never become a man. Fhassin I could have told. Fhassin had a thread of metal running through him when he was fourteen.

"She looks sick," Nabil whispers.

"We'll find a doctor," I say.

It's just words to push away the darkness. When you are a mother, though, you do things you don't know you can do. When I had four children and no husband, I did things I never would have thought I could do. And now I will again.

"Will you watch her?" I ask my sister.

"As if she were my own," my Zehra says.

Once Hariba said that she wished Zehra were her mother. I cried for nights.

Walking out into the sunlight makes me blink. It's the heat of the day and people are closing up until evening. Nabil follows me, hopeful and hesitant. "We're going to look for a doctor," I say.

"What if they call the authorities?" Nabil says.

"We'll find one that won't," I say.

My house is still cool and smells of rose perfume. For most people it's the smell of death, but for me it's the everyday smell of coin. I have a little money, some saved and some for the rent. I keep it in the wall, in a crack of a burial niche. People are too squeamish to reach inside and rob me. It doesn't bother me to reach inside—nothing there but dust and bone.

It's a pitiful amount of coin, but I have it tied up in a rag. Who would I ask to tell me about a doctor who would do something illegal? Not my neighbors. I don't know anyone who would know such a doctor, even if I could ask.

Fhassin would know, but not Nabil.

"We are going to talk to the dead," I say to Nabil.

He looks around him. We who live in the Nekropolis are always surrounded by the dead, and if we know anything, it's that they don't talk.

*   *   *

I've never been to prison. Never gone to see my son. I've sent money, if you don't send money to prisoners, they'll starve, but it felt as if I dropped it into the hand of someone outside the Moussin of the White Falcon. We take the underground outside of town, to where it comes above ground and the tracks have to be swept clear of sand. There isn't much sand to see. Most of the desert is bare, just rocky places and dead land. There are a couple of villages, marked by the green of a well or the fence of a military installation. I was born in a village by a well. I know what life is like out here. The train comes by, but the city is far away, as far away as heaven or hell.

Eventually we pass kilometers of fence. A single wire, that's all, just what is needed to disrupt a prisoner's brain. No people, no buildings, just the single wire swooping between each post.

The prison itself is more than one building and except for its size it could be one of the government buildings we'd passed on the train. It's the color of the soil, the color of emptiness under a blue sky. Three large buildings and then a dozen smaller ones. Men in army uniforms with guns, standing in the train station, apparently bored. Thank the heavens a lot of people get off the train.

I follow Nabil out onto the platform, and the hot dry wind tangles my robe around my legs, strong enough to push me forward. Is it the will of Allah? I balk anyway, pulling my headscarf around my face to keep the grit out of my eyes. I pretend to be looking for a sign to tell me where to go, but I want to get back on the train.

"This way, Mama," Nabil says.

I follow him through the turnstile. Most of the people coming to the prison are women. Young women, old women. A river of women whose men are in this place. Nabil stops at a stall that sells fruit and candy. "What?" I say.

"We need something to take him," Nabil says.

He's been here before. I didn't know. Nabil is short, like Rashida, but stocky. A bulldog, a turtle, with curly hair tight against his head and a flattened nose. He is a man when he's not with me, I suppose. Do I turn him into a child? Just by being his mother? He is bigger than me. What is this that we do to our children, to make them always children until we are so old we become children?

I think about putting my hand on his arm and telling him that I see he's grown up. But I don't know how to tell him, so I just watch him buy oranges and chocolate. As if we're visiting the sick.

I give myself over to him, to his expertise in this place, and it's as if I've been holding my breath. For years I have been holding my breath. Since Samil died, I have been doing all these things myself, with no man to do for me.

We walk a few meters from the railway station and we're at the prison gate. More army men in uniform. They check Nabil's string bag of oranges and chocolate and wave him through. Nabil is wearing a shirt and trousers and already the heat has made half moons under his arms. Anything he puts on is wrinkled as soon as he touches it. It's been that way all his life.

We walk up a long, rutted dirt road toward the big buildings. Women are chattering, holding on to their children. What is worse, a husband killed in an accident like Samil or a hus-

band in a place like this? At least I am an honorable widow
and I get to wear black. I feel the protection of my black chador
now. My husband is dead, he is not here. I've always had a
kind of secret pleasure in being a widow. When Samil died, it
marked me as someone outside of life and it answered questions. Then, later, it let me be a man when I wanted to be.

This place is the end of the world. Or the rest of the world
is gone. Only the train tracks go back across the desert, an in-
sect line rising and falling across the rocky hills until finally
they disappear. Nabil waits while I look back, but his hand on
my elbow is a subtle pressure to go on.

We go through another gate, this one in a low wall, and a
guard with a clipboard takes our names. And then in twos
and threes we pass through a doorway. When Nabil and I go
through the door, it closes behind us and we are in a place
with high walls and no windows and a closed door in front of
us. Above us, men with rifles stand on the high walls.

Nabil murmurs, "This is the dead man's gate."

I cannot bring myself to open my mouth. I wait mute for
the gate in front of us to be opened.

Then we're in a courtyard, where families are talking to
their men, and other men squat, waiting, their eyes on us. I
look for Fhassin. Will I know him?

"He's not here," Nabil says. "We didn't let them know we
were coming. I'll have them go get him."

The desert-colored walls of the prison rise before me. The
windows are long grates, broken a bit in some places, but too
shadowed to see into. In the places where the breaks are large
enough, a hand reaches out into the sunlight. I look away
from the hands, perched in the windows like birds.

The men are frightening, broken-toothed, raw. They crouch

and smoke, or eat oranges. Some of them don't have shirts. A few have fantastical mustaches and some have shaved their heads, as if they were holy men. One man's shaved head has writing tattooed all over it and he is talking to a thin-faced young woman whose veil is skimpy and whose hair is dyed red. I'm afraid. There are guards, and I don't know why any of these men would pay any attention to an old widow, but I feel like a rabbit.

I glance up at the wall, wondering if one of those hands belongs to Fhassin, if he can see me here. One of those hands is moving, cutting the air, birdlike but decisive. Swoops and chops. Is it Fhassin? I raise my hand, tentatively, but the bird-hand just continues its strange flight.

Nabil comes back. "Fhassin will be here in a few moments." He glances up. "That's one of the men who are sentenced to die."

"What's he doing?" I ask.

"Talking to her," Nabil says.

A young woman stands in the yard. Her hand is flickering, too, in the same birdlike movements.

"Condemned men aren't allowed to have visitors," Nabil says. "That's the only way they can talk."

"Who is she?"

"His girlfriend. His wife. I don't know."

She's a pretty thing. She looks like anyone—not cheap like some of the women here. I feel as if I should look away, but if she's embarrassed, I can't tell. She seems intent. A stubborn flame.

"Is it a code?" I ask.

He shakes his head. "She is shaping letters in the air."

I don't know how to read, but all my children do.

I watch her hands dance in this strange place.

Will I know Fhassin?

And I do know him, the moment I see him. I know from his smile he is being brave. I know that this matters to him and he would like to pretend that it doesn't.

"Don't cry, Mama," he says.

I hide my face in my veil.

Nabil and Fhassin stand awkwardly when I have composed myself. Nabil starts and remembers the bags in his hands. "Here," he says, and hands Fhassin the oranges and sweets. They're embarrassed.

Fhassin is wearing a tight shirt, stained and yellowed with age. He's older, harder-looking, but he's still Fhassin. I had imagined him in a dark place, alone, but here he is, surrounded by all these men. One of them.

"Are you well?" I say.

"Sure, yes," he says. "You look well, too."

"I am."

Fhassin looks at the bag of oranges and sweets. "This is great. Really good."

He needs a shave. "At least you haven't grown a beard here," I say.

He looks around. "Those men are fundamentalists. They band together. It helps to have someone stand with you here."

"You have friends here?" I ask.

He shrugs and glances away. "I'm not by myself."

Secret Fhassin, who never ever told me things. When he was a boy, he would answer in just the same evasive way. "Where were you after school?" "Where I could hear Hariba call."

He's the one I always worried about. The one who was always thinking.

"Hariba is home," I say.

"Hariba?" he says. "But she was jessed. Did she buy her way out?"

"She ran away," I say. The bitter taste in my mouth makes my lips purse, like lemon on my tongue.

"Good for her," Fhassin says. "Getting jessed was stupid."

"Not good," I say.

"Mama!" Fhassin says, "Going by the rules isn't always the best thing, you know?"

"You should talk," I say. "Look at you."

"Look at me," he says. "I made a mistake. But you always went by the rules and look at you."

"I sleep in my own bed every night."

He laughs, a short hard sound. "So your prison is the Nekropolis. So it's bigger than this prison. How much bigger?"

"Hariba is sick," I say. "She is dying. From the jessing. I need to find a doctor for her. I thought you might know one."

His jaw clenches with anger, but he laughs again. "That's why you came. Not because of me, because of Hariba."

"Fhassin," Nabil says.

"That's right, isn't it, Mama," Fhassin says. "You came for Hariba."

"I did," I say, because what else is there to say? It's true. And the Mashahana says that truth may be the longer way, but it is the way out of the labyrinth. So much truth I can't say, though. Fhassin, you were my favorite. And you were the one I lost.

"You wouldn't come for me," Fhassin says.

"I was afraid to look at you," I say.

He frowns.

"Don't fight!" Nabil says. "Mama, just once would you be fair to Fhassin!"

Fair! To Fhassin! I who have never been fair to Fhassin, who has always secretly favored him! I gape at Nabil.

"Fhassin," Nabil says, "listen to me. She can't eat, she can't sleep. She ran away with a *harni*."

"A *harni*?" Fhassin shakes his head. "No, not Hariba."

"Yes, Hariba."

"Nabil, a *harni* is something grown in a machine, it's not just a servant. You mean Hariba ran away with a servant?"

"No, a *harni*. The wife of the man she worked for had one. Then they sold Hariba's contract to someone else and she went back and got the *harni* and ran away to the Nekropolis. She was living in a death house down where Ibrahim has his shoe place. We didn't even know where she was."

"A *harni*," Fhassin says. "Why did she do it?"

Nabil shrugs. "No one knows."

"Because they are seductive," I say. "That's why they shouldn't be allowed."

"You're sure it was a *harni*?" Fhassin says.

"I've seen it," Nabil says. "She wanted it to come with her to Mama's."

I cannot read Fhassin's face, but I'm afraid that Nabil shouldn't have told him. What if it brings back memories of Fhassin's own crime? Since he could not have his adultery, will he be bitter about Hariba's? Will he refuse to help us?

"I don't know a doctor who can help you," he says finally, slowly. "But I know someone who would."

He tells Nabil about someone named Hassein. It is apparently someone whose brother Nabil knows, but I'm looking around the prison yard.

A bell rings, like a school bell, and the guards straighten up.

"Two minutes," Fhassin says. "Goodbye, Mama."

"What do you need?" I ask.

He's casual. "I'm fine. But if you could send some medicine. For headaches."

"You have headaches?"

"Sometimes," he says.

"I'll be back," Nabil says.

"Tell me what Hassein says. I had better go back." He needs to escape us. His body is tense, like the little boy I remember, ready to burst from me.

And he is gone back inside.

My sister Zehra looks up at me, then back at the pot of couscous she is stirring. Everything is neat in this house, even Hariba is washed. When we were growing up, there were five of us: Raschid, my older brother; Lida, my older sister; me; then Zehra, my younger sister; and Hamedi, my little brother, the baby. When I was twelve, my mother died and our life was nothing but shame. We were children who no one watched. No one paid for our school. I know my father was with us when he came home from work, but in my memory it is only Zehra and me, trying to be women, trying to keep a home. Lida didn't care. Lida had beautiful fat little hands and feet, but she was solid, and if Zehra and I didn't make her, she wouldn't even bother to clean herself.

Zehra and I chased her out of the house with a broom and a dustpan full of coals one time because we were trying to make the house nice and she wouldn't do anything. We were awful. "Do you remember when we used to go to Lida's and clean?" I say.

Zehra shakes her head. "What are you bringing up old things for?" But then she shakes her head in another way, in memory. "Those babies in wet diapers."

"We would push the trash out into the street," I said.

"Lida would sit there with a baby on her lap and just watch us," Zehra says.

"We were prideful," I say.

Zehra laughs, "We were, but Lida was awful. Somebody had to be prideful!"

I wanted a house that would not make me ashamed. When Samil was alive, after the first two babies were born, he would come home and find the house neat and dinner cooking and me there with a baby in my lap and I would think of what he saw and the smell of mint and onion and it would all be there. The sun would be going down outside and inside would be a house that did honor to Samil and to me. Sometimes I could barely hold the feeling in, I wanted to burst into tears from the strength of my happiness. I would kiss Rashida's toes and bury my face in her belly and make silly noises until she laughed.

"Where did you go?" she asks.

"To see Fhassin," I say, pretending I'm calm, that saying those words does not make my heart flutter like a trapped bird. I am sick, saying those words.

My sister Zehra, who is taller than I am and whose back is always straight while I've been bony and bent since I was in my thirties, looks at me and purses her lips. "Good," she says. "How is Fhassin?"

"He's in prison," I say.

"That's not an answer," she says. "You are exasperating."

"He's all right," I say.

To hide my agitation I go and kneel down next to Hariba. I think she's sleeping, but her eyes are open and glittering in her wasted face. "You went to see Fhassin?" Hariba says.

"I did," I say, trying to soften my voice for her. I am angry at her, but she is sick and charity given is for the giver, not the receiver.

She closes her eyes. "Then I am going to die, aren't I?"

"Not yet," I say. Her face, empty of responsibility, empty of care, makes me angry.

"Mama," she says. "Can I see Akhmim?"

"Who is Akhmim?" I say, but then I realize. "You mean the *harni.*" She would have it in my sister's house. I rise up and walk outside.

Children are a blessing. They are a happiness so sharp that it feels like pain. It slices your fingers like the razor I use to cut paper.

Zehra comes out to stand next to me.

"Dinner is ready," she says. "Will you stay and have something?"

"I should go home," I say. She thinks I am being hard. Zehra thinks I am a hard mother. Always did. When they were little, she used to tell me to be softer with my children, but then she had a man. She didn't know how it was. I told her that and it was true. Now that Driss, my brother-in-law, is dead, she has family all around her still. Not that she didn't help me. Sometimes the only reason my babies had anything in their stomachs was because Zehra had us come and eat dinner. And Driss never resented us. Zehra and Driss had a good marriage, I think, but now that he's gone, Zehra has come into herself. She is different without him, more the way I remember her from when she was a girl and she was bold. She has given back to herself that part that she gave up to be a wife.

"Why did you go to see Fhassin?" she asks.

"Motherly concern."

She laughs through her nose, a funny snort. "Did you tell him Hariba is home?"

"I told him."

She waits.

"I asked him if he knew of a doctor, someone who could help Hariba. He said he didn't know of one, but he knew someone who might know. Did you know Nabil has been going to see him all this time?"

"He is his brother," she says.

"So you knew?"

"No," she says. "But I am not surprised. Is Nabil taking you to see this person or do you want me to go with you?"

"Nabil will take me," I say. "Zehra? Should I go?"

"What do you mean?"

"Hariba broke the law. The Mashahana says that the law is the house in which we live—"

"I can't believe you," Zehra says. "I can't believe you are talking about your own daughter!"

"If your own eye offends you—"

"Don't spout holy words at me! That's Hariba in there!"

"If I told the police about her, they'd cure her," I said.

"And put her in prison," Zehra said.

"She took something that belonged to someone else."

"She was seduced by something that should never have existed in the first place!" Zehra said. "This is why there should not be *harni*! The sinner is the man who she worked for, the man who bought the thing."

"So you think Hariba has no responsibility? And I have no responsibility?"

"You are a mother," Zehra says. "That's your first responsibility."

I don't think Zehra's right. Zehra is speaking with her heart, but what Hariba has done is willful. "If she had stolen money, would you say the same thing?" I ask.

"She would never steal money," Zehra says.

"But she did steal. It's the same as if she stole money."

"But it isn't. Don't you see? Because she wouldn't steal money, because she is a good girl, then there must be something else. That's the *harni*. It shouldn't exist. They should be against the law."

"What if she'd stolen something else, something from the west, a piece of sculpture or a painting that was blasphemous, then you'd say she was guilty."

Zehra sighs. "You're being obtuse on purpose. I'm not going to argue with you, but I will tell you this: If you turn that girl over to the police, it will be on your head. Now come and eat."

To her back I think, and if I do not turn her in, it will be on my soul.

Nabil isn't home when I get there, but I hear him come in and lie down before very late. I get up early, before it is light, and make tea. Old women don't sleep very well. To my surprise, Nabil sits up, rubbing his eyes.

"What are you up early for?" I ask.

"Hassein," Nabil says. "Last night I found out where he is and I have to go early to catch him."

"I'll go with you," I say and give him tea. The smell of mint makes the morning comfortable.

"You can't," Nabil says. "He works at the horse track."

"I'm not a thirteen-year-old girl," I say, irritated. I don't trust Nabil to handle this. "I can go with you."

So we do, and the sun is just up when we find this Hassein, standing at the fence at the edge of the track, watching horses run past.

Hassein is dressed like a Berber, with a white and blue scarf wound around his head and neck, and his sunglasses, and sticking out, the tiny mouthpiece of a headset. He leans against the fence, holding a tiny thing that flickers with writing, and he watches a particular horse, following it around the track. Everything about him says that he handles foreign things like this all the time.

Young men like this. This was what I feared for my children, that my boys would become like this, that my girls would get mixed up with this. And here is Nabil, saying, "Hello, Hassein."

Hassein nods, without appearing to take his gaze off the horse, although who knows what he is looking at behind those glasses? His eyes are invisible.

I find I cannot speak, that I have grabbed my veil and pulled it tight under my chin. There are other men like Hassein, most of them dressed like Berbers, too, watching horses. There are no women here at all.

"This is my mother," Nabil says.

Hassein turns his head and smiles at me. "Good morning, ma'am. How do you like the horses?"

"They are very nice," I say, and against my will I lower my eyes. "The gray one," I say, forcing myself. "Is that the one you are watching?"

"Yes, he is. Isn't he a beauty?"

I look out over the fence and the green grass and fountain in the middle of the oval track, to the other side where the gray horse runs, the rider just a tiny figure in black clinging to its back. It's too small for me to see, and I've never seen a horse close up before. We had chickens and goats when I was growing up, and an old two-stroke machine for pulling that ran on solar and ethanol. But we didn't have money for anything but what we needed, and other than barn cats, no other animals. Some people we knew had a pet donkey that their children used to ride.

We stand and watch while time passes and Hariba wastes away. Hassein whispers into his headset.

They're fast and healthy. Aristocrats with shining coats. The gray horse and rider come past us, the rider standing in the stirrups and the horse rocking underneath him, not running hard now. They slow to a stop, farther down the track.

Hassein says in his headset, "Salty."

The rider doesn't respond, except to turn his face toward us.

"Salty," Hassein says again. "How's the tendon?"

The rider is only a boy. He isn't ignoring Hassein, but he isn't answering, either. He just smiles. The horse lowers its head, its neck a taut bow, and snorts loudly.

"Salty," Hassein says a third time. "Come here and let me look."

The rider doesn't seem to even twitch, but lazily, the gray horse ambles our way. The horse's legs are long and fine, with the muscles bunching under the skin. It stops not too close to us.

"Come on, princeling," Hassein says.

"He's not cooperative today," the boy says. "He's no princeling, he's dog meat."

The horse's ears flicker as if it is listening and it paws the track.

"Salty, you are a paranoid infidel," Hassein says, "and if you bow a tendon, I'll sell you in a heartbeat. You won't be a princeling then, will you?"

The horse snuffs and shakes its head. I realize "Salty" is the horse. They're talking to the horse. It sidles alongside the fence and when it gets to us, it places a black shining hoof delicately on the lowest board of the fence.

Hassein runs his hands over its joints and lower leg and the horse regards us with its black eyes, arrogant and curious. "Not too hot today," Hassein says. "I guess you're safe from the knackers."

The horse nips at Hassein's face, teeth clicking in the empty air.

"It understands you," Nabil says.

"Salty and I have an understanding," Hassein corrects.

The horse shakes its head as if shaking off water and the boy, tucked high in the saddle, laughs.

"Salty knows that the world is no good," Hassein continues, "and that I'm going to make him do things he doesn't want to do, and so he attempts to disobey at any opportunity, while I treat him like the prince that he is"—here the horse stretches his lips back from his teeth, as if he is jeering Hassein—"and he deigns to occasionally win a race, providing his owner with just enough cash to keep me employed."

The horse has taken his hoof from the fence and now he capers, flashing his tail. I cannot tell what it means. Is he angry? Laughing? Excited?

"Ice down the leg," Hassein says to the boy, and the animal trots off, the boy clinging like a monkey, his smile bright white in his dark face.

"How much does the horse understand?" Nabil asks.

Hassein shrugs, watching after them. The horse's tail switches back and forth like a girl's hips. "Sometimes I think it's all just tone, you know? I mean, of course, he understands when I say, "show me," and ask him about his tendon. We've been worrying about his tendons and his sore feet and his back. He knows all those words. But the insults? Does he have any clue what I mean when I say I'm employed? I don't think so. Or maybe he changes it all into some sort of horse society. Maybe he thinks we're in the same herd and he's a yearling or something." Hassein looks at us, his face still rendered expressionless by his glasses. "So, Nabil, are you here to buy a horse?"

Nabil laughs weakly. "Of course, I have a million lying around I want to throw away."

Hassein spits onto the track.

"I'm here, by the grace of Allah, to ask if you know someone who could help me," Nabil says.

"Walk with me," Hassein says.

They walk ahead and I follow behind in this strange place that smells like a barnyard but where horses live better than people. In Hassein's office Nabil explains to him about Hariba; that she's jessed and has run away. It's a little office, not nearly as big as the stalls where the horses stay. I sit on a chair and drink mint tea.

Hassein takes off his dark glasses to reveal very young eyes, and stares at the papers piled on his desk like rugs in a bazaar. "I don't know," he says. "We jess the horses. You could talk to Tahar."

"Tahar is a doctor?" Nabil asks.

Hassein smiles. "He thinks he is. Come."

The barns are a maze of long, low buildings, white and new in the early morning sun. Hassein wanders among them, asking after this Tahar, and Berber boys look up and point or shake their heads or grin and shrug. A lot of Berbers, desert dark and dressed, many of them, as if they've just walked out of the mountains.

Hassein finds Tahar leaning on a stall door, watching a horse eat. Tahar is long-jawed and needs a shave, but at least he isn't a Berber. His horse is as well groomed and shining as he is disheveled, but at least he doesn't look as if his family lives in a mountain fortress with their sheep.

"How is the mare?" Hassein says. "Is she ready?"

"Ready," Tahar growls. "She's been ready for days. The boy has been on foal watch so long he had to go tell his wretched family he was still alive." A boy sits in the corner of the stall, chewing on a long stem of hay. He is as dark and barefoot as any of the boys here.

"Is she waxing?" Hassein asks.

"Two days, now. Mares wax and within hours, they give birth, except the rajah-mistress here."

The horse lips at her hay, not really eating, letting it dribble onto the floor of the stall. She stares off into the distance, shifting from one foot to the other. I wonder if she understands us.

"This is my old friend Nabil. From childhood. He is looking for some help, and I thought of you."

Tahar looks Nabil up and down. "You need help with a horse?" he asks, looking sour.

"No," Nabil says, "with my sister."

Tahar looks at Hassein, a look full of meaning I can't understand, then he sighs. "Tell me about your sister."

"She is ill," Nabil says. "It's a delicate matter."

"It's always a delicate matter," Tahar says. "Come on, you can talk here. The boy won't tell anyone and the mare can't."

She doesn't even as much flicker her ears, but gazes dreamily off.

"My sister is a servant, and there was some difficulty with her employment—" Nabil says.

"Is she pregnant or jessed? What's the problem?"

"Jessed," I say. I am furious with this man. "And she is dying."

He raises an eyebrow at me. "You are who, her mother? Her grandmother?"

"Her mother. And luckier, I think, than your mother."

Nabil says, "Please, excuse my mother, she's worried about my sister."

Tahar looks at me and we have an understanding: We hate each other.

Nabil says, "Mama."

I leave the three men and go to the stall door and duck in. The mare is big, taller at the shoulder than I am, and once I'm in, I'm afraid. But she doesn't care. She doesn't even look at me. I inhale the smell of her, clean—healthy horse. Her beautiful pink and black feet are clean, her pink nose with its old man scattering of whiskers is clean.

"Mama," I whisper. "I'm a mama, too." I lay my hand against her huge belly. "Your poor back, your poor sprung ribs. You're tired, aren't you?"

She looks around at me now. She has a brown face with a white streak down the middle and wise eyes.

"Men don't know," I say. "But we know, don't we."

I can't say in words what we know. But that's all right.

Tahar says he'll come when he can. His racehorse is more important to him than any person could be. When I think of the mare, waiting for the coming of her foal, I can almost understand. But at home, there's my daughter.

Nabil sells paper funeral arrangements for me and I go to tend my daughter.

My sister's house smells of sickness.

"She's been vomiting all morning," Zehra says. "There's nothing in her stomach. She can only retch and bring up bile."

Hariba is curled up on her side, whimpering. "Mama, can Akhmim come? He'll make me feel better."

"Shhh," I whisper, stroking her forehead. She retches again and I grab the bowl. She brings up a little green bile and some strings of mucus. "Hush," I say. "The doctor is coming."

"Mama," she whimpers. "Mama, I feel really bad."

She retches again.

This is what it's like, all through the rest of the morning and the afternoon. My sister watches her granddaughter and two grandsons while her daughter works. They complain that it smells. When my sister cooks for them, Hariba is even more nauseated.

Nabil comes by in the afternoon and I send him home to get some of the oil that I use to scent the flowers.

"It smells like a funeral in here," my sister says.

"Isn't that better than sickness?"

Rashida, my other daughter, comes and sits with us. She is the one most like me—short, with my face. She's big with her baby. Two months left and she's already so ungainly that I'm sure she's miscounted the months. Or maybe it's twins.

"How are you?" I say.

She frowns. "I wish I could sleep, but if I lie on my back it hurts and I can't sleep any other way. But really, I'm fine."

Hariba opens her eyes sleepily and smiles at Rashida. They always fought, but they are sisters.

Rashida is still there when the doctor comes.

He's contemptuous of my sister's home. Her home is as clean as he is slovenly and poverty is no shame, but I keep my tongue.

"What's her name?" he asks, crouching.

"Hariba," I say. I stroke her forehead. "Sweet, the doctor is here," I say. Her forehead isn't even damp anymore.

"How long has she been like this?"

"She's been sick this way since before dawn," my sister says. "She can't even keep water in her."

"I have to give her an injection to stop the nausea and let her keep some liquid down. It'll keep her from dehydrating." he says. He names a price.

I feel, beyond my fear for my daughter, nothing but contempt for this man. I find my money and I pour it into his hand. "This is what I have," I say. "Can you cure her for it? Because if not, you'll have to take my word that I will pay you or you'll have to let her die."

"Take her to the hospital if I cost too much," the man says.

We can't. He knows that. If we take her to the hospital, they'll arrest her.

He gives her the injection and in a moment I see her relax.

Her eyes cloud. I think for a moment that he's killed her and my heart all but stops, but Hariba is breathing slowly.

He gives my sister patches to use when the injection wears off. A flutter of packets. "Cut them in half and then in half again," he says. "They're too strong, otherwise. Give her too much and she'll forget to breathe."

"Why do they make them that strong?" I ask.

"Because a horse is bigger than a person," Tahar says, irritated.

"These are for horses?" My sister picks one up.

"It's the same thing they give to people, only less expensive because it's for animals."

"You're giving my daughter horse medicine?"

"I'm giving your daughter medicine," he snaps. "A chemical is a chemical, it doesn't care what label you put on the package. How long has she been jessed?"

I'm speechless. I thought the mare he was watching was his horse, that he was a rich doctor who raced horses. But of course not, why would a rich doctor come here? "You're a horse doctor," I say.

"Horses are jessed, too," he says. "More often than people. In most countries it's illegal to jess humans."

I'm shamed. I can feel my sister looking at me, and my daughter. I can't think of what to say or do—I can't take Hariba to a hospital, but I've brought a man who doctors horses to cure my daughter. And given him all my money. My stupid pride.

Rashida says, "Can you release her from the jesses?" Her voice is calm, as if having her sister attended by an animal doctor is normal.

I cover my face so no one can see me cry. If I'd known he was a horse doctor, I'd still have had him come. What else could I do? It's my daughter.

"How long has she been jessed?" Tahar asks again.

"Five years—" Rashida pauses. "No, six years."

Tahar frowns. "That's a long time to reverse."

No one says anything. I keep my face covered and my eyes closed, choking on my own tears.

"I'll give her an injection. It will reverse the instruction, but I don't know if it will reverse all the jessing."

I don't understand what he is talking about. I'm too old, I never had any schooling. I don't know enough to help my children. There's some more talk and the horse doctor gives her the injection and leaves. Rashida puts her arm around my shoulders. "Mama," she says, "you're tired, let me take you home."

I wake in the night, not sure where I am. I build my home around me—Nabil is asleep here, I am here, the door is here. I've lived here for thirty years. Where do I think I am?

In the morning Hariba is awake and sipping mint tea, propped up on her blankets. She is a stick puppet—her upper arms are as thin as my wrist and although she holds the cup in both spider-fingered hands, it looks too heavy for her.

"Daughter," I say and sit down next to her. "You look better."

She nods on her stick neck. "Aunt Zehra says I have to drink a lot."

"You do," I say. Illness has made her simple—Hariba, who was always thinking and planning.

"I have to get a message to Akhmim," she says.

"The *harni*?" I ask, startled.

She is guileless. "I have to, he is worried."

I take the cup from her and put it down with a clink and hold her thin hand. "Don't worry," I say. I can feel the fragile bones of her hand, the skin dry and hot like paper. "Don't worry about the *harni* or anything."

"You'll make sure he knows how I am?" she asks.

"I'll tell Nabil," I say. I will tell Nabil, but we'll have nothing to do with the *harni*.

She drinks some more tea and sleeps, and drinks a little more and sleeps, until I tell my sister that I'm going home for lunch.

I walk home thinking of law and of justice. Of Hariba. The Mashahana says that justice is water in the desert, sweeter than love. Hariba has suffered; is it just to give her to the police? I'm supposed to protect and care for my children. I'm supposed to honor the law. Which is more important?

Nabil is sitting in the house with two men I don't know. "Mother," he says, starting to rise as I enter, but one of the men gestures for him to stay sitting.

"Ma'am," the man says. They are the police, I can tell, even though they wear dusty djellabas and not uniforms. My knees shake and I pull my veil across my face. People who run afoul of the police disappear. "We have been talking with your son," the older man says.

"Has he offered you tea?" I ask.

"No, thank you," the man says.

He is almost my age, this man, and he's lean and hungry-looking. The other is barely older than Nabil. "Have you heard from your daughter?" the old lean one asks.

"Rashida? I try to go and see her, she's pregnant," I say.

"Your other daughter," he says.

I shake my head and I think Nabil relaxes a bit. They have been asking questions, and now they want to see if Nabil and I give the same answers. Prophets and angels walk with me. "Please let me make you some tea," I say. "Nabil, how could you not make your friends tea?"

Nabil opens his mouth as if to speak, but the man cuts him off. "Your son has been most polite, ma'am."

"He's my youngest and I've spoiled him," I say. My voice rattles around like a single pistachio in a jar. "Sometimes he forgets." I can pretend they are friends of Nabil. I can be a dotty old lady. Then if I say something that contradicts what Nabil has said, it'll be because I'm confused and old. I pour water into the teapot and light the stove.

The lean one frowns. "Please, ma'am, about your daughter."

"Are you and Nabil looking for my daughter?" I ask. "Nabil, what have you been doing? I told you, she is dead to me."

The young one looks a little surprised.

"We're looking for your daughter," the lean one says, "but not with Nabil. There's been a report that she stole something. That she ran away. You knew this?"

"Did her employer send you?" I ask. I allow myself to sit down tiredly. "She didn't answer my letters. So we called." It's true. Rashida writes my letters for me, and Hariba has always answered, then for three months we didn't hear anything, so Nabil called and the man she worked for told us her contract had been transferred and that she'd run away with the *harni*. I didn't believe it until Nabil brought her to my sister's. "I'm sorry. If my daughter came to my door, I'd turn her away."

The lean one says, "Has she been here?"

"No." I shake my head. "She knows better. She is a thief and what she's done, the thing—" I hide my face in my hands. It's easy to be disgusted if I let myself think about it. "She's not my daughter anymore. I have one son and one daughter now."

My pleasure is a thing I can hold in my hands, but I don't think it shows in my face. It's almost true, and that makes it easy to say. I look up at the two men. They don't care about what I've said. In the young one's face I see Fhassin. It's an odd thought. Whatever else Fhassin has done he's never given me any reason to think he might want to be police—and certainly not police such as this, men who wear normal clothes and who spy on people. But it's there. That same glitter, that same cynicism. Policemen probably think that there are no innocent people. What does it matter if they spy?

Fhassin never had much faith in innocence, either.

I feel as if fingers walk up my back and I shudder.

"Come with us," the man says. "Both of you."

"Come where?" Nabil asks.

The young one takes Nabil by the upper arm and pulls him to his feet.

"But the tea!" I say, a foolish, ineffectual thing. I know it's stupid, but my mind stutters on it. "The stove," I say. "The tea!"

"It's all right," the man says and puts it out.

He's lying.

They take us to the police station, in full daylight, where anyone might see us go in and assume we are criminals. But I'm lying about Hariba, so I am a criminal.

They take us to a room with a table and some chairs and that's all and they lock the door from the inside.

"Where is your daughter?" the older man asks.

"I don't know. I told you," I say, "she's no daughter of mine."

He gestures to Nabil to sit down. "Where's your sister?" he asks.

Nabil sits down and stares at the table. "I don't know," he mumbles.

The man leans across the table and pushes him so the chair tips over backward. Nabil cries out as he falls to the floor. It's so quick I can't even think of it. The younger man pulls a length of fiber hose out from under his robes and strikes Nabil.

"No!" I say, reaching my hand out, although I'm nowhere near enough to touch my son.

Nabil covers his face with his arms, and the young man strikes again and again. Nabil is tangled up in the fallen chair. "Stop! Stop! O Prophet, stop!" I'm thinking that a good mother would throw herself across her son's body to stop the blows. I'm thinking that a good mother would at least try to grab the arms of the boy with the hose.

I'm not a good mother. I make funny noises and then I bite my fingers. I do, I stick them in my mouth and bite on them. Not so I won't cry out, but for no reason at all. Then I cover my mouth with my hands and cry.

Nabil! Nabil! My baby boy! He isn't good at the world, he doesn't have Fhassin's wit. Don't beat him. He's too good-natured. I've brought him to this, for Hariba, who's brought this on all of us. The black hose whistles through the air but, the sound it makes when it hits Nabil's forearms and side and shoulders is dull, a *thwack,* like someone beating laundry.

The older man raises his hand and the younger man

stops. "So," the older man says to me, "have you seen your daughter?"

"No, no no no," I say.

The young man pulls the chair away from Nabil, sets it at the table, helps Nabil up, and sits him in it. Nabil cringes from the help. Nabil looks at me. He has round dark eyes and his mop of hair has a clump of dust stuck in it near his eyebrow. He opens his mouth, maybe to say where Hariba is, maybe to say something to me, but I think it's to call, "Mama," and I can't help him. He closes his mouth without saying anything, but I hear my baby boy calling me in my head.

"You haven't seen her or heard from her?" the older man asks me.

I shake my head.

The young man grabs Nabil's hands and wrestles them behind the chair and snaps the bracelets on him.

"Wait!" I say. "I haven't seen her! Why are you doing this?"

"We know you have," the older man says simply.

My heart sinks. The ground is gone beneath me.

The younger man hefts the hose, watching me. The older man is watching me, too. But not carefully.

The most frightening thing is that they don't care. If we say something, if we're silent. If we die, if we live. These men will go home and sit down to dinner and not think of us again. The older man will go home and his wife will ask him how was his day and he will shrug and say, "You know how it goes," and she will put the platter of couscous down and the family will eat and talk of other things, like whether his daughter will have a boy or a girl, or about the job that the neighbor's boy has gotten, or even how much cumin is in the

couscous. The young man will go home to his young wife
with lips like berries and they will have sex when they go to
bed, his muscles will ripple in his shoulders when he takes
her in his arms and she'll think of what a handsome, wonderful animal he is, and not once will anyone think of us.

"No, no no no," I say, because it doesn't really matter
what I say.

The younger man raises the black hose and Nabil watches
it with his eyes, then turns his face away. The younger man
swings it, without rancor. Efficiently, like a soccer player or
like the long-legged horses we saw at the track, confident in
the play of bone and muscle. He strikes the side of Nabil's
face again and again as Nabil tries to get out of the way,
struggling until the chair clatters over.

The young man reaches down and grabs the back of the
chair and hauls it upright again, then hits Nabil some more.
The older man raises his hand and the younger man stops.
The younger man is breathing a little heavily from exertion.
Maybe the older man has stopped him so he can have a little
break. The kind of thing that one thinks of for one's partner.
Nabil's head sags forward and he is bleeding from his fore-
head and around his eye.

"So you say you haven't heard from your daughter?" the
older man says.

I cannot say anything. I cry into the palm of my hand, covering my mouth. I'm rocking back and forth. I can't speak for
crying and I'm afraid because they will kill Nabil and they
will kill me because in their eyes we are nothing.

The older man sighs. "Let them go," he says, irritated.

*   *   *

They dump us out a door and I sit with Nabil's poor bleeding head in my hands for a while. No one helps us. I don't blame them. I didn't even help Nabil and I'm his mother.

Eventually I can get him to stand up, although he says he is dizzy and everything is blurry. We stand in the dirty alley and he retches and throws up. I hold him standing because if I let him down, I'm afraid I won't be able to get him back up, so he vomits down his front and down part of my chador. Then I try to steady him and we walk like two drunks, swaying from one side of the alley to the other.

People stare at us in the street. I'm ashamed. But we can't stop and there's nowhere to go except home. Even if my sister Zehra's house were closer, I wouldn't go there. It's time to start making dinner by the time we get home.

I lay Nabil down on his own pallet and I take his shirt and pants off him as if he were a little boy rather than a grown man, and I wash his face clean.

"My head aches," he says.

I brew him mint tea and he drinks it at my urging, and then I let him doze. I change and clean up and sit in the gathering darkness. I will wake him every hour. Old women don't need much sleep.

I don't know if they know that Hariba is at my sister's. I don't think so. If they did, they would just arrest Hariba, wouldn't they? Maybe they want to catch the *harni*, too. But Hariba would probably tell them, she's weak and sick. I can't go see her, though. What if they're following Nabil and me? It is impossible to know what to do.

I wake Nabil and make him drink some more tea. "I feel sick," he says.

"Lie still," I say.

"I feel as if my head were at the center of something and my body were spinning around like the hands of a clock," he says.

I get a wet rag and lay it on his forehead and hold his hand until he falls asleep.

I nod during the night, and wake up not certain where I am, but each time I wake up, I wake Nabil as well. "Mama," he says one time, "I keep having bad dreams."

I sing to him until he falls asleep.

Zehra, my younger sister, comes the next day, bearing soup for breakfast. It's harira, full of chickpeas and onions, *kusbur* and tomatoes and salt butter.

"I heard," she says grimly. "The police, they're like vultures. People are murdered in the streets and what do they do? Beat innocents. Sister, you look exhausted, go to sleep."

"I can't sleep in the day," I say, irritable. "And you shouldn't come here. What if they're watching us?"

"Then they will see me come to visit my sister and nephew." She looks past the partition to see Nabil, and I have the bitter pleasure of hearing her gasp when she sees his face. "Poor baby," she says, whispered like a prayer.

Maybe now she'll stop thinking about Hariba as a victim and see what the girl's done to her family.

"It's okay, Aunt Zehra," Nabil says. "It looks worse than it is."

Zehra feeds him soup and then makes me eat some, too. Her harira is very good, but I like it with more cumin than she does. Still, it's good. It's good.

She beckons me to go outside with her, where Nabil can't hear. There she strokes my cheeks and the tears stand in her eyes. With my sister, all her emotions are there. She's strong, angry when she wants to be and sad when she wants to be. "Hariba," she says.

"What?" I say, and fear clutches at my chest. "Did they come for her?"

"No, no, no," she whispers. "But she's not as well today as she was. She has a bit of a fever. You need to come to her."

"Come to her? They might follow me! They might be watching!"

"Take your wreaths and go to the Moussin," Zehra says. "Watch everything. If you think you are being followed, come back here, otherwise go to my house."

"I can't leave Nabil," I say.

"I'll stay with Nabil. Go see your daughter."

"The doctor—" but I have no money for the doctor and he's a crook anyway.

Zehra shrugs. "He said it could be a few days before she improves. Maybe this is nothing."

I don't have very much to sell. I've been sitting with Hariba instead of making wreaths. But I pack what I have and trudge off to the Moussin. I spread them out. The police, if they have followed me, would expect me to. The Moussin is a crowded place, I don't know how I can tell if someone is following me. There are people who are here all the time, but that doesn't mean they aren't informers. And there are people who come once or twice.

I've brought paper, so I start making flowers. I'm tired, but my fingers think for me, and the sun isn't so bad. I can barely hear the drone of prayer being sung from the Moussin, and I lift my face for a moment to feel what breeze there is. A beautiful young man looks at my wreaths. He has hair that falls in looser curls than Nabil's, and he wears it a little long. He looks almost womanly.

"These are lovely," he says.

"Thank you," I say. "You are mourning someone?"

He shrugs, which is an odd sort of answer. "I'm looking for someone. I have a friend whose mother makes wreaths."

I'm frightened. "Most of us here are mothers, fathers, daughters, and sons," I say.

He nods. "My friend is in trouble and I'm worried about her."

He's secret police, of course. I can't think of what to say. I don't say anything.

"Her name is Hariba," he says.

What do I say? What do the police expect me to say? "I used to have a daughter named Hariba, but she is dead."

"Dead?" he says.

"Dead to me," I say.

"What do you mean?" he asks. "Did she die?"

He's not the secret police. He's someone she knows. But maybe not. I don't know how clever the police are. "What is it to you?" I ask.

"It's nothing," he says. "It's nothing." He sits down in the dust of the plaza and hides his face in his hands. His shoulders don't move, although he might be crying. But when he takes his hands away, his face is desolate but dry.

"You're a friend of hers?" I ask. "How do you know her?"

"I'm the *harni*," he says.

No, he isn't. He's human. He looks human, he acts human. I study him. I've never seen a *harni*, but I imagined they would have a falseness about them. His humanness, if he is the *harni*, is the most frightening thing about him.

"She wanted her mother, so I thought she should go home," he says.

"She's a thief," I say. "And you are blasphemy." I collect my things. "I wouldn't have her in my home."

"Is she still alive?" he asks.

I won't speak to him. I could call for the police right now, except he would tell them that he contacted her family. "If you have any feelings for Hariba," I say, "leave this city. Go far away, where no one will ever find you."

"So she's not dead." He scrambles to his feet, brushing away the dust. "How is she?"

"Get away from me," I say. "You've brought nothing to me and my family but pain. Get away from me!"

He bites his lip.

Very human. Very beautiful. Like the big gray racehorse. I can almost understand Hariba. Such pain in his face. I don't dare look at him. I walk away.

I take a long way from the Moussin to Zehra's house. Maybe the young man who claims he's a *harni* is sent by the secret police. Maybe he's really a *harni*, but not Hariba's *harni*. Or maybe the police have caught him and are using him to find Hariba. Wheels within wheels. I don't know what to think, but I walk forever. My poor old feet hurt and my heels are sore, but I cut through alleys barely wide enough for me, and then I watch to make sure no one comes out.

I don't tell Hariba what I saw. She's dozing, fitful, but it's enough for me to sit down and let my niece Husniya bring me some mint tea. Husniya whispers, "How is Nabil?"

I shrug. "I think he'll be all right."

I drink my tea and doze.

"Mama?" Hariba says after a while.

"Hmmm?" I say.

"Is Nabil all right?"

"Nabil is fine," I say. Who told her?

"It's my fault," she says.

I don't know what to say, so I give her a sip of my tea.

"Poor Nabil," she murmers. "Poor Mama. Poor Akhmim."

"Hush," I say.

While I am sitting there, Ayesha comes in. Her daughter is with her mother and she has brought tamarind drink to tempt Hariba. Ayesha has grown up to be a pretty woman. When she and Hariba were young, Ayesha was the follower, but now that she has a husband and a daughter, she's somehow left Hariba behind. Hariba, for all her experience in rich people's homes, is still a girl, artificially preserved in the way spinsters are.

I get up, ready to go home and see to Nabil, and let Ayesha take my place.

4.
The Invisible Rule

My daughter, Tariam, cries when I leave to go to see Hariba. She loves my mother, but she loves to go out with me and she hates it when I leave her behind. Her red furious face is the last thing I see, and I'm really glad to get out of the house.

Hariba always wanted to be a saint. It's been her downfall, I think. We were best friends, I suppose we're still best friends, so I know her better than anyone. I don't mean that she wanted to be a religious saint, although she was always pretty religious, like her mother. She wanted to be right. She wanted to be with *qi'aida*, the invisible rule. I just want something other than the Nekropolis. I hate the Nekropolis. Alem, my husband, is looking for a flat in the part of town called Debbaghin. We haven't found one that we like that we can afford. But my aunt Chama lived there for a while before her husband divorced her and she says we will. It just takes time.

The Nekropolis is all right, it's where I grew up, but I want Tariam to grow up in a place that's safer.

I'm not particularly thinking about anything when I see the *harni* standing there, at the end of my street. For a second I assume he's a beggar, then I realize who it is. He sees me and comes toward me. My blood just freezes, I'm so frightened. I know he's not going to do anything. The three times I've met him before he was nice. Today he has this hangdog way, as if he expects to be kicked.

"Ayesha?" he says.

I can't think of what to say or do, so I say, "What do you want?"

"Is Hariba all right?" he says.

"Hariba is fine," I say.

"Her mother said she was dead."

The *harni* talked to Hariba's mother? I love Hariba's mother dearly, she's almost a second mother to me, but she's as old-fashioned as they come. I can't imagine her with the *harni*.

"Hariba's not dead," I say. "She's getting better, I think."

His face opens up with relief and I feel sorry for him. "I have to go to work," he says, "but can I talk to you a little, tomorrow? Here?"

"No!" I say. He's the cause of all this. Where we're standing, no one in the little shop across the street can see us, thank Allah. Old Miss Nessa is a terrible gossip.

"Please," he says. "I just want to know if she's all right."

I go around him and walk as fast as I can. I'm afraid to look back. I almost expect him to put his hand on my shoulder, but of course he doesn't. When I finally can't stand it anymore and look back, he's still standing there.

"I'll be here tomorrow!" he calls after me. On the street. I'm so embarrassed I pretend he isn't talking to me and keep walking.

It's halfway across the Nekropolis to Hariba's Aunt Zehra.
Hariba's Aunt Zehra is like my own aunt, we spent so much time
there when we were growing up. Everybody watched Hariba
and her sister and brothers because their father was dead and her
mother had to work. For the first few minutes, my face is burn-
ing from meeting the *harni*. But then the walk helps me calm
down, and my new sandals hurt where the strap rubs across my
heel, which is a small and petty thing to think about compared
to Hariba's troubles, but it still hurts. My mother's always com-
paring hurts that way. If I said I was sad because we were poor,
she'd say, "But think how lucky you are that you have a roof over
your head, not like the old man under the bridge who doesn't
have any place to go." I was a married woman when I finally
thought of something to say back: "Just because some man's
worse off than me doesn't mean that I'm not poor, and I'm certainly not going to be happy about it." I never have the nerve to
say it to my mother, though. I just look at my husband, Alem,
who knows what I'm thinking, and he tries not to laugh.

Zehra's neighbors are an old couple. The old man is sitting
outside, watching the world go by. He nods at me. I wonder
what he thinks of Hariba.

Hariba's mother is sitting with Hariba. She doesn't look so
good, Hariba's troubles have made her face pull in and down.
Even when Fhassin was in trouble, she didn't change, she was
always little and neither young nor old, but now she's lined
and tired. What could the *harni* have said to her? Did she even
know what he was? Well, if she told him that Hariba was
dead, then she did know who he was, and I probably
shouldn't have told him it wasn't true.

She gets up when I come in. "I have to go and see to Nabil,"
Hariba's mother says. "Now that you're here, I'll go on

home." Nabil never left home, and Hariba's mother takes care of him as if he were still a boy.

Hariba's feverish. She opens her eyes and smiles at me. "Hi, sweetie," I say. I can't tell her about meeting the *harni*. "Tariam drew a picture for you."

She holds it in her trembling hand. "Give her a kiss for me," she says.

I think Hariba regrets giving up children the most. It's not as if being jessed means she can't have children, but who would marry her? Unless she could buy back her bond, and Hariba always said she was saving her money to have a little when she was old.

"Have you seen Akhmim?" she whispers.

I'm so startled I don't know what to say. How could she know?

"Ayesha," she whispers, looking to make sure Zehra's niece can't hear us. "I need to see him."

"He got you into trouble," I say.

"No, no, no," she says. "It's not like that. Can you find him? Have you seen him?"

I shake my head, lying.

"Please, please. I need to see him."

"Zehra would never let him in here," I say.

She sighs and surrenders, closing her eyes. After a moment I realize she's crying.

"Oh, honey," I say.

"I'm so scared," she says. "Ayesha," she says, "you're the only one I can trust."

I'm scared, too.

*   *   *

The next day he's there, waiting, of course. It's a place where beggars sit, but his clothes are too clean and he looks too nice to be a beggar.

Mrs. Ibraham is out on the street behind me. I walk past him, ignoring him. He looks terribly sad. At least he has the decency not to say anything to me with someone watching.

Can *harni* be sad? They're like AI, and some AI is sad and some isn't. Some doesn't have emotions like us at all, even if people like my mother don't believe it. I don't know anything about *harni*, though.

I look over my shoulder.

"Ayesha," he says.

If it's an act, or programming, it's very good. But I keep walking. If my little girl, Tariam, comes out to play, will he remember she's mine? Tariam would not know to be careful. But she doesn't come to the end of the street, my mother will keep an eye on her. Tariam would like the *harni*, but she is shy and he's a strange man. I can't believe he'd take her.

Although he took Hariba. But not like that. Hariba is a grown woman. He didn't just pick her up and walk away with her.

I could turn around and tell my mother to keep Tariam inside all afternoon, but I'd have to walk back past him.

I stop at a shop and buy a card phone. Calls are cheap, only a bit of silver. I call the shop near home—my mother always has a card phone around in case of an emergency, but she never remembers to put her number in so no one can call her. "Addi, sir," I say to the shopkeeper, "it's Ayesha, Zeinab's daughter."

When we were children, we were all in awe of Addi, who was so serious when we bought chocolate from him. But he's just a poor man with a tiny shop.

"Yes, miss?" he says. "Is anything wrong?"

"Nothing wrong, Addi, sir," I say, "but would you send a boy with a message to my mother? I saw some older boys I didn't know at the end of the street and they looked a little rough, so could she keep Tariam inside this afternoon?"

He'll send a boy to my mother. I could have told him I saw the *harni*, to call the police, but I didn't. What if Hariba found out? And the *harni* looks so sad.

I'm soft-hearted. My mother, who used to visit family on the farm, says I'd starve to death if I had to butcher my own food and she's probably right.

Hariba is better. She's sitting up again. The first time I came to sit with her she was so sick and there wasn't anything I could do. I kept asking her if she wanted a cool cloth, some tea, anything. I wanted to do something. There was nothing to be done, and I suppose I was one more problem for her, with my wanting. I told my mother I wouldn't go back.

She said I most certainly would, that Hariba was my oldest friend. I said I didn't know what to do.

"You don't do anything," she said. "You are just there."

So I tried to just be there. But seeing Hariba sitting up is wonderful.

Zehra and Hariba's mother are arguing about the doctor. "He didn't do anything," Zehra says.

"She's getting better," Hariba's mother says.

"That's because someone's taking care of her," Zehra says. "That horse doctor was a crook."

"The patches helped," Hariba's mother says.

"Horse patches," Zehra says.

"I want to sit outside, in the sun," Hariba whispers. "Help me."

She puts her bony arms around my neck and I pull her up. She leans against me and totters outside to sit in the doorway on her sharp-boned bottom. "You need a cushion," I say. She gets bruises.

"It will get dusty."

"I'll dust it off," I say, and get a cushion. "Have they been arguing all day?"

"All day," she sighs. "Oh, Ayesha, I forgot my tea."

I fetch it for her. Today Zehra's old neighbor is either inside or gone to a café, and except for some children playing, the street is quiet.

"I make you run around like a servant," she says.

"It's about time someone waited on you," I say. "You've waited on other people for years."

"Oh, I didn't wait on people," she says. "I cleaned and kept accounts."

Which didn't sound any better to me. "I hate cleaning."

"It's not so bad," she says. "Cleaning other people's dirt is not like cleaning your own. I don't know why. And you get to snoop." She laughs at my expression. "I used to clean closets, hampers, drawers, everything. I knew everything about the mistress."

"Like what?" I say.

"Like that she has to shave under her chin. And she's worried about having a fat neck, she has this special antifat cream she uses, as if it ever did any good. And Mbarek-salah has this, um, device, that he can put his, you know, his thing in."

"What are you talking about?"

Hariba looks around to make sure none of the children are in earshot. "It's from outside of the country, you know." I know. It's forbidden. "It's sort of like a plastic bag," she says, "only it's more like one of those floats children use when they can't swim? And it's shaped like a woman's, well, you know."

I know, but I can't imagine it.

"It's not filled with air, it's filled with this, um, gel," Hariba says. "So it's more like a real woman. And when you turn it on, it sort of ripples, you know?"

I can't help laughing.

"Really," she says, laughing, too. "And it gets warm and it's like rippling, and he sticks his, um—"

"I know what you mean," I say, nearly helpless with laughter.

"Well, you can't blame the poor guy, it's not like he ever got anything out of the mistress."

"You saw this thing? You cleaned for Mbarek-salah? I thought you were over on the women's side."

"One of the men on the men's side was having an affair with one of the girls in the kitchen, and she told us about it. She got him to show it to her."

"I don't believe it," I said. "No one would do that."

"It's true," she insisted. "And think about it, it's the perfect wife."

I hold my hands up to my hot face, laughing. "You are wicked, Hariba!"

"No, really," she says, "I'm not making it up!"

We laugh and then a silence comes.

"What was he like?" I ask.

"Mbarek-salah?" she asks.

"No," I say, "the *harni*."

"Why do you want to know?" she says, irritable.

"I don't know," I say.

She looks suspicious. "He's good," she finally says. "Better than anyone else I've ever known."

Which doesn't tell me anything about what he was like.

"You don't believe me," she says. "None of you believe me. This place is so backward, you all think he's some sort of abomination."

"Hariba!" I say, furious. All my life I have been trying to get out of the Nekropolis. She's the one who was willing to stay here, and she would have if Fhassin hadn't ended up in prison, if someone would have married her. She'd have stayed in the Nekropolis, had her babies, and made her funeral wreaths until she got old before her time.

"It's true," she says. "Just because he wasn't born, you all hate him and you don't even know what he's like."

"I'm *asking* what he was like," I say through gritted teeth. "Listen, girl, I've been trying to get out of this cemetery my whole life and you know it, so don't punish me because your aunt and your mother are living five centuries ago." Of course, I do think he is an abomination—well, not an abomination, but something that should never have been. Look at what he's done to Hariba's life. But I'm not some stupid, superstitious old woman who can't even read.

She snakes me a look.

I shrug. "Fine."

"What do you want to know?" she says.

"What he was like. I mean, how was he different?"

She rolls her eyes. "He's like a normal person, just nicer. He's just a person. You met him. You liked him."

I did like him, but mostly because Hariba was treating him so badly. "I met him for an hour one afternoon," I say.

"Did he act different than a human?"

"He was awfully nice, for a man," I say.

She laughs, a short sharp bark like a dog.

"I was only with you two for a little bit of time, and you didn't even want me to talk to him."

"I didn't care if you talked to him," she says.

"You acted as if I'd catch something if I looked at him."

"I did not," she says.

I'm too irritated to say anything, so I cross my arms and watch the street.

"I don't know how to say what he's like." Hariba finally says. "He's like a regular person, only better."

I roll my eyes.

"Like that," she says. "Just like that. Akhmim doesn't do that, he isn't sarcastic. I'm trying my hardest to tell you what he's like and you just roll your eyes."

Her voice is loud. I glance back into Zehra's house, afraid that Hariba's mother will hear. She's looking over her shoulder at us. I smile and look back at Hariba. "Your mother is listening," I say quietly.

"I don't care," Hariba says, but quietly.

We sit and don't say anything. I have better questions in my head: Is he smart? Is he ever angry? Does he feel the same things we do? How is he different from us? But I can't ask them now.

"I'm tired," Hariba says, petulant. "I want to go in."

I come to see her, and she gets mad at me. You'd think she'd at least have the decency to recognize I didn't have to come see her.

The *harni* is waiting at the same spot. He doesn't say anything as I come closer. I'm nervous. He doesn't look any different than a person, except that he's handsome, like a foreigner who has had his genes enhanced. I want to speak to him, but I'm afraid to. I could just keep walking.

"She's getting better," I say.

"Did you tell her I asked about her?" he says. "Did she send a message?"

"No," I say, and walk past him.

I can feel him looking at me, through my veil, like his eyes are heat on the back of my head.

The next day I don't go to see Hariba, because my husband wants me to look at a flat in Debbaghin, but to get to the train I have to walk past where the *harni* waits. He's not there.

Is he still in the death house where he and Hariba were living? What's he doing, is he sick? *Harni* probably don't even get sick. If I was going to make a creature, I'd make them so they didn't get sick.

I am glad he's not there. Or maybe not, I don't know.

If I left the Nekropolis, then I could just lose track of Hariba and her *harni*. Things would take their course. When my cousin moved out of the Nekropolis, I stopped seeing much of her. Not because either of us meant to, but she had to work and her son was in a crèche in the day and we tried to get together a couple of times for tea. It would be like that. Alem isn't really pleased with this flat, but if I got a job, we could get a better one. I could work in a tea shop or something.

The flat is on the fourth floor, up under the roof where it's hot. The air cooler is on, but it doesn't do much good. There's a way up onto the roof, a trap door, but when I ask if we could sleep on the roof, where it would be cool at night, the landlord says he doesn't want it unlocked, because thieves could get in.

"We would be on the roof, we'd hear a thief," I say.

"You don't want to sleep on the roof here," he says. "Anyway, what if you forgot to lock it and you were gone? Anyone could come in my building."

For some reason I think of the *harni* waiting on the roof.

It isn't a very nice flat, it doesn't have very much space. I thank the man and wonder why Alem wanted me to see it. Sometimes Alem just needs me to agree with him so he feels better about something he's decided. He's been complaining about how hard it is to work and then look for places to live and about how he's seen so many places he can't tell a good place from a bad one. I like it that he does that. At first it made me nervous, I think because of my father—my father never wanted my mother to have a single thought. And I wanted a husband who would be a real husband. I'm not so old-fashioned as most women in the Nekropolis, but that's just the way I am. Alem isn't weak and once I realized what he wanted, I found I really liked it. If he ever made a decision, for instance, if he decided that we should take this flat, I would do what he wanted.

I walk back to the train so disappointed. I want to live here so bad. Every flat has water and cool air. The markets are not just carts and stalls but shops on the corners, bigger than Addi's shop at home, with dates and oranges in bins out front. Cool air comes out the doors.

The buildings are tall. On the first floor of one there's a sign in a window that says FOR RENT and two men are sitting in front with a paint can. Their clothes are paint-spattered. I stop and tug my veil closer around my face.

One of the men looks at me and says, "Miss? Are you here to see the flat?"

"No, sir," I say.

The other one shrugs. "I don't think she's coming," he says.

"I'm looking for a flat," I say boldly. "My husband just sent me to look at one he had seen," I add, so they won't think I'm too forward.

"Where?" the first man asks.

"Around the corner," I say.

"Jamal's flat? Up under the roof?" He shakes his head. "Jamal's a crook. Come look at my flat, I've just painted it."

It's on the second floor, and smells strongly of paint. It's clean and white. The rooms are not very large, but there are two bedrooms, one very small, but enough for Tariam. The windows look down on the street and it's deliciously cool. It has shutters, which I love, they're so old-fashioned.

"How much?" I ask. It's the same as the other flat, the one Alem wanted me to look at. "We'll take it," I say.

"Your husband allows you to speak for him?" the man says.

"He'll talk to you, but I'm sure he'll say yes," I say. What if it's rented today? I dig in my purse and find my bankcard. "Here's our bankcard," I say. "I can give you a deposit."

He takes the card thoughtfully. "All right," he says. He puts the amount in, and presses his thumb against the pad. "It's yours. When do you want to move in?"

"I have to talk to my husband," I say. Such a big decision, made so fast. I look around the cool rooms and they seem even smaller. What have I done?

But I smile and thank him. I hope Alem isn't angry.

I take the train home.

The *harni* is back in his spot, which irritates me. I wish he would disappear. I have to put a stop to this. He doesn't see me, he's watching the dust, leaning against the wall like any man with no job. I try to think of something to say, some way to tell him to leave me alone.

"What do you want from me?" I say.

He glances up and sees me and straightens up off the wall. "Did you see her today?" he asks.

He's so single-minded about her that I'm invisible. Which I should admire, it should be romantic but it isn't, it's annoying and short-sighted.

"No," I say. "And I didn't want to see you. What do you want, why do you wait here?"

"I want you to take a message to her," he says.

"Go away," I say. "Leave her alone. Leave *me* alone."

"Just one thing," he says. "Ask her for me."

"Why would I take her a message?" I ask.

"Ask her, what does she want me to do? That's all, just ask her that."

"I won't ask her anything," I say. "You should go away."

He nods, not at all angry. "I should," he says, "but I can't." He's not like a real man at all, he has no pride, to stand there in the street and be told off like a woman.

"You're not good for her," I say. "You're not human."

"I told her that," he says.

"I am not going to talk to you," I say.

I haven't told Alem about the *harni* because if I did he would tell the police and they would arrest him. I'd like it if he were arrested, but I don't want to be the one who causes it. If he keeps hanging around, somebody will say something to somebody, I'm sure.

I could tell Alem about the *harni* after he's arrested, but then

I'd have to explain why I didn't tell him before. I would like to tell someone about the *harni*. I'd like to ask someone about *harni*. I don't know how Hariba stood it.

Not Alem, though. He doesn't talk about things. He tells me about his day and every little thought that passes through his head, but he doesn't really talk about things. My mother always said, "Men don't have to know every little thing."

I'm afraid of what he will say about the flat.

Alem comes home in his blue coveralls, so Tariam can see him from far down the street. She runs into the street without a veil, in the short dress she wears in the house so her legs are bare, shouting, "Papa! Papa!"

But Alem just laughs and scoops her up and kisses her curly head. "Princess!" he says.

She grins at me, knowing she has gotten away with something. He spoils her so bad. It makes me mad because he spoils her and then it's up to me to try to correct her. "Tariam!" I say. "Look at you running naked in the street! Come in here!" I hate that, making me the bad one. But I know I'm too critical of him.

"Alem," I say, my face very grave, "I have to tell you something.

"What?" He carries Tariam in, her long brown legs hanging down. She's getting too big to carry, my baby.

"I saw the flat and I didn't like it."

He holds his face still, so I don't know if I was supposed to like it or not. Is he angry?

"I found another one," I said. "It's very nice, very clean and cool.

"Where?" he asks.

"Closer to the train," I say.

"Okay," he says. "When do you want to go see it?"

"Tonight?" I say. "I mean, they were painting it when I saw it, that's how long it's been available, and it's really very nice. I was afraid it would be gone, so . . . so I put a deposit on it," I finish in a small voice. I'm hoping he will hear how nervous I am and not be mad at me.

He frowns a little. He doesn't like that I put a deposit on it without him seeing it, but the truth is, he hates looking for a flat. It took him months to even start looking, and then he would only look once in a while. So part of him is relieved I've found something and he doesn't have to look anymore, and part of him is worried he won't like it, and part of him—I know this—wishes we didn't have to go through the bother of moving at all.

"What about dinner?" he asks.

"My mother and I made couscous," I say. "It's ready."

It's early, but we sit down to eat. Tariam crawls into Alem's lap and he feeds her. "I'm not hungry," she says, but when he offers her couscous with zucchini and carrot, she eats it. Then I change her into street clothes, just a simple blue dress and a scarf for her hair—she has a wild head full of hair, curly like Alem's, and it stands out like a halo away from her face, so she's glad to get it tied back.

"Where are we going?" she asks. "Where are we going?"

"To look at a flat," Alem says.

"Are we going on the train?"

"We are," he assures her solemnly, and she skips, holding his hand.

"Hurry up!" she says. "Hurry up! I want to ride on the train!"

It's cool underground, but Tariam fidgets on the train and wants to hang on the pole. Alem gets up and stands with his feet wide so his legs are on either side of her while she clasps the metal pole in the middle of the aisle and sways back and forth. The lights flicker and they disappear and reappear and I'm happy to see them there. It's going to work out, I think.

And it does. We find the man who has the apartment. Alem likes the apartment. The landlord likes Alem. We can move in three weeks.

Tariam goes from room to room, singing a popular song I always hear playing on the street, "Silly boy, silly boy, you want to be my lover?"

"I saw him," I tell Hariba. It just pops out. I think about saying it and I know I shouldn't and *pop,* I say it. I won't have much time to see Hariba anymore, not with moving and all, and I'm relieved about that. I hate coming to see her, I hate passing the *harni*.

"You saw him?" she says. She doesn't ask who.

"I was going to catch the train. Alem and I are renting an apartment in the Debbaghin," I say.

"Where did you see him?"

"At the end of my street," I say. "He was waiting for me."

"Did he have a message for me?" she asks, her hollow face hungry and alive. We're sitting outside the door to her aunt's house.

I try to think of a lie, but my mind is blank. "He said to ask you what you want him to do." It occurs to me that I could lie, tell him she said to go away.

"I need to see him," she says.

"For what?" I say, exasperated.

"To figure out what we're going to do," she says. "Where is he?"

"I don't know, he's always waiting at the end of my street."

"You've seen him before?"

"Yes," I say. "And I shouldn't have told you."

She covers her mouth with her hands. "O Holy One," she finally breathes between her fingers. "I was afraid he was gone."

"You're just going to get in trouble."

She shakes her head. "You don't understand. Tell him, no, wait, you said he's at the end of your street? The end of our street? When? When you're coming here?"

"You can't go meet him," I say, aghast.

"I have to."

"I'll tell your mother. I'll tell Zehra. They won't let you out of the house."

"Don't," she whispers. "Please, Ayesha, don't."

"You can't go meet him on the street, you'll get arrested. You'll get him arrested."

"They'll kill him," she whispers. "Won't they? They'll put him down."

Which maybe they should do.

"They want to arrest you; look what they did to Nabil. You have to get better and then decide what you're going to do." We've all been talking about what she is going to do and we all think she's going to have to run away. She can't stay here.

"I have to see him again," she says. "At least one more time. You've got to help me see him one more time."

"Then you promise you'll decide what you're going to do?"

She nods. "I will. What do you think I should do?"

"Go abroad," I say.

She nods. "Okay, I'll plan it out. I'll decide where to go and I'll go away."

"Start a new life," I prompt.

She nods.

"So your family won't be in danger anymore."

That's hard for her. I can see it hit her. But she nods slowly. "Okay. Maybe he could meet me in a tea shop? Do you think?"

An unmarried woman meeting a man in a tea shop is going to attract stares. "Don't be stupid," I say.

She bites her lip."

"I know a place," I say. "You could meet in our new flat."

Tariam says, "Are you going to the new flat?"

"No, baby," I say, "I'm going to see Aunt Hariba."

"Can we go to the new flat?"

"No, you stay here with Grandmamma."

"No," Tariam says, looking down, her fat baby lip poking out. "I don't want to stay with Grandmamma."

"Mama has to go see Aunt Hariba," I say.

Tariam fusses. She's my guilty conscience. Sometimes she looks so—not frail, so provisional, as though I love her so much I shouldn't be allowed to have her and someone's going to take her from me. She's too tiny, too perfect in every detail, down to the utter loveliness of her teeth. Tiny white teeth like corn kernels. She wants to go on the train. I hear her wail as I leave my mother's.

I'm clutching my veil so hard it pulls across the top of my head like a band. I make myself relax. Maybe the *harni* won't be there. Sometimes he isn't.

But I see him loitering alone at the corner. Why doesn't anyone ever call the police on him? A strange man standing there.

He lifts his head from where he's been tracing the dust with his shoe, his face open to me.

"She wants to see you," I say. Until I actually say it, I've been pretending to myself that I might lie, but the truth is I never really would have.

"Where?" he says, as if this has been a foregone conclusion, and his easy assumption makes the anger rise up in me. What right does he have to assume!

"At an empty flat in Debbaghin. Do you know where that is?"

"I know," he says.

I tell him the address.

"Thank you," he says. "Thank you so very much."

"Don't thank me," I say. "If I had my way, you'd never see her again."

"You do it out of love for her," he says. "I can thank you for that."

It was the way he was so unmanly that made me so uncomfortable. If I had spoken to any man that way . . . I think Hariba had raised her brothers and she had always been bossy, so that was why she liked the *harni*, because she wanted a man like that.

"Hariba and I thought maybe she could go out with me today," I tell Aunt Zehra.

"She's not very strong," Aunt Zehra says.

"I can go in a pedicab," Hariba says. "It would be good for me."

I can see Aunt Zehra doesn't like the idea. "What if some-one sees you and calls the police?"

"She could dress like a new widow," I say. I have brought my mother's chador and I unfold it.

Zehra blinks and pulls her head back, startled. "Well," she says, "at least you didn't decide to use mine."

Zehra is as big as Hariba's mother is little and Hariba would have been lost in the folds of her chador, like Tariam in something of mine.

"We are just going to go around a bit," Hariba says. "Stop in a tea shop, go to the Moussin."

Zehra is not the kind of person who goes to the Moussin ex-cept when called to worship, but maybe she thinks Hariba has been so frightened by her sickness that she wants to go. It will certainly explain why we're gone for a few hours.

Hariba holds her thin arms up like a child and Zehra and I throw the chador over her head and help her straighten it so she can see. My mother is bigger than Hariba, but it's not so bad. One woman in a chador looks like another.

Zehra lets us use a card phone to call a pedicab and to-gether we bundle Hariba out the door and into the seat. She leans over and kisses her aunt on the cheek. "If my mother comes by, tell her I won't be long," she says.

Now that we have actually succeeded, I feel terrible about lying to Zehra. But Hariba doesn't seem to have any second thoughts. She seems as natural as if we weren't sneaking off to see her lover. She lies so easily and so well. It even seems to fill her with energy, but maybe that is just the anticipation of seeing the *harni*.

We take the pedicab to the train, and Hariba leans on my arm to get down the steps. She's full of questions about what the *harni* said and how he looked. The more she chatters, the angrier I get about how thoughtless she's being.

"I can't believe you," I finally say.

"What?" she says.

"The way you can lie to Zehra."

"You didn't seem to have any trouble," she says.

"But you don't even care," I say.

"Of course I care, but I have to see Akhmim."

"I shouldn't be doing this," I say.

"If you didn't help me, I'd just do it myself."

"You shouldn't see him," I say.

"You don't understand," she says.

I can't think of anything I could have done different, except maybe tell Zehra. Then Hariba would have just run away, she's so obsessed. I don't believe that she thinks this is the last time she'll see him.

The train comes in and both of us are angry so neither of us says anything and then it's off the train and Hariba hanging on my arm to get up the stairs. We stop a couple of times for her to rest, and she's shaky and sweaty when we get to the top. Luckily there's another pedicab. I'm spending so much money on pedicabs today. But Hariba doesn't have any money and she can't walk to the flat.

I hate having them meet in my flat. It's so clean, so nice, I want it to stay that way in my mind.

The *harni* is waiting across the street from the flat and when he sees the pedicab he starts forward to cross, but I put my hand up for him to stay where he is. Hariba doesn't see him until I move my hand, but then she tenses as if to cry out and I put my hand on her arm to stop her.

"Wait," I whisper.

I help her climb down. The *harni* stands on the other side of the street, watching us. He's so stupid. Can't he pretend not to notice us? And Hariba's as bad, watching him. I'm so embarrassed I could die.

The owner has left the door set to my thumb—I called and told him I was bringing a friend to see the flat today. What if they're working on it? Some painting, something with the cooling system? What will I tell him? That the *harni* is my cousin. And that he's going to help us move, so he's meeting me to see the flat, too.

But the flat is empty. Hariba says, "I need to sit down," so I help her sit on the floor. Then I go to the window and wave to the *harni*.

"Is he coming?" Hariba asks.

He comes up the stairs faster than I expect.

"Akhmim?" she says.

He kneels down next to her and her hands flutter around his face, across his shirt. It's as if I'm not even there. I wish I could leave. I could die at the way they act—I would never, ever have believed Hariba would act this way.

I turn my back and look out the window, but then I can't stand it and I look back at them. The *harni* isn't saying anything, but Hariba keeps saying over and over, "It's all right now."

"What do you want me to do?" he finally says.

"We need to get away," she says.

I am furious. She promised me that all she wanted to do was see him one more time. Hariba was never a liar, but she lied to me about this.

I have a silly thought, a thought that shames me, but Alem will never treat me this way. Not that I would want him to, not really.

I walk through the other three clean, cool, light-filled rooms of my flat. It feels as if we have dirtied this place. I wish we'd never come here.

"I can't believe you," I say on the train.

Hariba is worn out, her eyes look bruised. I should feel sorry for her, but I don't.

"What?" she says.

"You lied to me," I say. "You said this was the last time you would see him."

"No, I didn't," she says.

"Yes, you did," I say. "And you never intended not to see him again."

"Ayesha," she says, "I can't leave him. Look at him, he needs me."

"Well, sell him to someone else."

"Sell him! I can't sell him! He's a person," she says.

"Then let him get over needing you like any other person."

"He's not like any other person," she says. "You know that. But he's a person. He's intelligent. We love each other."

"Holy One protect us," I say. "Well, do what you must, but I'm done with you."

"Ayesha! No!" she says. "I need your help! You're my best friend!"

"Was," I point out. "But you've changed, Hariba. You lie to me now, and you use me."

"That's not true," she says. "I didn't tell you everything because you wouldn't help, that's true, but that's because you won't listen."

Is that true? "I'm listening now."

"If I love Akhmim and he loves me, what's so bad about our being together?"

"It's illegal," I say.

She pauses. Finally she says, "You're right, but—"

"But nothing—" I say.

"Listen to me! Okay, maybe what I did was wrong. Maybe I should have left him a slave to that woman, who treated him like a footstool, but—"

"That woman owned him," I say. "Just like she owns the footstool."

"All right, and I think that's wrong, and you don't. But now that it's done, I can't just give him back. He's unstable. They'll kill him."

Maybe they would. I didn't know what they would do with him. I nod.

"So why shouldn't we both run away together and be happy?"

"Because it's wrong," I say. "Suppose you run off and live happily ever after in some western country where people eat pork and drink all the time and are unhappy and frenzied. You can't have children, you have no family or friends."

"Do you think I'm going to have children if I stay here? Jessed women don't have children. I'm not going to be hired by some rich man whose wife died and who is lonely and falls in love with me and buys me out and marries me. That only happens in films."

"At least people here speak the same language as you."

"But I'm still alone," she says. "At least with Akhmim I'm not alone."

"At least here you have your family. What are you going to

do when you're alone and there's no one like me to do things like this?"

"The same thing I'll do now," she says, "since you won't help me."

"What's that?" I ask.

She turns her head and won't answer.

I wish I had someone to talk to. The person I would normally talk to about this is Hariba, so I can't, and I'm trapped. I should tell her mother and her aunt, but if I do, I know Hariba will run away. And she'll run away with the *harni*. I don't know any way that things can get back to normal.

"Mama, can I have an ice?" Tariam asks.

"We don't have any ices," I say.

"I want an ice," she says.

Alem wanted me to find a flat, so I did. Now he wants me to do all the packing, so I'm collecting boxes from stores that are going to throw them away and bringing them home. Hariba wants me to help her find a way out of the country. Tariam wants everything all day. Who is there for me? Who gives me what I want? Not Alem. I mean, he's a good husband, but there's no romance to him. I thought I didn't need romance, but I need something.

"Mama?" Tariam says. "Take me to the store and buy me an ice?"

"No, Mama can't right now," I say. "Mama has to pack."

Tariam whines, with her voice full of tears, "I want an ice."

"We can't always have what we want," I say sharply, and she bursts into tears. She might as well learn now.

I stolidly pack blankets and linens while she stamps her

feet and cries until I can't stand it anymore. "Tariam," I say, "that's enough. Stop it now or you'll have to lie on your bed."

"I won't," she says.

I grab her arm and swat her and then pick her up and put her on her bed while she howls. We've only got two rooms, so there isn't very much space to get away from her. When we move, we'll have four rooms, I remind myself. She'll have her own room.

"I wish you weren't my mama!" she shrieks.

I don't say anything, no matter how much it hurts. Alem will be home in another two hours. Although that won't make so much difference, since all he does when he's home is complain.

When he comes home, he starts in.

"How are you?" I ask.

"I had a terrible day. I can't believe they don't fire that dispatcher," he says, and then he launches into a long story about how this dispatcher sent him to someplace in the city, even though someone else was closer, and how if he doesn't get enough jobs logged in a day, then he gets a bad evaluation.

Just when we're moving to a bigger apartment and need money, he's going to get a bad evaluation.

I have chickpea soup for dinner. We haven't had it in a while.

"I've been so hot all day," Alem says. Meaning he doesn't want hot soup for dinner. But he just sighs and sits down, cross-legged, on the carpet.

"I don't want it," Tariam says.

"Why not, sweet?" I ask.

"I don't like it," she says.

"Well, that's what we have for dinner," I say, trying to be good. "Have a spoonful?"

"No," Tariam says.

I coax until finally Alem says, "Either feed her something else or let her not eat."

Of course, if she doesn't eat, she'll be hungry in half an hour, and I'll be doing this again.

"I want couscous," Tariam says.

"I didn't make couscous," I say.

Tariam starts to cry, and Alem gets up, disgusted, and takes his soup into our room. Nobody notices I cooked this food and haven't even gotten a chance to eat any of it myself.

Tariam finally sniffles her way through half a cup of soup, and I eat mine, and then I send her out to play until it gets dark. I go into our room and take Alem's bowl. He's lying on our blankets with his coveralls off.

"I just had a bad day," he says.

"You go on out and see your friends," I suggest. I don't want him underfoot anyway, it's like having two children instead of one.

"I'm too tired," he says.

I take the bowl back and clean up the dishes.

Alem comes out of the bedroom, wearing a djellaba. "I think I will go out, maybe just for an hour or so," he says.

The frustration comes up like bile, which isn't fair, because I told him to go out. But I didn't want him to.

The *harni* is waiting at the end of the street again.

"What do you want?" I ask.

"Have you seen Hariba?" he asks.

I shake my head. I haven't seen her in four days.

"Are you going to see her?"

"I'm shopping for vegetables," I say. "Do you know what the best thing you could do for Hariba is? Never see her again."

"It's too late for that," he says.

"It's only too late when you're dead," I say.

"I wish that were true."

"It's scripture. You're blaspheming."

He smiles. "You're like Hariba. Do all the women of the Nekropolis quote scripture?"

"I don't know," I say. He's infuriating. "I'm moving out of the Nekropolis."

"That's right," he says. "You have a beautiful flat."

I wish he didn't know where I was going to live. Not that he seems as if he's going to hurt me. In some ways it's hard to imagine anyone more harmless. Maybe it's because I look at him this moment and I wonder if he has a penis like other men. My face heats up. I don't know why I'm thinking of this, or of Alem's penis, inflamed and dark with blood. Alem's testicles like dark leather sacs. The *harni* doesn't need testicles. He's never going to have children. Maybe that's why he's so gentle; he's a gelded bull. Oh, my thoughts!

"You shouldn't talk to me," I say.

"I'm sorry," he says. "I'm just worried about Hariba."

"Hariba is fine," I say. "She's with her family. Leave her alone."

"I can't."

"You can."

"That's not the way I'm made," he says. "Hariba is my . . . I don't know how to explain it to you. My superior complement."

"Is that why you got her to run away?"

"I didn't get her to run away," he says. "I can't make Hariba do anything she doesn't want to. I don't know anyone who can."

That sounds true, but I know it really isn't. Hariba ran away because of him. Hariba is headstrong, but she has always been dutiful.

"If you see her, ask her what she wants me to do," he says.

"I'm going vegetable shopping," I say.

"I'll try to be here most afternoons," he says.

I want to run away from Hariba and her *harni*. For that matter, I want to run away from Alem, and Tariam, and everything and start over where I wouldn't feel so mean all the time, and where somebody thinks about me once in a while.

I shop and then stop by my mother's. Tariam is playing with her cousins. "Can I stay at Grandmamma's tonight?" she begs.

My mother is delighted. "It's wonderful to have a child in the house." My mother lives only a couple of blocks from us. So I get some things for Tariam and bring them over. When I leave, the girls are squatting by my brother's house, building something with strips of plastic, and Tariam is so engrossed she can barely manage to wave goodbye to me.

I make dinner more spicy than I can when Tariam is eating with us.

"Where's baby?" Alem says when he gets home. When he hears that she is at my mother's, he is pleased. "I like your mother," Alem says.

We never see his mother. When Alem was growing up, his parents were always fighting and his mother would go off and stay with her family and it would be just Alem and his brother and sister and their father. Then his mother would come back and everything would be all right for a while until the fighting started again and his mother left. Now she lives kilometers south in Youssoufia. We've visited her twice and I like her well enough. I like his father, too. Sometimes people are just oil and water.

"Alem," I say while we're eating, "were you ever in love with me?" It is a stupid question because, even if he answers that he was and is, I'd only believe it if he told me without my asking.

"Ayesha," he says, "I love you so much. You know that. You are my wife, the mother of my beautiful daughter."

"I know you love me, but are you 'in love' with me?"

"I don't understand," he says. "Do you mean do I feel about you the way I did when we first met? People can't be like that all the time. What we have is true love, not infatuation."

I nod as if that answers my question, but of course it doesn't. Alem's a good man, and he does love me. He loves me more than my parents ever loved each other. But it's because of what I do for him and his life. It isn't love for me.

We're quiet a while, both unsettled.

"Have you seen Hariba?" Alem asks. He's trying to make conversation.

"No," I say. "She's so difficult to be around. She's changed so much."

"Maybe it's just because she is sick. Now that she's getting better, she should be more like the Hariba you know."

"Maybe," I agree.

"What are they going to do? Her family, I mean?"

"She's thinking that maybe she can smuggle out of the country."

"Where would she go?" he asks.

"North, I suppose."

"To the E.C.U.?" He's surprised.

"That's what I said. Really, though, where else can she go? But I don't know how she can get there."

"I might be able to find a way she could get there," Alem says, "but I don't know why she would want to go."

"What do you know about smuggling?" I ask. Alem does the virtual guidance for a couple long-haul lorry drones.

"Sometimes we ship E.C.U. goods," he says. Most E.C.U. goods are illegal, but there are a lot of them that nobody cares about, like the cardboard phones. I knew they had to be smuggled in, but that's not real smuggling, not like getting a criminal out of the country.

"I thought a lot of that was copies," I say.

"Some of it is," he says, "but the originals have to come from somewhere."

"Smuggling entertainments isn't the same as smuggling a person."

"I know," he says, irritated. "Why is everything I say wrong? I said I *might* be able to find out."

"I don't want you to get in trouble," I say. Especially not for Hariba. "If you lost your job or something—"

"If you don't want me to ask around, I won't," he says. "I just knew you were worried about her."

"Hariba got herself into this," I say. "I don't want anything to happen. Look what happened to Nabil. And it's killing her mother, you can just see it. She looks twenty years older." I just want him to understand that it isn't worth it, but I feel as if I sound accusatory. What if he got in trouble? Doesn't he think about that, about Tariam and me?

I know he thinks I'm such a nag, but sometimes he's such a little boy.

"Hey," he says. "Let's not waste the evening."

I know what he means.

He leans over and kisses me.

"Oh, you," I say. "Is that all you think about?"

"Yes," he says. "All day I think about you." I give him a kiss back. Alem likes me to be forward.

"You look so handsome, tonight," I say. He does, he always looks good to me. What I love most is when he puts his hands on me. I like when he's above me and all his weight is there, against me.

And afterward we lie together, sweaty and happy, and I feel like hot bread, all soft and airy inside.

"Why don't we do this more often?" I say. Like I do every time.

I keep a cardboard phone with my key in it and sometimes Alem calls me at home, so when it chirps, I assume it's him. But it's Hariba's key that shows up. "Ayesha?" she says.

"It's me," I say.

"I need to talk to you," she says.

I want to say that we're talking now, but I know what she means. I tell her I'll come over and at least she gets off the phone quick. This one still has most of thirty minutes' use left on it. Tariam spent the night before at my mother's, so I feel as if I shouldn't take her there. "Come on, sweet," I say. "We're going to go visit your aunt Hariba."

She hates being dressed to go out, hates having her hair covered and is always pulling at her veil, but she likes the idea of going to see Hariba, so she's patient while I dress her in bright yellow. Maybe seeing Tariam will remind Hariba that I have a life of my own.

The *harni* is waiting at the end of the street, but he just nods at me when he sees Tariam, thank merciful Allah. I don't want her thinking it's all right to talk to men when she's un-escorted.

She's worn out by the time we get to Zehra's, but delighted to see Zehra and Hariba. "So big!" Zehra says.

"You're big!" says Tariam.

Zehra just laughs.

Hariba is sitting up, and her face has a bit of flesh. "You look better," I say politely.

"I *am* better," she says. "Come outside and sit with me."

"Me too," Tariam says.

"All right," I say. I don't want more secrets and I'm willing to use Tariam to keep Hariba from scheming.

Hariba frowns. "No, baby," she says. "You stay inside with Aunt Zehra. I want to talk with your mama."

"I want to talk with you," Tariam announces.

I know Hariba didn't call me all this way to give in to a child, and Tariam's presence probably won't stop her from whatever she wants, but I refuse to make it easier for her. "Come on," I say and lift Tariam onto my hip. She's not so small anymore.

Hariba follows me outside and I glimpse Zehra's face for a moment—stiff and expressionless. At least Zehra suspects Hariba is up to something.

"Can we ride the train?" Tariam asks.

"No," I say. "The train doesn't go the way home from here."

"I need your help," Hariba says quietly.

"For what?" I ask.

"I need to get out of the country," she says.

"Why can't we ride the train to the new flat?" Tariam whines.

"Hush, baby," I say.

"We could go to the new flat," Tariam says.

I put her down and she reaches up for me to pick her back up. "You're too heavy," I say.

"Why don't you go inside and see if Aunt Zehra has a cookie?" Hariba says sweetly.

"I don't want a cookie," Tariam says. "I'm hot." She pulls at her veil. I can feel mine hot on my hair.

"Don't pull on it," I say.

"I'm hot," she says and starts to cry.

"Hush, little girl," I say. "We'll get some cold water from Zehra."

Hariba scowls while Zehra fusses and gives Tariam some cold tea. "Look here," Zehra says and opens her sewing kit. "Help me match up my buttons."

As soon as we're back outside, Hariba says, "I need you to take a note to someone for me."

"Who?" I say.

"A man Nabil knows. He might be able to help me get out of the country. Nabil can't go because he's afraid the police might be watching him."

"You're going to get Nabil put in prison or killed," I say.

"What can I do!" she whispers. "Should I just go to the police and say, 'Arrest me'?"

Maybe, I think. But that's just anger talking. "Alem may know someone."

"Alem?"

"Sometimes they ship smuggled goods." Why am I saying this? Because I'm afraid of this man Nabil knows. Zehra told me about the track and the horse doctor—this is probably just as bad.

She chews on her thumbnail. Hariba looks frightened and tired, even if she is getting back a little weight. What a stranger she's become with lines around her mouth and her thin face, like those women begging at the Moussin. She looks like a divorced woman with no family.

"I told him not to ask," I say. "You know Alem, he doesn't have a devious bone in his body. I was afraid he'd get caught."

"Would you please take the message?" she says. "If you don't like it, then maybe ask Alem? I know it's a lot to ask . . ."

How can I say no?

"Where is he?" I ask.

I want to take Tariam. Hariba is sending me to the new part of town, but a bad part of town, and I'm thinking that maybe people would be nicer to a woman with a child than a woman alone. Of course, I can't take Tariam there. I don't really want to. What if something happened? I don't want to go with Tariam, but I want to go with someone.

I should ask Alem. I've already volunteered him to look for a smuggler for Hariba, so I can't pretend I'm keeping him uninvolved, but I just can't tell him. This whole business with Hariba has gotten so complicated. Maybe I won't have to involve him. Maybe this person I'm meeting can help Hariba. He's certainly got to be better help than Alem. Alem doesn't know anything about smuggling, couldn't smuggle oranges into a restaurant. There's no sense bringing Alem in on this unless I have to. Things like this sometimes just work out. This man will smuggle Hariba and maybe the *harni* out of the country, and Alem will never have to be involved. Or maybe if this man doesn't work out, Nabil will know someone else, or even, Holy One forgive me, the police will find Hariba.

I don't want Alem to do me a favor, certainly not a big favor like this. I don't want to be in his debt.

I decide the only one I can ask to go with me is the *harni*.

He's there at the end of the street, as dependable as the sunrise.

"I need you to do something with me," I say. "It's for Hariba."

Of course he is willing. He has such a soft look about him. "Do you want me to be your escort?" he asks. "Do you want me to pretend to be someone?"

"Pretend to be my cousin," I say.

He falls in step with me, and I can't help looking around to see if anyone I know sees us. My veil makes it impossible to look without turning all the way around, but luckily there's no one around. Maybe it's a sign things are going to be okay.

"Once," he says, "Hariba and I had to pretend to be characters in the mistress's *bismek* game. I was terrified, I didn't know how to pretend that way. But now pretending is easy. I pretend all the time. I pretend to be human."

I don't want to talk to him, but I feel rude. Although I'm rude to everyone anymore. "Do you like it?"

"It doesn't matter. I realized that *harni* pretend all the time."

I've never heard him say *"harni"* before and it sounds ugly when he does. Or maybe I have heard it and never paid attention, I don't know. "Hariba wants you both to get out of the country, to go across to the E.C.U."

He shakes his head. "I don't know. There aren't any *harni* there, are there? But I don't know that there is any place for me."

"Are you lonely?" I ask.

He nods, thinking of Hariba, I guess. But then he says, "I don't know why they make us so we need other *harni* and then send us out to be alone. It's very cruel."

"Don't you miss Hariba?"

"Of course," he says. "But that's different. She's human."

He sounds human. It's strange to hear him talk about humans as if we were different. I want to know what's different about us, but I'm afraid to ask.

It's a long train ride west, away from all the parts of town I know. Not south into the desert, but into sprawl. The buildings on the west side of the city are a hodgepodge. Some have blank walls to the outside and courtyard in, and some have shutters on tall windows, but in the new city a lot of them are concrete buildings from the years after colonialism, clean-looking even when they're old. Some neighborhoods are kept up and the buildings are whitewashed or painted blue. Some of the signs are in French. I can't read French, but I like the way it looks. It's too expensive to live out here, and too far from Alem's work.

Farther beyond that the buildings are made of trash or foamstone and they all look raw and ugly. We get off the train in a neighborhood where the buildings are all foamstone, the walls tinted desert red or yellow, the doorways, added after, are blue. Cheap colors.

I give Akhmim the address, and he asks a woman sitting on a dark red foamstone bench in the train station. She looks

Berber. She pulls her blue and white veil around her face and points but doesn't answer. Akhmim looks at me and I shrug. We walk that way. "Maybe we'll see the street name," I say.

The street is called Tel el Amar. We come to it, and it isn't nearly as exotic as it sounds. The first block is all two-story foamstone warehouses with chrome plastic laminate doors, stained-looking. The buildings run one into another, and there's no feeling of neighborhood. Nowhere to go, no door to knock on if we get in trouble. I find myself clutching my veil.

Akhmim doesn't seem comfortable, either. He checks the address against numbers above the doors. Dried mud shows where the street puddles when it rains.

We walk through more blocks of warehouses, and see only two people, both short, gnarled dark men who look like Berbers. They stare at us. I'm glad I brought Akhmim. He looks young and strong. Past the warehouses there are some empty lots and smaller buildings that sit plunked down in the middle of gravel and dirt. A lot of them are empty to the dry wind. A few of them seem to have something to do with fixing machine parts. Other than the woman we saw at the train station, the only people around are men.

"Is it much farther?" I ask. If he says yes, I'm going to suggest we just turn around and go back, but Akhmim says no, maybe just a block.

The address is a green foamstone building. It has a big open chrome door, as if cars or tractors or lorries are supposed to pull in, and there are dark stains on the slick concrete floor. There's some sort of machine and a lot of dark, greasy parts and electrical wires. A man and a boy are sitting there, looking at the machine but not working on it. They watch us walk across the lot without saying anything.

I take the paper from Akhmim and look at the name on it. "I am looking for Khalid?"

The older man says, "He's not here," and the boy, who looks about seventeen, thinks this is funny, showing white teeth. The older man doesn't say anything else, and doesn't look at the boy. Some sort of joke is being played on us.

"Ah, when will he be back?" I ask.

The older man shrugs, and the boy laughs. Is Khalid dead? Moved away? In prison?

"I'm here for a friend," I say. "Nabil sent me."

"I'm Khalid," the boy says and the older man grimaces in pleasure.

This is another joke.

The boy grins at us. "How do you know Nabil?" he says.

"I know his sister."

"Rashida?" he says, and I realize he really does know Nabil.

"No," I say, "Hariba."

"Who's Hariba?"

"His older sister. She was jessed." Maybe the seventeen-year-old will take us to Khalid?

"Ah. You know Rashida?"

"Yes," I say.

"Rashida is a sweetie," he says. "I've got to do some business," he says to the older man.

The older man nods and raises his hand. We walk back across the lot and when I look back, holding my veil with one hand, I see the old man still sitting there, looking at the dismantled machine.

"How's Nabil?" the boy asks.

"Not so good," I say. "He got beat up by the police."

The boy whistles through his teeth.

"What for?"

"Because his sister, who is jessed, ran away. They thought he might know where she was."

"Holy Name," the boy says meditatively. He looks at Akhmim. "Who's this? Your husband?"

"My cousin," I say.

"Hello," Akhmim says.

The boy snorts through his nose, obviously unimpressed.

We walk down the street for a bit, then the boy says, "So why did Nabil send you to me?" and I realize he really is Khalid and we're not going to meet someone else.

"He is trying to help someone get out of the country."

"Two people," the *harni* says.

"His sister?"

I don't know what to say.

"And whoever she ran away with, right?" Khalid says. "She wants to go north to the E.C.U.? Do they want papers? Or how do they want to go?"

"I don't know," I say. "How can they go?"

"They can go with false papers, but that's really expensive. Or they can go as cargo. That's cheaper. We take them across to Málaga or Cádiz. Then they can claim asylum or whatever they're going to do. Personally I recommend Málaga." He looks at Akhmim. "You ever been to Málaga?"

"Not yet," Akhmim says.

"It's a nice town, I like it very much. I'm thinking of going to Málaga myself and staying there. You can get augmented, get a good living, live in a nice place."

"You should go," Akhmim says politely.

"My mother would die if I left her," Khalid says.

"How much would it cost to go to Málaga or Cádiz?" I ask.

He says, "Six thousand." It's more than Alem makes in a year.

Akhmim shrugs. "Oh well, so much for that idea."

I open my mouth, as shocked by Akhmim as by the amount.

"You think it's too much," Khalid says, defensive.

Akhmim shrugs. "It's probably a fair price, but you know Nabil. You know his family. His mother can't sell enough funeral wreaths to pay for that."

Khalid frowns and hunches his shoulders, looking very much as if he's seventeen. "I don't know. Maybe, for Nabil, if I don't take a cut. Normally I have to take my cut, you know? I have a business. I have to keep up appearances. These boots, do you see these boots?" He holds up one foot. They're ugly; they look like the military boots all the boys are wearing. "These are E.C.U. Do you know what they cost?" He names a fourth of what Alem and I will pay for rent for a month in our new flat. I try to look impressed. "But for Nabil," he says, "maybe I could do a favor, you know? Nabil is a good guy. Good to his mother. He does good business for me."

Khalid looks at his expensive boots for a minute. "Half," he says finally. "That's the best I can do, even for Nabil."

"I'll tell him," Akhmim says. "He'll be grateful."

"Yeah," Khalid says, sullen now. "He better be."

"We'll see if they can get the money," Akhmim says.

"Okay," Khalid says. "You know where to find me, right?"

I show the piece of paper.

As we are walking back, I ask the *harni,* "How did you know to do that?"

"We're good at bargaining," he says. "Humans are easy to read."

"What did he say?" Hariba says.

"He said he would take you and Akhmim for a price." I tell her the price.

"You asked about Akhmim?" she says, eager.

"I took him with me."

"Oh, Ayesha! Thank you!" She grabs my hand.

"Be quiet," I hiss.

We glance at the door. I didn't bring Tariam this time, but Hariba's mother is visiting and we can hear the low murmur of Hariba's mother and Zehra talking.

"So much money," Hariba says. "How can we get so much money?"

That's up to her family. I can't help her—after we put the money down on the flat, Alem and I don't have enough to get through the rest of the month. We're eating with my mother more times than is decent and she doesn't understand why we're moving away, so every dinner is strained. When I told her we were moving for better schools, she said I had gone to school here and turned out fine.

"Are you going to tell them?" I say as softly as I can, cocking my head at her mother and aunt inside.

"I have to," she says miserably. "Maybe Zehra could help us? Maybe we could pay it back, send it from the E.C.U.? Everybody's rich in the E.C.U. I'm going to send money back to my mother and to my aunt Zehra and to my sister Rashida for the baby and to Nabil. I'll make up for all the trouble I've caused."

I nod. I don't believe her, but I'm not going to argue with her. I don't think Zehra has money to loan her.

"I will even send the money to Mbarek to pay for Akhmim."

It's difficult not to comment on that, but I don't.

"What does she want me to do?" Akhmim says. He's waiting at the end of the street like he always does.

"Is this what you do all day?" I ask. "Wait for me?"

"Only in the afternoons," he says, "and only until three. You're always home by three to cook dinner."

I shudder. "She doesn't know how she is going to get the money."

"I've got the money," he says, the same way I would say, "I've got some tea."

"Where did you get it?" I ask.

"Some of it's mine," he says, "from work. Some of it was loaned to me by a woman named Tabi, where I work. Most of it's from a *harni* called Ebuyeth. She doesn't have much to spend money on, so she gave it to me."

"You know another *harni*?" I ask.

"Three other *harni*," he says. "What does Hariba want me to do?"

"I think she wants to go," I say. All that money. I've never seen that much money at one time. I didn't believe Hariba would go because of the amount of money. With that money, Alem and I could buy a co-op. With that money, Tariam could go to a private school.

"Will you ask her for me?" the *harni* says.

"Are you carrying this money around?" I ask.

He shakes his head. "Ebuyeth is keeping it until I need it."

"I think we need to go and see Khalid. Can you go tomorrow?"

He nods. "Should I have the money then?"

The next day I don't even go to Hariba. I meet Akhmim and we get on the train and head west. The ancient Egyptians considered the west to be the land of the dead. I can't stop thinking, "land of the dead, land of the dead," although it's a stupid thought that pretends to mean something. How long until Akhmim and Hariba are gone? It could all be over so soon, please, Allah. I try to remember my life before I spent all this time going to see Hariba. I told my mother that was where I was going today. I'm tired of the lying, I want it to all be done. But I couldn't tell Alem where I am going, he'd forbid me to go. Or at least he should.

It will all be over. Hariba and her *harni* will disappear to the E.C.U. and I can go back to my life.

There's no one in the train station this time. The walk is even longer than I remembered between the foamstone warehouses. Then we walk for blocks until the numbers say we've passed the shop where we can meet Khalid. "We've gone too far," I say.

"Let me see," says Akhmim.

We walk back and pass it again before we realize. We find it the third time and see the reason that we passed it is that it's all boarded up. It looks abandoned, but the pale boards are new.

Akhmim walks up to the big garage door and tries to pull it open, but it won't move. He strikes the door with his hand. "Hello?"

We wait and the wind sighs down the empty street.

He hits the door a couple more times with his fist. "Anyone here?"

No one answers. It's so creepy I feel sick.

The *harni* walks around the building and when he comes back, he pulls on a board and tries to pull it off. Then he looks around until he finds a rusted length of re-bar, the metal bars that reinforce concrete, and pries at the board until he gets it lifted off. I watch him disappear inside.

I'm afraid he won't come back out.

No one is on the street. It's as if no one lives here, as if we were in the desert.

The *harni* comes back out. He shakes his head. "No one here."

"This is the place," I say.

"I know," he says. He dusts his hands against his pants.

"Where could they go?"

"I don't know," he says, as if it were a real question.

We stand for a while. I'm trying to think of what to do next, and then when I don't know, I'm trying to decide how long I should stand here before I say we might as well go back. I look up at Akhmim and he's looking up the street.

A boy on a dirty bicycle pedals towards us.

"Excuse me," Akhmim says.

The boy looks at him, but shows no sign of stopping.

Akhmim steps into the street, "Excuse me. Do you know where the people who were here went?"

The boy slows down, passes us, then does a slow, lazy semicircle in the street and stops, one foot down.

"What?" he says.

"The people who were here two days ago," Akhmim points to the boarded-up building. "One of them was named Khalid. Do you know where they went?"

"Khalid?" the boy says, and my heart starts to race. Then he says, "I don't know any Khalid." He waits there to see what we'll do next.

"Thank you anyway," Akhmim says.

"Are you looking for Khalid?" the boy says. He looks about fourteen. His hands and face are dirty, his ankles are black, and he smells. I think maybe he's a little crazy. It's the way he stares. He doesn't blink, he just stares at us with this funny kind of smiling expression. "Do you want me to look for him for you?"

Akhmim shakes his head. "No, that's all right."

"I could look for him for you," the boy repeats.

I want him to go away. "Let's go," I whisper.

Akhmim and I start to walk. "Thank you, but no," Akhmim says.

The boy shadows us, pedaling slowly. "You want me to look for him?"

I'm afraid of this boy. I don't know if Akhmim would help me if the boy did anything crazy.

"I could look for him," the boy says.

Akhmim says softly, "Don't answer him."

"What?" says the boy. When Akhmim doesn't answer, he says, "You want me to look for him?" again.

He shadows us all the way back to the train station, although he finally stops asking us if we want him to look for Khalid.

There's no train scheduled to come for another forty minutes. The boy rides up and down the platform for a while, then he sits down next to Akhmim on the bench where we are waiting. He doesn't look at Akhmim, just sits there, with his tangled ratty hair and his black fingernails. I try not to look at him.

After a while he starts singing a pop song about a girl who tells a boy no. His voice is flat and hoarse, but he sings with great energy. He gets up and sings to the empty tracks and then sits down again. I'm sitting at the end of the bench and Akhmim is between me and the crazy boy. The crazy boy gets up and picks up his bike where he left it lying on the platform and goes and puts it on the train tracks. "Should I leave it here?" When we don't answer, he walks away, leaving the bike there. He walks behind our bench so I can't see him without turning my head, so I'm trying to listen for him and I can hear the sound of my veil rustling. I turn around and he is across the street, peeing against a garage door. I turn quickly back around. I stare at the dirty bike. It has dirt crusted on the sides of the wheels and on the chain and the spokes and the handlebars. He comes back after and picks up the bike and rides up and down the platform for a while. Finally the train comes in. He stands, one foot on the ground, and watches us get on the train.

We sit down, the train pulls out, and I burst into tears.

The first place we go is Hariba's mother's house, to see Nabil. I leave Akhmim in tea shop with a glass of mint tea—I don't know how Nabil feels about the *harni,* but I know how Hariba's mother would. Hariba's mother should be selling wreaths right now outside the Moussin, but who knows? And my mother lives right across the street. I couldn't explain a strange man to her.

Only Nabil is there. He's recovered from his beating, except for the yellow bruises. "Ayesha?" he says, standing up. "How are you? Are you coming to visit your mother?"

"Not yet," I say. "Hariba sent me to see Khalid."

"You went to see Khalid?" he asks.

"I did. I went to the place she told me." I show him the paper. "I talked to him, and he said that he could smuggle them to Málaga, but it would cost three thousand. So I went back to tell her. And when I go back to Khalid today, this place is all boarded up. No one's there."

"Khalid is always there. He lives with his uncle, and that's his uncle's place," Nabil says.

"He wasn't there," I say. "There was no one inside. Ah, one of the boards was loose and I could tell it was empty inside. Do you know where else he might be?"

"You're sure you were at the right place?" Nabil says. "Those places, they all look alike."

"It was the right place," I say. "This number. I walked up and down the street. And I was there day before yesterday."

"I don't know," Nabil says.

"How do you know him?"

"Through Yusef, You remember Yusef? I went to school with him. He had a sister. He knows Khalid, a little, you know? Khalid said he needed somebody to do something for him. Sometimes I do, like, odd jobs for Khalid."

I can imagine what kinds of jobs. Delivering smuggled goods, probably.

"Would Yusef know how to find Khalid?" I ask.

"Yusef is in Cádiz," Nabil says simply. "It was that or prison."

There is nothing to be done there. I go across the street, check in on my mother and Tariam, and lie and say, "I just want to do a few errands. Can Tariam stay a little longer?" Tariam is playing, and she doesn't fuss. My mother asks how Hariba is, and I put on a sunny smile. "Better every day," I say.

Then I go back to Akhmim and tell him that there is no way
to find Khalid.

"What do you want me to do?" he asks.

Disappear, I think. "Wait," I say. "I'll ask Alem if he can figure anything out."

I wait that night until we are in our bed. "Alem?"

"Hmmm?" he says. Alem usually goes to sleep faster than
I do. It usually takes me a long time to go to sleep.

"Do you remember you said you might be able to find a
way to help Hariba?"

"Yeah?" he says, a little more awake now.

"Can you find out if two people could get to, you know,
Cádiz or Málaga?"

"Two people?"

"Hariba won't go unless the *harni* goes with her." My heart
hurts when I say this and his silence frightens me more.

"The *harni*," he says.

"Yes," I say. "I'm so mad at her I could spit in her face. But
she says she won't go unless the *harni* goes."

He sighs. "She's a disaster, isn't she?"

I feel as if I can breathe a little. "She is," I say. "She's crazy.
I hate to go over there."

"I wondered what was wrong," he says.

"I just want it to be over," I say. It is so nice to be able to tell
him that. "I just want her gone and out of our life. Can you
check?"

"I can check," he says.

"Be careful, Alem," I say.

"I'll be careful."

"I love you," I say, my voice sounding tentative and hopeful to my ears.

"I love you, too, Ayesha," he says, and puts his arm around me so I lay spooned against his side. I still find it hard to go to sleep.

It's two days before Alem finds anything. But finally he comes home and says, "I found someone."

Tariam is outside, playing with her cousin. I'm watching my sister's son, six months younger than Tariam. I can look outside and see them there. I don't like them playing outside, I keep expecting to see the *harni*, but he never comes here and I know it's just nerves.

"It will cost them money," he says.

"They have some," I say, thinking, More than Khalid?

"It will cost them eighteen hundred."

"Apiece?" I say. Ahkmim has borrowed enough to have 3,000; can he borrow 600 more?

"No," Alem says. "Eighteen hundred for both."

"Oh, good, they've got that."

"They have to go to Tangier, and then they are to wait in a tea shop called"—he looks at a piece of paper—"the Cockatoo." Someone will meet them there. I have it all here. I'll go with them."

"Why do you have to go with them?" I ask.

"Because I'm the one who set it up."

"Let them go by themselves," I say.

"It doesn't work that way."

The next evening I take Alem to the *harni*. Alem is a good-looking man, and in his djellaba he is quite distinguished. But he is not as tall as the *harni* and not as beautiful, of course. Men aren't supposed to be beautiful, not like that.

Alem says, "This is the *harni*? It looks really . . . human."

The *harni* puts his hands together and says formally, "I am called Akhmim."

Alem is nonplussed. After a moment, he says, "Let's go get Hariba."

The *harni* waits at the end of the street while Alem and I go to Zehra's. Hariba is ready, all packed. Everyone is there: her mother, her sister Rashida, Rashida's husband, and their new baby, Nabil, and Zehra and two of her sons. The little clump of death houses is full, with people spilling out into the street.

Zehra is weeping. She takes both of Alem's hands into her own and kisses them. Alem is grave and dignified.

Zehra kisses me and hugs me. "You are too good a friend," she says. If she only knew how I really felt. Hariba's mother cannot speak. Tears brim in her eyes, but she doesn't cry. She just holds my hands wordlessly.

It takes forever to leave. The street is dark, but light spills out of the houses all around us. I wonder how many of the neighbors know about Hariba and how many know it's Alem who's helping her.

Finally we can leave and at the end of the street, where we turn to go to the train station, the *harni* is waiting. I'm afraid Hariba will make a fool of herself, but she doesn't, thank Allah. She's quiet, but there's a happiness inside her that infuriates me. She has to realize the risk Alem is taking.

I have insisted on going to Tangier with them. I can't stand waiting at home. We don't have the money, I don't know what we'll do. I have to have us ready to move. But I can't. Everything waits on Hariba's troubles.

Riding the train is as bad as waiting at home. I want to be with Alem, but I can't say anything to him because Hariba and the *harni* are here and they're all I want to talk about. What kind of life does she think she's going to have? Does she think she's going to live with the *harni* like a wife? It's insane, all of it.

I fall asleep in the train.

Tangier smells of ocean. In the dark all I can see are white buildings. At least Akhmim pays for our two rooms at the hostel. I expect Alem to comment on the fact that Akhmim says to the clerk that he is Hariba's husband, but Alem just looks at me, then looks away. I should never have brought him into this. I should have let Hariba solve her own problems.

In our room we lie down on a strange bed, not touching, and pretend to sleep.

It isn't until afternoon the next day that the three of them go to the tea house, the Cockatoo. Alem says I can't go. Alem so rarely puts his foot down. I think about arguing, but I don't, although I don't know how I can stand it. I sit in our room and watch out the window. I watch for hours, until finally, around dinnertime, Alem comes back with a dinner of shaslik. He looks tired.

"Is it done?" I ask.

He nods. "They leave tonight."

I cry. He doesn't comfort me or anything. He just sits on the bed, holding the shaslik and waiting. I don't know why I'm crying. I'm not sad. Tension, maybe. It's embarrassing, and I'm afraid to scoot over next to him. I manage to stop crying and we eat without talking about anything but the train the next morning. I wonder what this has done to us, to our feelings about each other. You get over things, I know. My mother says marriage is work, that you work through bad times. This is certainly one of the bad times.

After dinner, he says, "Do you want to walk around a little? You've never been to Tangier."

We walk around and pretend we're on a holiday. I look at the sea. It's big, but I don't feel anything. "Everything will be normal now, won't it?" I ask.

"I hope," he says tiredly.

They're gone, I tell myself. At least they're gone.

Finally we decide we're tired and go back to the hostel. Lying in the strange bed, I can hear other people walking and talking through the walls. Death walls are so thick, but the walls of our new apartment are like these, will I go to sleep every night listening to my neighbors? Maybe moving is a mistake. Look what happened to Hariba when she left the Nekropolis.

In the dark I wonder, Are they gone yet? Are they on the water, on their way to Málaga?

When it finally starts to get light, that's when I can really be sure they are on their way, and I can finally sleep for an hour until we have to get up for the train.

"When we get home," I tell Alem, "we'll both take a long nap."

We are walking home from the train station. I feel as if someone poured sand in my eyes.

"I'll go get Tariam after we've had a nap," I say.

Alem takes my arm and stops me. He isn't paying attention to me, and I look up and see people outside our house. "What?" I say.

Some of them are in police uniforms. Oh, my heart.

"Go to your mother's," Alem says.

"No," I say, "it's a mistake—"

"GO TO YOUR MOTHER'S," he says.

They've seen us.

He pushes me away, back up the street. I can't figure out what direction to move, but Alem walks toward them, dignified in his white djellaba.

Will I ever see him again?

In the Land of the Infidel

Alem is our savior. In the tea shop he's as gentle as a brother, holding my elbow to seat me. When Ayesha married him, I was happy for her. "Hariba," she told me, "he's a good man." But he's the last person I would have expected to be able to arrange something like this.

Still, here we are in a tea shop, waiting to meet the man who will get Akhmim and me out of the country. I've said thank you so many times that Alem is embarrassed. He's a blessing from Allah. Allah watch over him for what he's done for us, because I know that Ayesha didn't want to be involved, I know I cajoled and guilted her into it.

The tea shop has a real bird in it, a white cockatoo with a headdress of feathers and scaly gray-blue feet. It shreds paper and screeches while we sit and sip tea, a harsh, shrill sound that makes me cross my ankles tight around each other and draws my shoulders up toward my ears.

A man comes in and sees us. It's easy to tell we're who he

is looking for. He comes to our table and says, "Ahmad Shipping?"

That's the name of the company that Alem works for. Alem nods.

"Please call me Carlos," he says.

I thought the person we met would look like a sailor, worn skin from sun and weather, or like a tough guy, but he looks young and smooth and his teeth are very nice. He's not E.C.U., he looks Arab, like us, but his name is foreign. Maybe he's from Málaga? Maybe he's a foreign? Or maybe he's like us, and he's not using his real name?

"You have money?" he asks.

"Half now and half on the ship," Alem promises.

Akhmim gives him 900. So much money. Akhmim won't say where he got it, just that he borrowed it from friends.

"There's no record of them," Alem says.

"No record," Carlos agrees. I'm thinking that he has an accent, maybe. A little bit.

"All right then," Alem says and stands up. He puts his hands together. "A pleasure," he says.

Carlos looks at him as if he doesn't know what to make of this man in his djellaba. "The same," he says.

Alem walks out the door and stands on the street for a second, looking up at the sky. Then he turns left, away from the hotel and toward the water, and walks. Where's he going?

I'll probably never see him again. Or Ayesha, or my mother or my brothers and sister.

Carlos watches him, too, then shakes his head. "All right then," he says. "Let's go."

I'm still shaky from being sick, but once I've stood up a moment, I'm all right. Akhmim is right there. It's wonderful how reassuring he is. It's wonderful to feel his hand on my elbow, just the way Alem held it, but different because it's Akhmim, who's part of me now. Since I'm not jessed anymore, I feel different in my head, as if part of me weren't there. I haven't told anyone, but I think maybe I'm damaged in my brain. Or maybe it's just like wearing a cast. You wear it so long it feels like part of you and then when you take it off, you feel too light.

I keep watching for Alem when we walk down to the water, but I don't see him. The Mediterranean is bright, bright blue. I never knew it was as blue as this. And it goes on out of sight, huge and full of water and air. I lift my face to the breeze.

Carlos takes us down to the docks, which are full of tar and dirt that clings to the hem of my gown, but I'm getting so tired I don't care. He takes us up on his ship and shows us a place where we can wait. "I need your thumbprint on the manifest," he says.

"Alem said I wasn't supposed to sign anything."

"It's just a manifest," he says. "No one looks at a manifest."

"I can't," I say.

There is a tremor all through the ship as if something deep inside had awakened.

"We're about to cast off," he says. "I can't land at Málaga if you aren't on the manifest. Nobody ever pays any attention to it." He shows me a slate, all electronic, with long forms and lists. "They're automatic and no one ever reads them. Sign it or I'll have to put you both off."

I look at Akhmim. We've already spent 900, if he throws us off, I don't know where else we can go. I press my thumb to the manifest.

Carlos says, "Sign for the *harni*, too."

I press my thumb next to his name.

"Okay," he says, "I need the rest of the money."

Akhmim hands him the other 900. Is he going to throw us off now? Are the police waiting onboard?

"Okay," he says, "we make landfall in about eleven hours, traffic allowing."

He leaves us in this little place, sitting on the bed. It's a small room with a bed that swings down out of the wall and a sink. It doesn't even have a window. The ship is alive and moving, I can feel it. I'm nervous. I put my arms around Akhmim's neck and lean against him and he puts his arms around my waist. I have forgotten the slightly musky smell of him.

The ship sails on the crayon-blue Mediterranean Sea, and no one bothers us at all.

We get to Málaga at three in the morning and someone other than Carlos comes and gets us. "Off," he says. I have been asleep and I can't figure out where I am or why everything smells like plastic and metal. The coverlet on the bed has a rough weave and it's imprinted on my cheek.

"Can't we wait until dawn?" Akhmim asks.

"Customs is here," the man says. He has a strong accent.

I stumble out of the bunk, feeling stained and dirty in the clothes I slept in. "What do we do?" I ask.

"Claim asylum," the man says.

He takes us up on deck. There's not much room to really stand, most of the deck is like a bunch of boxy buildings and ladders and antennae whipping around searching for signals, but there's a narrow place to walk, just wide enough across for one person. Akhmim follows me.

There are two men in uniform, and my heart starts beating too fast. I feel Akhmim, behind me, touch my shoulder. The ship stinks and the wind off the harbor smells like oil and garbage. I feel faint.

One of the men in uniform says something to me. The man who has taken us up on deck says from behind Akhmim, "He wants to know if you speak Spanish."

"No, sir," I say.

He says something to the man in the uniform—the customs official. The customs official frowns. He has a smooth face like a young man, but I think he isn't really young. He beckons us to follow him. We climb down a ladder. My knees are shaking and I have to go very slow, but the customs man just waits. Then we walk down another narrow walkway to the gangway, and from there onto the dock. The ship never felt as if it were on the water, it always felt stable, but somehow I can still feel the difference in the dock. At least it doesn't have the feeling of being alive. The ship's huge in the darkness beside us.

I turn around and look at the city. It's all lights, as if it were nine at night instead of three in the morning. There's a big sign near us all lit up with an image of a woman drinking something the color of pale tea and full of light and bubbles. "Akhmim!" I say.

"What?" he says. "Are you all right?"

"I'm sorry, it's nothing," I say.

The woman in the sign is drinking *beer*.

I knew they drank in the E.C.U., but I never thought they would be so . . . so public about it.

We go down to the end of the docks to an office. It's too bright. Everything in it looks so new. A woman is there with a spidery little headset, talking in Spanish, and a man looks up as we come in. The man bringing us in says something that sounds disapproving and this man frowns. He says something to us in Spanish and the first man says something in Spanish and they frown even more. This man points to two chairs, dark red and padded on the seat and back, and Akhmim and I sit down.

There we wait. People work all around us, but no one talks to us, of course. They're all Spanish people, although one of the men looks a little as if he might be Berber.

Akhmim holds my hand. I'm so tired and sleepy. I try to lean my head against his shoulder, but I can't get comfortable.

It's nearly dawn when the man who brought us from the ship comes back to the office. He talks with the man and woman there, and the woman says something that makes everyone laugh. Then finally he looks at us and beckons, and we follow him outside to a little gray bubble car that really only has room in the back for one, but Akhmim and I both squeeze in. Three people are too much for the little car and every time we hit a bump, the bottom scrapes against the road and I grip Akhmim's arm, but he just keeps saying softly, "It's all right."

It's not all right. This is where we're going to live and already I don't like it. It will never be all right again. But I smile every time he says it.

There're cars in the street, lots of little bubble cars and some sedans and even some lorries, although not any like Ayesha's husband Alem directs. These lorries all have human drivers. There are people on the sidewalks and they all have a lot of skin showing—legs and arms and women's faces. It's like the mistress used to watch. Somehow, until I actually see it, I guess I haven't believed it, not really, not in my heart.

You can never go back, says the voice in my head.

I can't dress like these women. I can't.

"Where is he taking us?" I ask Akhmim.

"I don't know," he says.

"Maybe they are taking us to a hotel, or someplace where we can sleep?" It occurs to me they might take us to jail, and I would be separated from Akhmim.

The city is hilly. There are old buildings on the tops of some of the hills and they are grand, lit from outside like monuments. They have steeples or towers. Down on the streets, though, everything is a mix of old and modern.

We drive into a narrow alley and park behind a big foam-stone office. It's nicer than the foamstone buildings at home, it has wavering balconies and it's got little decorations like stalactites. The building is yellow and the decorations are red and blue. It looks as if a child made the building. I think it can't possibly be a jail.

The man takes us in a back door and up some stairs. Akhmim holds my elbow. We fall behind because I get tired so easily and can't go so fast yet, but he waits at the door to an office when we get to the second floor.

The office isn't anything like the outside of the building. Where the building is playful, the office is full of desks and information consoles. There are a dozen people at the desks. Some are talking into headsets. At least they aren't wearing uniforms.

A woman takes off her headset. "Hello," she says in Moroccan. "I'm Miss Katrina." She has on a sand-brown dress with sleeves that come to between her wrist and elbow and a skirt falls to a few inches above her ankles, but she's not naked-looking like the women on the street.

"I'm Hariba," I say, "and this is Akhmim. He's a *harni*."

She has us sit down and she takes my whole name and where I used to live. I give my aunt Zehra's address.

"Does the chimera belong to you?" she asks.

I don't know quite what she means. "Do you mean Akhmim?"

"I'm sorry." She smiles. "We don't say *harni*. We call biological constructs "chimera." *Harni* is something of an insulting name." She has a Spanish accent, but she's easy to understand. I don't know why they don't use the word "*harni*," though.

"There are more like Akhmim here?" I say.

"Not so many like Akhmim. There aren't many places where it's legal to make people like that. But there are a pretty fair number of different kinds of chimera here. And there's a little community of chimera that were made to be slaves. Do you own Akhmim?"

"No," I say.

"Who owned you?" she asks Akhmim.

He gives her Mbarek's name and address. "Do I have to go back?"

She shakes her head. "We don't recognize ownership of people or chimera in Spain, or anywhere in the E.C.U. Do you want to go back? Have you been brought here against your will?"

He shakes his head. "No, Hariba brought me, but I don't want to go back."

"Are you impressed on Hariba?" she asks.

"Yes," he says.

I'm tired and nervous. The questions they're asking make me even more scared. "We love each other," I say.

This woman, Miss Katrina, nods her head. "All right."

She runs her fingers across the unfamiliar letters on the touch pad. She asks me some more questions: Do I have any family in the E.C.U.? Do I speak any languages other than Moroccan? Did I work in Morocco? What kind of work did I do?"

"I was a house manager," I say. "I was jessed."

She stops and says, "How long since you left?"

"About twelve hours," Akhmim says.

"All right, we need to get you medical help. You should have told me. Hold on." She puts her headset back on and starts speaking in Spanish. After a moment, she says, "Do you have a headache? Feel sick?"

"A little headache," I say, "but I'm not jessed anymore. I ran away over a month ago."

She covers her mouth with one hand. "What did you do? Did you get help?"

"Akhmim took care of me," I say, "and then my family did. My mother found a horse doctor who gave me some patches."

She talks in Spanish for a moment. "We're going to take you to the hospital anyway," she says. "The doctor wants to assess you."

"Can Akhmim come?" I ask.

"I'll take care of Akhmim, and then I'll bring him to see you in a few hours."

"Akhmim needs to go with me," I say. "He shouldn't be by himself."

"He'll be all right," Miss Katrina says, "and so will you. We'll take good care of you."

"Are you going to take him from me?"

"No, no," she soothes. But I don't believe her.

"I should go with her," Akhmim says. He knows how afraid I am.

"I'm afraid you would just be in the doctor's way."

I'm so tired I start to cry.

"Let me get you a cup of tea," Miss Katrina says. She gets up.

I watch her walk away and think, We should run. But run where? There isn't any Nekropolis here. I wouldn't even be able to ask for help. "They can't take you from me," I say to Akhmim.

He holds my hand. Miss Katrina brings black tea.

"We don't have any mint tea, I'm afraid," she says.

It is bitter but hot. The room is cold. I sip the tea and shiver.

People aren't looking at us, at least. Evidently in this office they're used to women crying. MISS KATRINA takes a card out of her desk drawer. "This is my card," she says. "It's a smart card, so open it up and it's a phone." She shows me. "I'm your facilitator. Let me write my name in Arabic for you." She writes MISS KATRINA in round, childish script. I can read the numbers but none of the other writing on the card, which is all in Spanish, of course.

A man and a woman in blue come in the door. They are carrying cases. Katrina waves to them. "These are the medics," she says. "They'll take care of you and take you to the hospital. They don't speak Moroccan, but they are good people and they'll be gentle with you." Then she talks to them in Spanish.

The woman kneels on one knee in front of me and smiles. Carefully, she takes my hand and turns it palm up, then she shows me a strip of plastic and puts it around my wrist. She takes some sort of slate off her belt, and shows me the numbers flashing on it. I think I recognize blood pressure.

Miss Katrina hands me a tissue and I take it in the hand the medic isn't holding.

Akhmim watches gravely. After a minute, he takes the tissue from my hand and wipes my face with it.

The hospital building is different. It's a long complex of dun-colored stone buildings with galleried arcades between some of the buildings. The truck with the medics and me stops at wide doors. The woman holds my arm as I climb down out of the truck. The back of the truck had made me nervous—it had a kind of huge black coffin. But the man had sat in the back with me while the woman drove. We'd sat in seats that he showed me could become a bed. He had pulled a belt across my shoulder and waist gently, as if he were a father and I were a child. Then he'd pointed to me and said, "Hariba."

I'd nodded.

"Gianni," he said and pointed to himself.

"Gianni," I'd said.

He'd been pleased. Then he'd checked the plastic band on my wrist again. I'd wanted to tell him that I wasn't sick anymore, but hoped maybe the plastic strip would show him that.

The hospital isn't like a hospital inside. There's a large room for a lot of people, and more of the black coffins. One is open and the inside is full of thick blue liquid. There's a face-mask hanging out of it on a long flexible tube that's ribbed like a windpipe. There are a couple of beds, too. But we pass through that room to a hall with bedrooms off of it.

The medics take me to one of the rooms. It's pretty, all old-fashioned-looking with yellow stucco walls. The woman pats the bed and motions for me to sit on it, so I do, and she takes off my shoes and brings me a blanket as if she were my servant.

The medics leave and I think I'm so tired I might go to sleep. But I can't. After a bit, another woman with a slate comes in and smiles at me. "Hariba?" she says.

I nod.

"Estanza," she says. Then she checks my wristband, the way the medics had.

She does something on the slate she holds and a pleasant voice announces, "I am your doctor." The slate takes her Spanish voice and repeats it for me in my own language.

"Doctor Estanza?" I say, forgetting that she can't understand "doctor," but she just nods and smiles. She taps something else.

"Are you comfortable?" the slate asks me.

I nod.

"Headache?"

I answer a lot of the same questions that I answered for the medics. I'd like to be able to tell her I'm not sick, but of course she doesn't ask me that.

"I want to do a test," she says through the slate. "It won't hurt."

She leaves. I look around the room to see if something is happening. Am I supposed to sit still? I can see the lights in the ceiling and beside the bed and there's an image on the wall, like a window on the ocean in a place where there are palm trees. Maybe the image is some sort of screen? She would have told me if I was supposed to sit still.

She comes back with something like a hat with a facemask and I realize she had just gone to get it, that the hat device is the test. She has me sit up and take off my veil and she sets the hat device on my head. It's a little heavy, a little unbalanced. It has a lot of weight on top toward the front of my head, and I feel that if I lean my head forward, it might slide off. The mask comes down over my eyes and rests against my cheekbones. There is nothing to see inside, no screen or anything.

The doctor asks me through the slate, "Can you hear me?"

"Yes," I say, but I'm not sure she understands me, so I nod cautiously.

"Good," says the slate. "Who are you jessed to?"

"Um, my mistress is named Zoubida," I say and I feel the hat get warm. "Oh," I say and reach up.

"Wait," the slate says and I stop with my hand halfway raised. I can imagine her fingers tapping across the slate.

I wait.

"It is all right," the slate says. "It will get warmer, but not much. Please describe your mistress."

"She's tall and middle-aged," I say. "She's not very well off, not like my first household." I don't know what they want me to say. "I liked her. She wasn't mean to me, and if it hadn't been for Akhmim, I don't think I would have left her." Although if it hadn't been for Akhmim, I would probably still work for Mbarek. "Um, I feel bad about leaving her because she paid a lot of money for my services." I can't think of what else to say. Maybe if I'd had some sleep, I would be able to think better.

I wait.

Finally the slate says, "Describe the best thing about the person you are jessed to."

"The best thing?" I say. Are they recording this? The whole test is very strange. Maybe the device is reading my thoughts? "She was very kind," I say. "And she was very appreciative. I guess the best thing was that she was easy to please, that she didn't expect more than a person could do."

I wait.

The slate says, more quickly this time. "Describe the thing you like least about the person you are jessed to."

I think a minute. "She didn't have very good taste," I say finally. "She was disorganized and she didn't have very good taste." When I was jessed, it was hard to think about the mistress this way. I think maybe thinking about her this way is giving me a headache, but I'm so tired that could be the real cause.

It's silly to dislike someone because they have bad taste. But it was true.

I wish I could take a nap. I wish Akhmim was here.

"All right," the slate says. Then I feel the doctor's hands lifting the hat. She smiles at me.

"Would you like some water?" she asks me through the slate.

I nod.

She gets me water and then she says through the slate. "Someone will take you to a room, and you will rest."

She leaves me. In a while a young man does come and take me to a pretty white room with two tall narrow shuttered windows. The room is small and nice. He opens the shutters and they look out on one of the connecting walks with their series of arches. The breeze comes in—it feels cooler than it should but very nice. When he leaves, I'm so tired that I cry for a while and that makes my head ache more. Then I do finally fall asleep.

*   *   *

I stay three days in the white room. Miss Katrina brings Akhmim to see me in the evening and seeing him is like going home for a moment. But she explains to me that when the horse doctor took care of me, there were things that he couldn't really do, so he has kind of made a little cage for the problem. Eventually, she says, the cage will cause other problems, so the best thing to do is to be cured.

Curing involves putting something else in me the way when I was jessed they numbed the roof of my mouth and injected the thing that jessed me. Then they keep me for two more days. Twice a day they bring in the device like a hat and ask me to talk about my old mistress.

On the third day Miss Katrina comes and gets me.

"How are you feeling?" she asks.

I don't think I feel much different, maybe a little stronger from the food they have been giving me, but I say that I feel very good.

"I've found a place for you and Akhmim to stay," she says.

"Where is Akhmim?" I ask.

"He's at your flat." She has a little gray bubble car and we climb in.

"How do I pay for the hospital?" I ask.

"Hospital care is paid for," she says. "We have hospital care for everyone."

"Who pays?" I ask.

She blinks for a moment. "Nobody," she says. "I guess you could say that the government pays."

It's obviously a very rich government.

"Tomorrow," she says, "you will need to come down to us and file your paperwork for asylum, then you can be granted residency status. We granted you emergency temporary status so you could be in the hospital, but we need to get that up-graded to permanent as soon as possible."

I nod. The little gray bubble car goes quickly around the corners and through the narrow streets of what looks like an old city, but then we climb up into the hills and the buildings get newer. It's like going through time, up from ancient to old to shabby to foamstone, and finally we stop at a building a lit-tle like the office where Miss Katrina works, yellow with blue balconies. Some of the balconies have plants on them.

They're so much prettier outside than the places back home, but I don't like the balconies. It feels like living your life in public. If they had a courtyard, a balcony would be all right. Upstairs inside the hallway is plain with a plain blue carpet on the floor. She stops at 216 and knocks on the sea-blue door and Akhmim opens it.

Our flat is empty. The rooms are square on three sides and bow out on the outside wall. The floors are dark, deep green foamstone, polished and grooved like tile. It's so empty. Akhmim doesn't even really seem to live here, there's nothing behind him but windows and air.

I walk through the flat with them. There are four rooms—the big room, the kitchen, the bedroom, and the bathroom. It's nicer than a death house and I think to myself that with rugs and a couple of chairs and curtains on the windows it would be nice. There are blankets on the floor in the bedroom where Akhmim has been sleeping. Our bags are there, looking small and dirty in the corner.

It's very foreign and bare. As if no one had ever set foot in-side this place before. Miss Katrina chatters a few minutes and then leaves.

"What have you been doing?" I ask Akhmim.

"Waiting," he says.

I can imagine him waiting, too. When I was sick, he had unimaginable patience. He could just sit.

"What do you think?" he asks.

I sit down on the blankets—there's no place else to sit. "It's nice," I say. I hadn't thought about what it would be like to get out of the country. I had the vague idea we would find other people from Morocco. "It's very foreign."

"How are you feeling?" he asks.

I shrug. "Better."

He seems remote. He wasn't distant when we were living in Mbarek's household.

"Miss Katrina said I have to go file some papers tomorrow to get residency."

He nods. "I know which bus to take."

"What about you, do you have to file papers?"

"I already have my residency," he says and shows me his smartcard with his image on it.

"You have residency?" I ask. Somehow I never thought about it, I thought Akhmim would have residency with me or something. I remember what she said about not calling him a *harni*. "Does it bother you when people call you a *harni*? Do you prefer chimera?"

He shrugs. "Not particularly. Whatever people call me, I'm still what I am."

"I don't see why it makes any difference."

"It's a human thing," he says. "Words shape your thoughts."

It's a human thing. I shudder and I don't know why.

"Do you want to rest?" he asks. "Or we could go shopping. I still have some money, and Miss Katrina helped me get it changed into E.C.U. units."

"We should probably save it," I say.

"Miss Katrina says we will get an allowance from the government until we can get training and find work."

"How much?" I ask. But I realize I don't know how much it is because I don't know how much anything costs. Akhmim doesn't know anyway.

"Come on," he says gently. "Don't be sad. Come pick out some things for your new home."

Miss Katrina calls on my little cardboard phone. "Miss Hariba," she says, "I was talking to someone for whom I used to be facilitator, and I mentioned you. She's Moroccan and she's having some friends over tomorrow evening. They are all Moroccan expatriates and she asked me to invite you."

And so Akhmim and I go to a party.

We go on the bus. The buses run past our flat until two in the morning, later than we'll stay, I think. I don't have anything to wear to a party. I brought some things from Morocco but not very much and the people in Spain are all so rich. Akhmim and I go to the store to buy something to bring the hostess. It is an astonishing place, the store. So big, and so full of so many things. There is a part of the store that is full of vegetables and fruit, and a part of the store that is full of different kinds of meat. I look at the pork because I've never seen pork before. It's pale and unwholesome-looking, but while I am standing there, a woman buys some. It is so expensive. These people have so much money.

A lot of the things in the store are in boxes or packages, sealed and bright and clean. There is an entire section of beer

and, I think, wine. I stand for five minutes and seven people
buy beer. I don't have too much trouble with couscous and
rice and vegetables, not even with meat and fish, but I can't
tell which boxes are soap. Nothing is in Arabic.

I buy figs for the party.

The party is in a flat in the old part of the city, in a stone
building. The woman who is having the party is Miss Aziza.
She opens the door and she is wearing a long dark-red dress
and has her long black hair in a braid that is hanging over her
shoulder. The dress is beautiful, but it isn't Moroccan, and she
isn't wearing a veil, so she must be very rich.

"Miss Hariba?" she says.

"Yes," I say.

"Welcome!" she says, and takes my hands between hers.
"Welcome to Spain, and welcome to a little bit of home!"

I smell familiar smells—mint and cinnamon and chickpeas.

She looks past me.

"This is Akhmim," I say.

"Oh," she says. She is startled, because he's a *harni*. Miss
Katrina must not have told her.

Akhmim bows politely, as if he doesn't notice. I thought it
was all right here. He's so plain in his white shirt and black
pants. He has the figs and he hands them to me and I hold
them out to Miss Aziza.

"Oh, figs," she says. "How sweet of you. Come in, come in!"

There are a dozen or do people standing or sitting and talking, and none of the women are wearing veils. The room is full
of rugs and chairs and pillows and drapes and it's beautiful,
more beautiful than anything at Mbarek's. There's a long table
and it is covered with food—couscous with vegetables and
bisteya and chickpeas with cumin, and little pastries. There are

pistachios and almonds and cheese and fruit—grapes and dates and figs and oranges. I'm even more embarrassed.

But it's still a little like home.

I drop my veil so it's not covering my hair, just hanging over my shoulders.

Miss Aziza turns to the room. "Everybody, this is Miss Hariba and Akhmim, just a few days from Morocco." She introduces people, a blur of names. "Get yourselves something to eat," she says.

There are plates at one end of the table, and people around the room are holding plates of food. I take a plate and get some bisteya. I haven't had it in so long and this pie has a beautiful flaky crust and smells of pigeon and lemon, ginger and almond. The wedges are dusted with cinnamon and sugar.

Miss Aziza is smiling. "I love bisteya," I say.

"Let me introduce you to someone," she says. "Professor Malik?" she says.

Professor Malik is dressed all in white. He looks like a distinguished man, except that he looks so young. "Miss Hariba," he says. "Welcome. And Akhmim." These people smile at Akhmim, but I don't think they really want him here. He's taken some bisteya and some fruit and a piece of cheese.

"So where are you from?" he asks.

"Fez," I say.

"Fez," he says. "I had a great friend in Fez. I'm from Marrakech."

"How long have you been here?" I ask.

"Twelve years," he says.

I don't know what to say. The idea makes me so homesick. "Do you miss home?" I ask.

"Of course," he says. "But this is my home now, and I don't think I would live in Morocco, even if I could. It's so easy here. Have heart, you'll get more comfortable."

"What did you do in Marrakech?" I ask.

"I was a professor of religious studies," he says. "But some of the things I published made people unhappy. How did you come to Spain?"

"I came with Akhmim," I say.

"Ah," he says to Akhmim. "You're a chimera."

"Yes, Professor," Akhmim says.

"How did you meet?" he asks me.

"I was a house manager, and Akhmim was, um, part of the household." I don't think I'm supposed to say "owned." I wonder what he thinks now that he realizes that he's talking to a housekeeper. But if he's appalled, he hides it well.

"It's good to have someone new come," he says. "We all see the same faces too much." He leans close and whispers, "And it doesn't hurt to see Aziza reminded about the rights of chimera."

"She doesn't like chimera?" I ask.

"Aziza is quite proud of her tolerance, but I don't think she expected your friend for dinner. You're quite amazing." He says it as if I should be proud of it, as if I did it on purpose.

"Me," I say.

"Oh yes," he says. "We all talk about how dreadful conditions are in Morocco, and about how horrible institutionalized slavery is, but we never do anything about it. You have."

"I haven't done anything," I say.

"But here you are, and here is Akhmim, who I assume you brought from Morocco."

"Yes, Professor," Akhmim says, "she did."

"How do you feel about having rights thrust upon you?" Professor Malik asks Akhmim.

"It's a little strange," Akhmim says.

"There are other chimera like you in Málaga," Professor Malik says. "I could put you in touch with someone."

"I would like that very much," Akhmim says simply.

"You must be very lonely," Professor Malik says.

"Very," Akhmim says. "But I've been lonely a long time."

"And you," Professor Malik says to me, "you must come and have tea with me."

Alone? I think.

"Don't worry," he says. "I am old enough to be your father. And my wife will be there."

I don't know what to think about any of this.

We're enrolled in language classes. Akhmim goes in a different class because *harni* learn languages differently than humans. Chimera. Spanish is difficult, mostly because of the alphabet.

Because I was jessed, I have political asylum, which Katrina says is the best kind, because in three years I can qualify for E.C.U. citizenship. I can't qualify for Spanish citizenship because I'd have to be born in Spain, but she says that would only matter if I wanted to be a politician.

Akhmim has political asylum, too, because chimera are enslaved at home.

I write my family and let them know where they can get in touch with me, and I include money for my mother and my aunt Zehra. Not very much, but some.

I'm also enrolled in counseling to help my adjustment to Spain.

I go to counseling at three in the afternoon, which is the same time that Akhmim has his Spanish course at the Instituto Internacional Alhambra. My counseling session is only an hour, but his class is an hour and a half, so I promise to meet him at the Instituto. I don't like riding on the bus by myself, though. We get on together at our apartment. Akhmim can recognize the bus, but not by the bus number. I don't know how he does it because a lot of buses run on our route, and some have our Centre Number, C2, and some have other letters and numbers but look pretty much the same. Akhmim doesn't know how he does it, either, but he's always right. We get on the bus together and then when we get to the Center, I stay on, but he takes the R16 out to the Instituto.

I have learned to say the name of my stop, Parque and Cinquente-Cinco. I tell the driver. I'm afraid that the driver will forget, but he remembers and calls it out.

I have a note from Miss Katrina saying that I don't speak Spanish and that I have an appointment with Dr. Esteban. I show it to the young man at the desk and he smiles and calls someone. Another young man with hair dyed yellow comes and gets me. "Hola," he says. I know that. "Hola," I whisper and smile. I stare at my toes in the elevator.

My doctor looks young like many of these people, but I know he isn't. I'm getting better at telling when people aren't really young. Something about the way their noses and ears and chins are. Something about the way their eyes are set in the hollows of their skulls.

"Miss Hariba," he says. He has an office with a big window, but it's covered in a heavy red patterned curtain, a little like the patterns on rugs at home. "We have many things to discuss."

He's Moroccan, but I don't think he was born in Morocco. "I'm here to help you with your transition to Spanish and E.C.U. culture. I'm here to help you with your feelings about the things that have happened to you and about your loneliness, and to help you resolve your relationship with the chimera."

"What do you mean, resolve my relationship?" These people talk about Akhmim in the oddest way. For all the unfairness with which people in Morocco treated *harni,* at least in Mbarek's household we didn't talk about him as if he were a problem.

"There's a basic inequality in your relationship with a chimera like Akhmim. Akhmim has no choice."

"Of course he has a choice," I say. "I didn't ask him to love me."

"That's what we'll talk about," says the doctor.

"You can't take Akhmim away from me," I say.

"No, nor do I want to," the doctor says.

I don't understand these people at all.

"So," the doctor looks at his slate. "You're taking Spanish classes."

"Why do I see you and Miss Katrina?" I ask.

"Miss Katrina is . . .?"

"My facilitator."

"Ah," he nods. "Good question. Miss Katrina is to get all the legal things straightened out. But I'm here to help you and your feelings."

I don't think Dr. Estaban is going to be much help. He makes me nervous. "Can you tell me what soap looks like?" I ask him. "I mean, I know what soap looks like, but in the store everything is in packages and I can't read them."

He blinks. "I can do that," he says. He opens up his screen

and types a couple of things. "Here," he says, and shows me the screen. "This is the soap that I use. I don't know if it's the best, but it's the one my wife always gets. You mean soap for washing up, don't you?"

I look at the blue and white wave and I think it's pretty clear. "Washing up, and washing clothes and dishes."

"Oh, the soap for washing clothes is different, and so is the soap for washing dishes." He calls up the labels for those and prints them all off for me. In his very neat hand he writes WASH-ING UP on the blue and white one, DISHES on the bright yellow one, and LAUNDRY on the red one with the big smiling sun. I thank him. Personally, I think soap is soap. I'll get the blue and white one.

Sometimes these people can get too complicated.

I take the bus to the Instituto Internacional Alhambra, where Akhmim is having class. It's as nerve-wracking as taking the bus to Cinquente-Cinco and Parque. The Instituto is a large place, crowded by other buildings in the city. I get very lost, looking for Akhmim's classroom. I'm afraid if I get there too late that he'll think I'm not coming and go home, although, I remind myself, Akhmim is very patient.

But I find the right floor and count the classrooms until I find his. The door is half open. Inside there is a teacher sitting at a desk and three *harni* and they are . . . entwined. Not as if they are having sex, but still sitting against each other, a leg thrown across another's lap, an arm around another's waist. Akhmim is in the middle and on one side of him is a beautiful woman and on the other is a young man, really a boy. Akhmim is holding a screen that they are looking at.

His face is remote and happy, terribly happy, like I have never seen it before.

I back away from the door and stand in the hall. When he finally comes out, I pretend that I didn't see anything.

"How's your class?" I ask.

"It's good," he says. "I like it a lot."

"Have you made friends?" I ask.

He nods. "What was the counselor like?"

"He told me what soap to buy," I say and show him the labels. I'm looking at his face, trying to see into it. He just looks like Akhmim, not like someone who would sit with two strangers as if they were all but the same skin.

"Are you happy with me?" I ask.

"I love you," he says. "You know that."

I do know that. I want to ask him if he would rather be with other *harni*, but I'm afraid to. Akhmim has a counselor, too. I wonder if his counselor needs to talk about Akhmim's relationship with me. I wonder if his counselor is human.

I get a letter from my mother. Her letter is short, of course, since she comes from the countryside and Nabil writes out what she says.

Dear Hariba,

Thank you for your letter and the money. I'm glad to know that you're safe. Your aunt and I are fine, but I'm sorry to tell you that Alem has been arrested. Ayesha and Tariam are staying with her mother. Your brother and sister are well. Please take care of yourself.

I call Miss Katrina. I have never used her little phone card before. She answers in Spanish, and then something must tell her who it is because she says in Moroccan, "Miss Hariba? Is that you?"

"Yes," I say. "Please, miss, I need your help!"

"What's wrong?" she says. "Are you hurt?"

"No, it's not me. It's my friend, in Morocco, who got us out. His name is Alem." Tears rise up, hot, as I say it. "My mother has written to tell me that he's been arrested!"

"Oh, Miss Hariba," she says, "I'm so sorry."

"What can you do?" I ask.

"I don't know. Hold on." As she mutes the phone, I hear her saying something in Spanish. I have probably interrupted her. It's foolish of me to feel such a sense of urgency, no doubt Alem was arrested days ago. My mother may very well have been arrested by now. And Aunt Zehra. I'm ashamed. "Miss Hariba?" she says.

I draw a shuddering breath. "Yes, I'm here."

"I can request that the Spanish government and the E.C.U. enter a protest with the Moroccan government. I don't know if they will, but the E.C.U. often does in cases like this."

"What will that do?" I ask.

"Probably nothing," she says. "It might put a little pressure on the Moroccan government, but given the North African Alliance's refusal to have any trade or diplomatic relationships with the E.C.U. or the North and Central American Unity, I don't see much that we can do."

"Oh," I say, because I don't know anything else to say.

"I'm sorry, Miss Hariba. Can you tell me his name and address and what he was arrested for?"

I don't know what he was arrested for, but I tell her everything else.

"Is there anyone you know who can intercede for him?" Miss Katrina asks.

"I'm a housekeeper," I say. "I don't know anyone important."

"Well, I'll let you know what response I get. I'm so sorry, Miss Hariba."

When she cuts the connection, I try to think of what to do. Akhmim is out at his counselor. He'd know what to do to make me feel better.

Professor Malik might know someone who could help, he was a professor in Marrakech. I call, but there's no answer, so I leave a message.

I walk from the main room to the bedroom and back again. We have rugs now, and some pillows. We're saving what little money we have left, although Miss Katrina has told us we'll get 2,000 E.C.U. units in less than a week. Everything is so expensive. For my Spanish class I had to pay over 200 E.C.U. for a slate and 62 E.C.U. more for an e-book. Soap was 4 E.C.U. units. The bus is 2 E.C.U. units every time we ride it. I sent 100 E.C.U. units to my mother and Aunt Zehra, which is more than I made in three months, but so little here.

One of the phone cards chirps and it takes me a minute to find it. "Hello?" I say, and then remember I am supposed to say, "Hola."

"Miss Hariba?" It's Professor Malik.

"Oh, Professor, thank all that's holy you called."

"Miss Hariba," he says in his beautiful, educated voice, "what's wrong?"

"They have arrested my best friend's husband for getting

Akhmim and me out of Morocco, and I don't know what to do!" Tears in my throat and in my breath.

"Oh, my poor dear. Oh, that poor man."

"Miss Katrina, my facilitator, asked me if I knew anyone who could help in Morocco, but I'm just a housekeeper. And then I thought of you. You're a professor, is there anyone you know?"

I hear his indrawn breath. "Miss Hariba," he says, "I have been gone from Marrakech many years. But don't cry, let me think, let me think. I know some people in the opposition, but this should be done more quietly. I'll tell you what, you and your friend, are you free for dinner tonight?"

"Y-y-yes," I say, trying so hard not to sob on the phone.

"Come to my house for dinner, and let me think what I could do. I'll send a *taxi* for you, all right?"

"A *taxi*?"

"A car for hire," he says. "It will just be dinner with my wife and me," he says. "Nothing fancy."

"Thank you, Professor," I say. "Thank you so much. I feel so bad. I feel so ashamed."

"It's not you who are to blame," he says. "It's the government. We'll talk it over, we'll think of something to do, all right? Now, see you in a few hours, dear."

I collapse on the pillows and cry until Akhmim finally gets home and wraps his arms around me and kisses my tears away.

Then I dress in my best blue, with a clean white veil. It's old and the hem needs to be resewn, but it's clean. Akhmim braids my hair in a thick single braid. I'm thinking that maybe Professor Malik's wife wasn't at Miss Aziza's because she doesn't approve. I can always take the veil off.

I can imagine her, someone like my aunt Zehra, only kept young like all these people are, like Akhmim and I will be. (A strange thought, that Ayesha will grow old like my mother and I will stay young—someday I will look like her daughter, like Tariam. Another betrayal.)

A little red bubble car pulls up while we are waiting outside, Akhmim and me, and the driver says, "Miss Hariba, Mr. Akhmim?" Professor Malik lives out east of the city, and we drive down almost to the sea before turning and heading east. I catch glimpses of the water sometimes, bright in the early evening sun. He doesn't live on the water, his house is a couple of streets back, but it's a little house crowded in with other little houses, not a flat. The bubble car pulls into a kind of courtyard with bricks for a floor and planters with olive and lemon trees and flowers spilling over them. Professor Malik comes out, dressed in unbleached linen that looks very elegant. I feel shabby.

Maybe here I can be made beautiful. So many people seem beautiful here. If they can make people young, how much harder can beautiful be?

"Miss Hariba," he says, "Mr. Akhmim. Welcome to my little house." There is a fountain and a pool near the door, all of brick, with lilies floating in it. "My wife gardens," he says. "She has the touch."

It isn't a big house like Mbarek's, but it's beautiful in a way that Mbarek's could never be. The floor is tiled in beautiful stones, and there is furniture everywhere, but light, graceful, and curved pieces of furniture that don't clutter everything up. The mistress had preferred projections of blue glass and silver, but the colors here are warm and each room is a little different. The main room is colored with wood and deep red and brown velvets, but there are splashes of green, as light as spring and suggesting rain.

He takes us through the kitchen, where the unexpected color is orange. The sink is the color of tamarind.

The room in the back is full of light from a huge window in the ceiling. The table is long and narrow and set as if for a party, with lots of yellow and bits of amethyst. It is all so vivid, but it looks handled and used, a bit worn, not too garish, as if all these things have been loved for years and years.

"Your house is beautiful," I say.

"My wife," he says, and waves his hand. "She does these things."

"Malik? Are your people here?" A woman calls from the hall.

"Claudia," he says. "This is Miss Hariba and Mr. Akhmim."

His wife is nothing like I expect. She is tall and as narrow as a stork, with dark red hair that frames her face and shines like a helmet. She is wearing a green tunic with a high collar and long sleeves, and white pants. Even her feet, in leather sandals, are elegant. She's not Moroccan.

I reach up and pull off my veil. I'm glad I braided my hair.

"This is my wife, Claudia," says Professor Malik. "She is a professor of mathematics."

Akhmim, unperturbed as always, puts his hands together and bows slightly.

"Claudia," Professor Malik says, "This is Miss Hariba, and Mr. Akhmim."

We sit down at the long table, all eating at one end. Professor Claudia brings in chicken and rice and vegetables. "I'm sorry it's all so plain," she says.

I can smell the lemon and garlic in the chicken. "Oh no," I say, "its wonderful." There are olives in the chicken, too. Professor Malik's wife asks me about how Akhmim and I like Málaga. Akhmim tells her that we are taking Spanish classes, and compliments her on her Moroccan.

"Claudia's mother is from Morocco," Professor Malik explains.

"Where is she from?" Akhmim asks.

"Fez," Professor Claudia says.

"That's where you're from, isn't it?" Professor Malik says.

I look at my yellow plate and my amethyst glass and my yellow napkin. No one mentions Alem. I wonder what Ayesha is doing at this moment. Eating with her mother. And Alem is in prison. Maybe with my brother, although more likely he would be in jail right now. I wonder if they've beaten him. Nabil said that they beat Fhassin.

But the chicken is very good and I'm hungry. I eat it, and the rice, yellow with saffron. After dinner, there's strong, sweet coffee and pastry with walnuts and honey.

"I've got some work to do," Professor Claudia says. "I'll leave you here to talk."

"It was a wonderful dinner," I say. "And you have a beautiful house."

She smiles. "The house has been in my father's family for over a hundred years."

"It's lovely," I say.

"We're comfortable," she says. I don't know if that means that they love the house, or if it means the house is not so much. They seem rich to me, but what do I know?

"Some more coffee?" Professor Malik asks.

"No, thank you," I say. "Thank you very much for the lovely dinner. I hope we didn't inconvenience you."

"Not at all," he says. "But let's talk about your friend, the one who was arrested."

Akhmim smiles at me. He's been holding up the conversation all during dinner because he knows I'm too upset to talk. I couldn't do without him, and he does love me, and he understands me better than anyone else, better than my mother or my sister or Ayesha.

"I've been thinking of who we could ask to help, but there aren't many," Professor Malik says. "Obviously, if I can contact them, then they're under suspicion because they have contact with the E.C.U. But I was thinking that we might be able to buy his freedom."

"Buy his freedom?" I say.

"The police are quite corrupt," Professor Malik says. "I think maybe ten thousand E.C.U. in the right place and your friend would be free."

10,000 E.C.U. is more money than I have ever seen in my life. I am not sure what the professor means. Is he offering to pay for Alem to go free?

"How much do you have?" the professor asks.

"Fourteen hundred E.C.U.," Akhmim says. "Maybe a little more."

Professor Malik sighs. "Not enough, I'm afraid."

"Professor Malik, could you help us, with a loan?" I say. Surely with this house, this life, it isn't so much to him. "We'll pay you back." I don't know how, but we will.

He sighs again. "I'm sorry, dear, I can't. I don't have a secure teaching position here, and everything we have, well, it is all my wife's . . ."

All his wife's? Then I understand. Professor Malik is a refugee, like us. He has nothing. He lives on the sufferance of his wife.

He's like Akhmim.

Akhmim and I send 600 E.C.U. to Ayesha. It's worth about 2,000 in Moroccan. She can use it to do what she can for Alem. I wait to get a letter back from her, but I don't. Eventually I get a letter from my mother telling me Ayesha says she received the money, but that's all.

I mean to send more. But everything is so expensive here. Akhmim and I have to have all new clothes. And school is expensive. It isn't like we didn't try, after all. And I also have to send money to my own family.

There's nothing I can do. I try not to think about it. It's all so far away that when I think about Morocco, it's like a pain in my chest.

Professor Malik gives Akhmim the address of another chimera, a man named Ari, but Akhmim doesn't mention him again. I don't think he gets in touch with him, either, because most of the time we're together, except for our classes and our counselors.

I ask the counselor about chimera.

"There are half a dozen kinds of chimera," he says. "Laborers from Brazil and Argentina. There is a whole caste of chimera in India. They're priests and it's considered good karma to raise a boy chimera and endow him a place in the temple. The Hindu believe that these boys are souls that are ready for enlightenment, that they are above humans. But there aren't very many of them, of course."

I don't understand what he's talking about.

"Prostitute chimera like Akhmim are pretty common in the Middle East and northern Africa," he says.

"Akhmim's not a prostitute," I say, shocked. "Men can't be prostitutes."

The doctor nods, as if thinking. "Why not?"

"Because women don't pay men to have sex with them," I say.

"What about your master's wife? Did she have sex with Akhmim?"

"No," I say, and I can feel myself flushing bright red.

"Are you sure?" he asks gently.

"Yes," I say, although now I'm not.

"And there are men who like to have sex with other men."

I can't think of anything to say to that. I mean, I've heard men call each other fags and buttfucks, but that's just low men talking. I couldn't say any of that to the doctor. I can't believe I even said "sex" to the doctor. I've never said "sex" to a man before.

"Even if Akhmim wasn't a prostitute," the doctor says, "the kind of chimera he is, what you call a *harni,* is designed to be the perfect concubine. They're the perfect lover, they put the needs of the human first and their needs second."

I think maybe I won't come here anymore.

"It's hard for you to talk about these things," the doctor says, "but I promise you, this is the one place you can ask questions and no one will think you are bad, no one will be shocked."

I nod. I think about the *harni* all sitting on top of each other in Akhmim's Spanish class. I almost ask about that, but I don't.

I make my next appointment. I can always cancel it.

*   *   *

We're studying for our Spanish. To have: *tenir*. I have, *yo tengo;* you have, *tu tienes;* he has, *el tiene*. I have a question. *Yo tengo un amigo.* "Akhmim?"

He's sitting across from me, working on his slate. The light from our main room lamp falls across his hair and his beautiful skin. Akhmim is the most beautiful man I have ever known. He looks up and his face is so much more beautiful than a housekeeper deserves that my heart breaks.

"Did you ever, you know, lay with the mistress?" My face grows hot.

"No," he says. "You're the only one. You're the only one I love. *Yo tu quiero.*"

"I love you, too," I say.

He smiles at me.

"Professor Malik said he knew some chimera you could meet," I say.

He shrugs and looks back down at his slate. "Eventually, maybe."

"Aren't you lonely?"

"I have you," he says.

"You told Professor Malik you were lonely," I say.

He shrugs again. "That was different."

I wait for him to explain, but the doesn't. "How?" I finally say.

"He has a romantic idea of *harni*. He wanted me to be lonely, so I said I was."

"How do I know you aren't just saying that you aren't to me?"

"Because I don't lie to you," he says.

I believe him.

*   *   *

Miss Katrina, my facilitator, calls me. "Miss Hariba," she says, "how's your Spanish class going?"

"Well," I say. I've been studying Spanish for six weeks, and for the last two weeks I have had to go to school five days, all day, and speak Spanish all the time with the other students. If I don't know a word, like when we are eating lunch and I want salt, then I have to point and say, "That, please give me that." I've learned a lot more than I ever thought I could.

"Do you have an address on your slate?"

"I do," I say. "It's Hariba635914." I send all my homework to my teachers on my slate. There are only three people in my class from northern Africa, and they are both from Tunisia. Everybody else is from somewhere else in the E.C.U. or from North America, and they do everything on their slates. They shop for things, they talk to other people. I like to shop in stores.

"I have a job if you are interested," she says.

"A job?" I ask.

"Yes. It won't affect your subsidy, in fact, it won't pay very well at all. Would you be interested in working with children at a school?"

"Children? I would love to."

"You'll have to do an orientation, but the job would be assisting at a childcare place. You'd help the people working with toddlers.

Children. I don't know whether to laugh or cry. I have always been afraid of being around children because I knew that since I was jessed I would probably never have my own, and now that I'm with Akhmim, we can't have children. But I love children. And I'm afraid to say no.

Miss Katrina is pleased. "I thought you would be perfect for this," she says. "I'll send you the information on your slate, all right?"

It comes just as my homework would. It's in Spanish, but my slate can translate it for me. A job with children will be good. Children won't care if I speak Spanish badly. I can imagine myself with them, holding a child in my lap, singing to him in Moroccan, while he looks up at me and people think, Hariba has such a way with children. I will be the most patient, even-tempered person ever and they will love me.

It's three days a week, which allows me to keep studying my Spanish and meeting with my counselor. My counselor and I aren't talking about Akhmim these days, we're talking about how scared I am to try to speak Spanish. How hard it is to understand when people talk to me. How much I feel that I stand out wherever I go.

For my first day at my new job I wear a long shirt with sleeves to my wrists and long pants. The shirt is almost long enough to be a dress, so it doesn't feel as if I am dressing like a man. The counselor and I agree that it's a good outfit, that it's modest without seeming quite so foreign. Akhmim braids my hair, but I don't wear a veil.

I look in the mirror in the bathroom and I wish I were pretty. So many people here are pretty. But even in this strange costume, I still look like me.

I go to work in the dark. People have to leave their children at the daycare before they go to work, so it opens early. I get off the bus, a little afraid that I've gotten off a stop too early, but then I see the sign. The daycare looks like a house, except that in front is a complex of tunnels and a fort.

The woman who meets me at the door says, "You must be

Miss Hariba." Her name is Isabella and she looks very Spanish. I feel small and dark next to her. There are seven women and one man working at the daycare. Miss Isabella has me set out juice and breakfast sweets for the thirty children who are coming. They come in dribs and drabs, their heads on the shoulders of fathers dressed for work or hand in hand with mothers in suits. They know how things work here. Some of them come up for juice. I say hello to the ones who do, and some say hello, some just take the juice and the sweet and wander off to Miss Isabella or one of the other caregivers. Miss Isabella is surrounded by children. She sits on the floor and they sit against her knees or her side, or reach over to pull on her sleeve. I can't understand them because they lisp in Spanish, but I recognize the insistence when they say, "Miss Isabella. Miss Isabella." They all want to tell Miss Isabella something.

I sit down and wait to be told what to do.

There are places all over the daycare where there are things to do and part of the day the children have to do simple tasks. Part of the day they have unstructured play and if the weather is good, they can go outside. Part of the day they do things in groups. First this morning they have to listen to Miss Isabella tell them a story and she does. It's a long story about a girl who lives in India and things she does in her day, but I don't speak enough Spanish to understand it. Miss Isabella keeps smiling at the children and at me as she tells it and I smile and nod back as if I understand. After she finishes, the children all take out their slates and whisper the story to it. This is one of their tasks, that they have to listen and then say what they heard.

Listening hard to the story makes my head ache. There are

a lot of words I don't understand, and the verbs are especially difficult for me. My eyes feel heavy, and the sound of children whispering makes me even sleepier.

After the story, five of the children and I go and make bead necklaces. Miss Isabella takes us over. "Here are beads," she says. There are bins of beads. Big wooden beads and little stone and plastic beads, lots of colors, and some are smooth and some are bumpy. People in Spain have so much money that they can let children have these things to play with. My mother spends less on paper for wreaths than it costs people to bring their children to this daycare to make necklaces.

I hand out string and we sit down on the floor with the beads. I don't know what to do, but the children do.

"Show me," I say.

"Get a piece of string," says one.

"Miss Hariba," says a little girl, and then she tells me to do something, holding her string out to me. I don't understand.

She says it again.

Miss Isabella is taking five children out to the garden. Everyone else is busy.

The children are all holding their strings out to me. Finally one little boy tries to make a knot in his string and I realize what they want and I tie knots in all their strings.

"Miss Hariba, look!"

I look, I *ohhh* and *ahhh*. I make mine of blue and yellow beads alternating, with a couple of big beads for emphasis. Am I supposed to try to teach them about patterns? I let them do whatever they want, and one boy makes his like mine, only black and red, but the other four do whatever they want.

"Look at mine."

Then one little girl wants me to wear hers, so I tie it around my neck. Then I have to wear everybody's. I'm not sure if I'm supposed to.

We're done before anyone else is done with their tasks. "Can we go garden?"

"No," I say. I try to think of what else to do. I tie another string for everyone and we make another one. Akhmim is at home right now, not worrying about if he's doing everything wrong.

That goes even faster. I go ask one of the other caregivers what I'm supposed to do. She says that they need to put the beads away.

So we sort out the beads, but before we get all the beads put away, everybody else is done with their tasks and gets to go outside. My children are the last ones to go outside.

It's a difficult day. I don't understand a lot of the things the children do and at the end of the day I'm sick to death of being touched.

The bus is full, and I have to stand. People keep brushing against me and I feel it each time they do. If I were a mother, I would be going home to my children. For the first time, I wonder how mothers can stand it. I think, Maybe if they were my own children it would be different.

Maybe not.

Akhmim gets a job serving in a restaurant. He is gone when I get home from work, and it seems as if I never see him.

Miss Katrina tells me that we're doing very well. I'm getting better at Spanish, although it seems to me that the only people I ever talk to are children.

I come home at night and get off the bus and go up to the empty apartment. There's nothing to do there except more Spanish, or entertainments on my slate. I can't think after a day of work, so I sit on the cushions and play games on my slate until I'm hungry, and then play more until it's time to go to bed. Once in a while I talk to Professor Malik or get a message from him, but that makes me think of Alem, and my chest tightens up, so often I don't answer when it's him.

I am sitting playing an entertainment called Opt Ciudad. I like it because I don't have to know a lot of Spanish, and it's easy for people like me who haven't done a lot of things on a slate—some of the entertainments go so fast that I always crash or get shot. But this one is about building a city, and about putting groceries where all the people in the city can get to them easily and roads and highways.

Professor Malik calls and I answer, a little out of guilt and a little out of not thinking fast enough.

"Miss Hariba," he says. "How are you? How are the children?"

I hate being interrupted in the middle of the game, but that's wrong. I tell him about the children.

"Did Akhmim get in touch with the chimera whose address I gave him?"

"Pardon me?" I ask.

"He called me and asked how he could get in touch," Professor Malik says.

"Oh yes," I lie. "He's at work right now. Since he works in the evening, I don't get to talk to him."

"You must miss him," Professor Malik says.

"When did he call you?" I ask, trying to sound as if I just forgot.

Professor Malik frowns, remembering. "Monday?"

"Right," I say. "That's right. I don't know if he's had a chance to call yet."

"I knew he was lonely," Professor Malik says.

I think this call will never end.

But at last it does and I sit there, thinking, for a long time, before I go back to playing Opt Ciudad.

I go to bed before Akhmim gets home—I always go to bed before Akhmim gets home because he gets home so late and I get up so early. I even fall asleep a little bit. He comes in so silent, so careful, as always, not to wake me. I think he can tell that I'm awake, but if I don't talk to him, he doesn't talk to me.

I should talk to him. I should ask him about it. But I know he has an answer and I can't ask him. I'm afraid of what he'll say, and what I'll believe.

It's like having a sore tooth, this idea of other *harni*. I worry at it and worry at it.

On Friday I work, and on Saturday I can stay in bed late, so I don't have to go to bed so early. I plan to stay up late. I want to talk to Akhmim. Of course, by Friday evening I'm so tired I think I'll never be able to stay up and at ten I go to bed. But I can't sleep. Akhmim didn't tell me he had called Professor Malik.

I'm going to ask him on Saturday.

I can't sleep and I'm still awake when Akhmim gets home.

He's quiet as a cat. When he gets into bed, I can smell his smell, and the smell of restaurant.

He never kisses me. We're like brother and sister. Maybe that's what he needs.

"Akhmim?"

"What's wrong?" he asks.

I don't know. "I miss you," I say.

"I miss you," he says.

"Do you remember how we used to sit in my room at Mbarek's and talk?"

"I remember," he says. He rises up on one elbow, barely visible in the faint glow of the nightlight in the hallway. "Are you sad, Hariba?"

"I am," I say. "I really am. I feel so bad about Alem. It's so hard here. It's harder than I ever thought it would be."

He leans over and kisses me on the forehead. I lift my face and he kisses me on the lips. I love when he kisses me.

"Kiss me more," I whisper.

He kisses me more, and I put my hand on his chest. What do people do when they want to make love? I put my arm around him, tentative. Doesn't the man usually do that? But I've never wanted to do more than kiss with Akhmim. It's like I've told him not to go any further, so now I have to show him.

He puts his arm around me and draws me close.

I'm so nervous. I've never seen him naked. I've never let him see me naked. Years ago, when Nouzha and I had talked, before I found out she was committing adultery with my brother Fhassin, she told me that the first time it hurt. I asked Ayesha after she got married and she said it was true, but then it got better.

Did Nouzha have to go through that again with Fhassin? Does it hurt at first with every man? Or just with the first man?

Akhmim strokes my back. It feels good. I don't know what to do, though, since he has me pressed against him and I have one arm around him. Surely, if this is what he wants, he'll take it. He kisses my jaw and my neck. It's like one of the entertainments that the mistress used to watch.

He lays me on my back and kisses me some more, and then strokes my breast through my nightgown and I startle.

He stops.

"It's all right," I say.

"Shh," he says, and kisses me some more. He doesn't touch my breasts, though. Is he supposed to? O Allah, what am I doing?

I'm supposed to wait until I marry. Will I ever be able to marry if I do this? Is Akhmim who I want to marry? Yes, I tell myself, I am already in love with Akhmim and I came all the way to Spain because of that love. (But the counselor's voice is in my head, telling me that our relationship isn't right.)

Akhmim lies down next to me and strokes my forehead.

"Are you tired?" I ask.

"A little," he says.

"Me too," I say.

"I love you," he says. And I didn't even ask him to.

He holds me against him until finally I'm too hot and I stretch out and fall asleep.

Saturday morning I'm all jittery. If he were a man, he wouldn't have stopped. Is it my fault? Is it Allah's will, protecting me?

I want to ask him if he *wants* to have sex. I want to ask him if he wants to marry me, but I'm not supposed to ask, he is. Maybe this is what the counselor meant about having to resolve my relationship with Akhmim. Maybe I have to learn different ways because he's a *harni*.

Instead, I say, "I talked to Professor Malik, and he told me you called and asked how to get in touch with a *harni*."

I want it to sound just curious, but it comes out sounding irritated.

Akhmim shrugs. "My counselor told me I should talk to another chimera."

Chimera, I think. *Harni* is a bad word.

"Did you call?" I ask.

Akhmim looks at me for a moment. "No," he says.

"Why not?" I ask.

He says, watching me steadily the way he always does, "I was busy. It's you I need."

"If your counselor says you should, then you should."

"Okay," he says.

He comes over to me and hugs me, and strokes my hair. "This is hard for you, all this change."

Normally I would just let him, but now it strikes me that he's doing this to change the subject.

"I think you should call," I say. "Why don't you call now? Maybe we could go and meet him. Or her."

"Him," Akhmim says.

Thank Allah.

Akhmim lets go of me and steps back. "Right now?" he says.

"Sure," I say. "Why not?"

"I'm tired," Akhmim says. "I have to work tonight."

"Just calling isn't so bad," I say, merciless.

He can't refuse me, I know that.

He finds his slate and looks up the number. "Hola," he

says. *"Me llamo Akhmim, yo soy una chimera y un amigo de Professor Malik."* His Spanish is better than mine. I can understand that he's said hello and introduced himself as a friend of Professor Malik's, but I have trouble following everything he says.

Sunday. He says Sunday afternoon a couple of times, and he smiles and nods. I wish I could see the face on his slate, see who he's talking to. He laughs, looking beautiful for the face I can't see. Who, I realize, must be beautiful, too.

Merciful Allah protect me.

"His name is Ari," Akhmim says. "He says we should come tomorrow at two o'clock. He says a lot of the chimera in the household will be around."

Akhmim's face betrays nothing. He seems perfectly at ease with the idea.

Oh, my painful heart.

Sunday afternoon and off we go, taking the bus past the bullring and then changing to another bus and then another bus because on Sunday some of the buses run and some don't.

I'm wearing my best clothes. As if I'm going to be able to compete with chimera. I'm sweating and so nervous I feel sick. Akhmim holds my hand tightly and chatters about everything that happened at the restaurant the night before.

Finally we get off at a little apartment building, only three stories tall, concrete, and old-fashioned. Akhmim knocks on the door, still holding my hand.

The chimera who answers is small and dark, flat-faced and bow-legged. I can't tell for a moment if it's a man or a woman, but I decide it's a woman.

"I'm here to see Ari," Akhmim says.

"This way," the chimera says.

Inside the apartment building has been changed so the first floor is all open like a house. In the back there are two more chimera working in the kitchen. They look identical to the one that let us in the door. The one that let us in takes us upstairs, and then up to the third floor.

"At the back," she says. We walk toward the back, passing an open door that looks in on a room where another chimera, this one small and Asian-looking, but ugly like the one that let us in the door, sits watching an entertainment. Every surface of the room is covered with something shiny, so the room glints and glitters. The chimera doesn't look up when we pass.

But there is space for four apartments at the back, and a door standing open. Akhmim calls hello, and a beautiful man comes to the door.

"Akhmim," he says, "and Hariba, hello!"

His hair is straight and black and he looks as if he comes from India, but even though they look so different, he and Akhmim could be brothers. They're the same height and they both have the same long legs, but it's more than that. It's the way they move. The way they stand, and both turn their faces to look at me.

Ari invites us in. There are six women all sitting there, all beautiful.

"This is where we live," Ari says. "All the pleasure chimera."

My Spanish isn't so good so Ari fetches a slate and translates for us. The first two floors are all labor chimera, mostly from South America, although some from Indonesia. And on this floor the front rooms are all Indonesian.

"Except for poor Anna," he says. He gestures toward a woman I didn't notice. She's standing in a doorway. She's tall and broad and soft-looking, pale brown with placid brown eyes. "Anna is a nanny chimera. She's only here until she can get work. But she needs a child, don't you, Anna?"

She smiles sadly and tears well up in her eyes.

Nanny chimera, he explains through the slate, are very uncommon.

"Would you like something to drink?" Ari asks.

The other women are all sitting there and they look perfectly natural and very beautiful—four shades of blond, one redhead, and one dark-haired—but they aren't doing anything and it feels as if they're arranged, as if for a play. Their faces are all turned to me.

"Do you want to see the rest?" one of them asks me. Her name is Maria Inez, she says. She has a beautiful voice and I can understand her pretty well when she talks. The rooms all connect to each other, but other than the sitting room and the kitchen, I can't tell what they're for. Some of them have big, huge beds, and one has a mat that covers most of the floor, and one of them has a bunch of chests of drawers in it.

"Which is your room?" I ask.

Maria Inez is blond and her hair is the hundred shades of honey—clover, buckwheat, orange blossom. She says, "This room." It's one of the rooms with a big bed, but it doesn't have anyplace to keep her things and it doesn't have a door. None of the rooms have doors.

She's . . . not watching me, exactly. When Akhmim looks at me, it doesn't feel as if he's watching me, but like Akhmim, she is always looking at me.

"You're very beautiful," I say.

"Thank you," she says. "But it's only because I'm a chimera. Your Spanish is very good."

"Not so good," I say.

When we get back to the sitting room, Akhmim is sitting, too, and they all look at me, and he's one of them. One more beautiful face. The he scoots over for me to have a place to sit down and he's my Akhmim again.

"Are you impressed?" I ask the woman sitting next to me.

"Oh yes," she says. She is the redhead. All the women have long hair and it is soft and beautiful and they wear it down like children. "His name is Enrique."

"Does he live here?" I ask.

"No," she says. "We decided it was better if we lived apart."

"Do you miss him?" I ask.

"Always," she says. Her expression is like Akhmim's. Calm, without pain. "But I'm happy here."

I look at Akhmim.

He is looking at me, patient, calm. They are all looking at me. All alike.

"Would you like to live here?" I ask.

"It's different for you and me," he says. "I love you."

It's not, though. And now I know it.

I need him. I'm alone in a strange country. That's the difference. I can make him happy, I know I can.

That night I ask him, "Do you want to make love?"

He sits down next to me on one of the big cushions we use and kisses me on the forehead. "My sweet Hariba," he says.

"I love you," I say. "You're everything to me."

"And you to me."

"Do you feel as if . . . I mean, I know, men have urges," I say.

"We're not like other people," he says. "Our love is based on what we have here." He touches my chest.

It's exactly what I would want him to say. Isn't everything exactly what I would want him to say? "You're saying that just for me."

He strokes my face, his fingers delicate and precise. "What do you want?" he says.

"I want to know what you want," I say.

"I'm here, I want to be here with you."

"Do you want to be with the other *harni*?"

"I want you to be happy," he says. "When you're unhappy, it makes me unhappy."

"I want you to make love to me," I say.

"All right," he says. He kisses my forehead, and then my mouth. "All right." He kisses me gently on the lips, and then on my neck.

It will hurt the first time, but then it gets better. That's what everyone says. But it will change us. It will be like a marriage. I can be a wife to him, I can give him what he wants. It can be as if we were jessed to each other—has anyone ever done that?

"Come," he says, taking my hand and leading me to our bed. He sets me on the bed and kisses me again. I don't feel anything. I'm waiting for some kind of feeling, some urge.

I like when he kisses me, but I don't know what I'm supposed to feel.

He takes his shirt off. "Do you want to take off your dress?" he asks.

"I . . . I guess," I say. "Can we close the curtains?"

He closes the curtains so the room is dim. It's not late enough that the sun has gone down, and the curtains let the light shine through so everything in the room is washed in red. I take off my dress, but I'm still wearing my shift. He's seen me in my shift before. When I was sick, he saw me in my shift a lot.

"Do you want me to take my clothes off?" he asks.

"Yes," I whisper. I wish he wouldn't ask. I wish he would just do it. My face is hot from embarrassment.

He takes off his pants, and his underwear, and I can see what he looks like. I've never seen a naked man before, and I want to look, but I don't, so I look at him a little, and then I look up at his face and promise myself I'll just keep looking at his face.

He sits down next to me on the bed and kisses me again. "You have such nice skin," he says. "And I love your hair, my Hariba. I think of you all the time."

"I love you," I say helplessly.

He kisses me and has me lay back on the bed. He carefully touches my breasts and I don't flinch this time. I won't flinch, no matter what he does.

He kisses me a lot, and strokes me with his hands. He kisses between my breasts, and then he has me sit up and he pulls my shift off me so I'm only wearing my underwear. He kisses between my breasts again, this time on the bare skin. I have goose bumps.

"Are you cold?" Akhmim asks.

"I'm okay," I say. I will make him happy. I try to smile as if I'm happy. When I get more used to this, I'll be better at it.

He touches my chest and my belly. He touches my knees and my arms and then my thighs. I try to smile at him.

"Does this feel good?" he asks.

"Yes," I say. I don't care what it feels like.

He lays next to me and takes my hand. "I like this," he says. "Just like this. I like being with you like this."

I glance down to see if he's aroused, and he is. I want to believe he likes lying here with me this way, but if he's aroused, then surely he wants to go further. I try to think of what to do. I kiss him. "I want you," I say.

He kisses me gently, and then he touches me. I don't flinch. He rubs me and after a moment it feels good and I can really smile at him a little.

"That's nice?" he says.

"Yes," I say. I'm not perfect like the *harni*. I have little breasts and my belly is flabby, a little. My thighs are thick and my shins are thin. He is looking at me and I know he must be thinking of the *harni*. "I love you more than anyone else," I say.

"I love you, too," he says. "We're together here."

I slide off my underwear, awkward, scooting up my butt. Finally he eases on top of me and, holding it in his hand, he searches where to enter me. There's not enough space for him to go in.

"Just relax," he says.

"It's okay," I say. It isn't, but I tell myself, Women have babies.

He pushes in. Who could imagine it would feel the way it does, all hard. It does hurt. All the good feeling is gone. He is in me for a moment, not moving.

I will make him happy. "Go on," I whisper. This will be over soon. He is in me and he moves, and it doesn't hurt so much, and then he groans and pulls away.

"Hariba, sweet," he says, "are you all right?"

"Yes," I say. "Was it good?"

"You are the loveliest," he says.

I don't feel different. Actually, I do. I feel as if I have done something wrong. But it's done.

My mother would be ashamed.

I'm ashamed. He puts his arm around me and I lie there, trying to go to sleep. After a while, I get up and put on my underwear.

On the sheets there's a spot of blood, like menstrual blood. I'm a little sore.

Akhmim raises up on his elbow. "Hariba?"

"I just want to clean up," I say. I go and take a shower. I can cry in the shower.

He's waiting in the now-dark room when I come back in. "Are you all right?" he asks.

"I'm okay," I say. "Just tired. I have to go to school tomorrow."

I get back into bed. He's changed the sheets. I lay on my side, a little away from him. I'm so lonely. Nothing has changed.

Well, something has changed. I'm not fit to marry now.

The next morning I go to school and everything is different and nothing is different. Except that Akhmim is more far away from me and I'm different inside and no one can see.

Monday night I wait for him to get home from work. "I've been thinking," I say without even saying hello. "I think you should go visit the *harni* during the day when I'm at work and at school."

He stands there, looking at me in his calm way.

"But I need you for a while yet," I say. "I'm all alone here."

"All right," he says. "You know I love you."

"I know," I say. "But it's not enough, is it?"

For once he doesn't answer.

In two weeks we arrange it so that he's only home on weekends—since we rarely see each other during the week anyway. I tell my counselor, Dr. Esteban, and he asks me how I feel.

"Lonely," I say.

"How do you feel when Akhmim is there?" he asks.

"Still lonely," I say.

After two months, Akhmim stops coming home. I talk to him a couple of times by slate, and after that he calls me almost every day and we talk. It's good to hear Moroccan.

He loves me. It's good to be loved. But it isn't enough.

About six months after Akhmim leaves, I decide that I'm going to learn accounting, because I like the numbers and the software, and one of my teachers recommends a book on business presentation. It talks a lot about professional appearance.

"Long hair," it says, "looks naive and immature."

For a week, I brush my heavy hair before braiding it and look at myself in the mirror, trying to imagine. I look at the other women on the street.

So finally I go to a place to get it cut, and Gabriel, the man who is going to cut it, puts my optical image on his slate and shows me different ways I can look. For the first time, the face staring back at me looks different.

"A haircut is a new beginning," Gabriel says.

My Spanish is getting a lot better.

I choose a haircut that makes my hair slide in waves and rounds my face, a shining helmet of hair.

Gabriel gathers my hair in his hands. When it isn't braided, it is long enough that I can sit on the ends. "You need to cut off the old hair," he says. "Either that, or you need to make it healthy. But all this hair, it makes your face so tiny, and you will be pretty, I promise." He cuts a long length of it off, and then he coils it and puts it in a box. "For you to have."

He cuts and looks in the mirror and cuts and my head feels oddly light. I watch the new girl in the mirror. She looks like a Spanish girl who has Arab parents. She looks modern.

When he is finished, he shows me the hair all around, and I look so different. I shake my head and the hair falls back into place.

"So pretty," he says.

Not pretty, I'm not pretty. I wish I were pretty. But maybe I look as if I am part of this place, even if I am not.

He puts the box of my old hair on my lap. It is coiled in the box like a wreath. I touch and I try to think of what to do with it. I could send it to Akhmim, but I don't know what it would mean to him. It probably wouldn't be a reproach. It probably wouldn't even be a message.

I could send it to my mother, but it would break her

heart. I could send it to Ayesha, but if I were Ayesha, I'd just burn it.

I think it belongs to no one at all, this smooth coil of black hair, and I run my fingers over it. My tears are so hot, they're as hot as blood.